A V O I D A N C E

Also by Michael Lowenthal
The Same Embrace

AVOIDANCE

—◦—

A novel

Michael Lowenthal

[handwritten signature: Michael Lowenthal]

For Lys,
With warm memories
and love. Mike

Graywolf Press
Saint Paul, Minnesota

Publication of this volume is made possible in part by a grant provided by the Minnesota State Arts Board, through an appropriation by the Minnesota State Legislature, a grant from the Wells Fargo Foundation Minnesota, and a grant from the National Endowment for the Arts. Significant support has also been provided by the Bush Foundation; Marshall Field's Project Imagine with support from the Target Foundation; the McKnight Foundation; and other generous contributions from foundations, corporations, and individuals. To these organizations and individuals we offer our heartfelt thanks.

Grateful acknowledgment is made to Barry Louis Polisar for permission to reprint lyrics from the song "I Wanna Be a Dog," words and music by Barry Louis Polisar © 1979.

Published by Graywolf Press
2402 University Avenue, Suite 203
Saint Paul, Minnesota 55114
All rights reserved.

www.graywolfpress.org

Published in the United States of America

ISBN 1-55597-367-1

2 4 6 8 9 7 5 3 1
First Graywolf Printing, 2002

Library of Congress Control Number: 2002102974

Cover design: Scott Sorenson

Cover photograph: Stephen Sheffield/Photonica

*This book is for Dan Wolfson
and the other camp counselors who raised me*

And for Scott Heim

Oh, to be emptier, lowlier,
Mean, unnoticed, and unknown . . .

—Amish hymn

A V O I D A N C E

PROLOGUE

—◆—

Try to imagine not even knowing how to fall, because a hand was always, always there to catch you. Two sisters, five brothers, a hundred cousins. At her one-room Amish school, built on Uncle Christian's farm, a third of the pupils shared her surname. Her plain, aproned dresses and organdy prayer caps were her sisters' hand-me-downs, sewn by their mother. The clothes of every girl she knew were stitched identically, right down to the width of their *Kapp* seams.

But that was Beulah Glick's life before. What I wanted to know was why she'd left. How?

We were sharing a booth at the Plain & Fancy Diner, in blink-and-miss-it Gap, Pennsylvania. My first field interview, four years ago. Twenty-five and enthused about my new research topic, I'd read Hostetler, Kraybill, Huntington; I'd browsed the Pequea Bruderschaft Library. I'd never spoken with someone "in the ban."

Despite Indian-summer heat I was dressed in blue chinos and a buttoned poly shirt that showed my sweat—not too city-slick, not too academic. Beulah sat rigid, arms locked to her sides, as though the booth were a plunging roller coaster. She wore a gray blouse and a brown knee-length skirt, misfitting store-bought clothes. Her hair was still yanked back, Amish-style, from a center part. The bald streak from years of tightening looked painful.

I ordered the farmer's special: three pancakes, three eggs, a side of scrapple. (In Lancaster County, appetite trumps diplomas.)

Beulah asked for coffee—no sugar, no cream—and, as an afterthought, two eggs. Waiting for the food, she barely spoke. Shy-
ness around an unfamiliar man? Maybe shame? Or the meek
temper of *Gelassenheit*. It's the personal submission the Amish
strive for—self-denial for community's sake—and a lack of it was
Beulah's supposed crime. To me, she could hardly have seemed
more yielding. When her eggs came, she only poked them with
her fork.

I can't bring myself to touch my food, either. Why'd I bother
smuggling it into the library? The air in here, freeze-dried, feels
worse than outside's scorch. Saturday evening. Most of Harvard's fled.

Congealing in Styrofoam, shrimp pad thai fouls my carrel;
Thai iced tea glares the shade of fake tans. And what I'm craving,
believe it or not, is a hot dog. A humble hot dog, third-degreed
on a stick. Let it fall from the stick, even; spice it strong with ash
and mulch. I'd eat it anyway. That's the spirit—summer camp!

Who'd have thought I'd wax nostalgic for wieners? Or
s'mores? Or bug juice, toxic with red dye? First-night fare I used
to rail against in staff meetings. ("Why pander to kids' precon-
ceptions of camp? Ironwood's different. We should show them
from the start.") But Charlie Moss was director; he called the
shots. Comfort food is always best on first night, he insisted. We
had all summer for Camp Ironwood values.

Not this summer. Not for us. Not for Max.

Max's cast—well, half of it—sits up on the shelf, propped
against the tools of my trade (*The Riddle of Amish Culture;
Habits of the Heart*). And where is Max himself, his wrist now
healed, strong again? I haven't heard anything since camp ended.

The diner stank of cigarettes and fake maple syrup. Sugar-drunk
flies sputtered low. Between sips of coffee, Beulah eked out her
story in a jumpy Pennsylvania Dutch–trained voice.

Her sheltered childhood had stretched to adolescence. She
rarely ventured beyond Quarryville, her hometown. At seven-

teen she was baptized, at twenty-two she was wed. Only then did her troubles begin.

Her husband, Jonas, worked on an Amish building crew, saving cash till he could buy a farm. The steady jobs were over the border in Maryland, where subdivisions tumored on the land. The Amish can't own cars, but they can hire them; the crew enlisted a driver who collected them each morning and shuttled them the fifty rolling miles. At day's end, he returned again to fetch them.

But the driver was sometimes thirty, even forty minutes late. The Amish sat and waited at his mercy. Jonas got sick of wasting time. He wanted to get home, to be with Beulah. He hired a neighbor, Steve Hutchinson, to retrieve him in a private car: an old convertible with room for just them. Steve, too, commuted from Quarryville to Maryland. It seemed a perfect mutual arrangement.

But there was talk in their church district. The sports car was worldly, it was "English." Going separate wasn't the way of *unser Satt Leit,* our sort of people. Was Jonas too proud to wait with the group?

He was visited by the deacon and asked to confess his wrong. Start going with the crew again. Be Plain.

Jonas balked. What could be wrong about getting home to his wife sooner?

Hiring Steve might not specifically have violated the *Ordnung,* the church's unwritten set of rules, but disobedience was a gross and flagrant sin. Now Jonas was called into church to kneel. The community required his contrition.

That Sunday Jonas stayed at home.

Beulah was shocked by her husband's selfishness. She pled with him to yield, to be patient. "Maybe the crew can find a different driver," she told him. "And you won't be working away much longer, ain't? Soon we'll have our farm, and you'll stay home."

But for Jonas it was a matter of principle. The ministers themselves were flaunting pride, he said. As if *they* had created right and wrong, not God.

Bishop Mose Ebersol called for *Meidung*—social avoidance—
a temporary ban at first, six weeks. He quoted Romans: "Mark
them which cause divisions and offenses contrary to the doc-
trine which you have learned, and avoid them." He quoted First
Corinthians, Second Thessalonians.

Even Beulah was supposed to shun Jonas, because shunning,
the bishop reminded her, is an act of love, and who loved Jonas
more than his wife? Avoidance was the strongest way to show
care for his soul, the best means to hasten restoration.

And so, hoping to turn him, she complied. She ate at a different table, took nothing from her husband's hands, slept in a separate bed. Fellowship required giving up of will.

Her sisters Sadie and Ruth visited, bringing quilts and tea to
take her mind away. They held her hands, one on either side.

Then the worst: four weeks into the ban, it was discovered
that Jonas had paid for Steve's convertible. (Steve told a friend,
who told the seed salesman, who let it slip to an Amish cus-
tomer.) In all but title, Jonas owned the car.

The minister asked again for a confession—if Jonas knelt in
church and "put away" the car, he would be fully reinstated.
But still Jonas wouldn't show contrition. Mose Ebersol came to
their house, weeping, and read a curse, delivering Jonas's soul
to Satan.

Now Beulah, too, risked expulsion if she didn't join the ban,
didn't treat Jonas as a stranger—her own husband! Such a mar-
riage was unthinkable. Could they be "one flesh" when they
weren't allowed to touch? Yet she couldn't leave; the church for-
bids divorce. The only Amish way was to keep living with Jonas,
but with a world's frigid distance between.

Complicating everything was what she'd known as she pled
with him, but hadn't told him or anyone: that inside her grew
their child, three months to term.

She prayed. At her empty table every morning, and at night in
her lonely bed, she prayed to Jesus Christ for guidance. And
what she finally knew—thinking of God who was the Son—was

that a child needs above all else its father. The child needed Jonas, and thus did she. After a full month of *Meidung,* Beulah woke one rain-whipped morning and set their places together at the table.

Soon her choice was known in the community. The deacon summoned her as, before, he had Jonas, but Beulah, too, stayed clear of church. Her mother and father begged her not to be headstrong; Ruth and Sadie cried that they would lose a sister. When Beulah revealed her pregnancy, they clucked their tongues and asked, "Will you raise your baby in a worldly hell?"

But hell was a home where the parents couldn't touch.

Next Sunday, the bishop called for expulsion. When he asked if all in the fellowship were agreed, everyone nodded, even Beulah's mother. The curse was delivered. They put her out.

Beulah had tried to prepare herself for the pain, but the truth was beyond imagining. When she passed her friends on Horse-shoe Lane—friends she'd known since infancy—they turned away and walked silently by. Her family's circle letter stopped arriving.

She gave birth to a boy and named him Benuel, for her father, but her father never came to see the baby. No one did. No one helped her with the wash.

One morning she took Benny to Musserman's Dry Goods, to buy diapers and laundry detergent. Unloading her cart, she saw Ruth come through the door with her four-year-old twins, Abie and Ruben. The nephews smiled and waved, but when Beulah asked, "How are you?" and showed off her apple-cheeked infant, Ruth said only, "We wish you patience and grace." She hustled her boys down the nearest aisle.

We wish you patience and grace.

"It's what the Amish say," Beulah explained, "when someone in your family has died. My own sister. To her, I was good as dead." Beulah blotted her coffee mug on the Plain & Fancy place mat, where her grief showed in a hex of muddy rings. "I thought Jonas and Benny would give me strength to live. But being put out? Losing everyone else? Well, it's just a slow death anyhow."

The air conditioner, a pious library worker, shushes me. My computer's glow is mealy, stifling. All I've typed, these long hours? The title page.

I try to read—a *Mennonite Quarterly Review* article about Amish Church Aid—but my pulse beats, relentless, in my ears. The tempo's exactly that of the camp song.

> *Roots firm in the ground, Ironwood.*
> *Toughest tree around, Ironwood.*
> *Unafraid to bend, every limb a hand to lend—*
> *Ironwood, the best camp in the land!*

They'd be done with their cookouts now, I figure, their sticks snapped and fed into the fire. They'd be getting to know each other, playing Truth.

If I were there, this opening night, how would I play? One: *I know I made the right decision.* Two: *The one I blame most is myself.* Three: *I would never harm a boy.*

But which statements are true, which the lie? All three seem just about as false as true.

I think of Caroline—of all the counselors—stuck in Vermont for the summer. Barely paid, barely time to breathe. And Max, on an island far away.

Me? I'm free to write—or not to write—my thesis. Free for anything, which means nothing. Just like Beulah.

ONE

◄◯►

Max clocked a record for broken bones.

We'd sustained early mishaps before. One year, a boy named Chip or Chad (or some anachronism of the privileged) rolled from his bunk on camp's opening night. He landed headfirst on the rude rough-plank floor and merited six stitches in his scalp. Another summer, a twiggy overeager twelve-year-old, assigned to crafts for his first activity, missed a finishing nail and hammered his thumb instead; the fractured finger swelled kielbasa-sized, bruising every lurid hue of a sunset.

But this! A cracked wrist at three o'clock on arrival day, before we'd even lit our welcome fires.

I was stationed on the main downhill path—the one we'd gussied with sawdust, as if wood chips could mask the muck of coming months—supervising the haul of trunks from cars to cabins. On the road, Mom and Dad reigned absolute. "Son, grab the handle," they'd bark, hoisting a trunk from the Volvo wagon's hatch. "No, not that way—*that* way!" Then the awkward waddle to the cabin area. The adults remained in charge for the first yards. But as paths steepened, complicating footholds, the boy nimbly asserted his domain. Like a creature released from captivity, he thrilled to this new habitat. "Over here," he might call, forging a shortcut. "Are you sure?" Dad would ask gingerly. "Yeah, come on, it's, like, totally faster." And by the gaining of their destination, the camper would have scored a full reversal. "Watch that ceiling," he'd say. "Don't bang your head."

9

That's how fast boys transformed at Ironwood. This was their place, and they sensed it from the start.

I was directing a newcomer to his cabin, scanning my clipboard checklist for his name, when Simon came wilding up the path. Simon had been a runty ten-year-old in my maiden summer as a counselor, and now, at nineteen, in his own counseling debut, displayed the jumpy zeal of a Seeing Eye dog in training. He was broad-shouldered and on his way past six feet tall, but still walked with giant overcompensating strides, as if afraid of being left behind.

"Jeremy," he panted, more panic than voice. "He fell. The back stairs. Rotted through. Arm, I think. Or wrist. I heard the pop."

Only then did I register Max's presence. Simon had the kid cradled practically off the ground, as you might carry a car-hit dog to the vet. I'm tempted to describe Max for you now, but when I looked at him that first time—not yet knowing his name—I catapulted into crisis mode. I glanced only the quickest inventory.

Max's right arm lopped at his side, the wrist already gut-colored and swollen. A raspberry scrape painted the right side of his face, which was tight with the strain of not crying.

"What's your name?" I asked.

He grunted a response, but through the clenched jaw his answer was unclear.

"Max Connor," Simon offered on his behalf.

"Parents here?"

"Came on his own. Bus."

"All right then. I'll take him up to Caroline. You better stay here, direct traffic." I held out my clipboard.

Simon stared a second, disappointment and relief fighting on his brow. His retriever-golden hair briefly wavered in a gust, then fell back to its opening-day spiff.

"Go with Jeremy," he said, unlatching Max. "You're doing great. Just, um, you know, just keep breathing."

I hooked a half hug around Max and carefully grabbed his

arm, bracing the elbow and letting the rest droop. He was all rib cage, skinny as an unstuffed scarecrow. I could count his frenzied pulse in my fingers.

"We're going to the infirmary," I told him in my most measured assistant-director voice. "We'll find Caroline and she'll take a quick look. Then to the doctor. Think you can handle that?"

Max whimpered assent.

"Good. Then we're in business. My name's Jeremy. I'll be your host for this afternoon's cruise."

Not even a hint of laugh, but I tried not to take it personally.

"How old are you?" I asked.

"Fourteen."

"Yikes—exactly half my age. Which I guess makes you twice as likely to get hurt?"

Still no response.

"All right. Relax. I might ask you every now and then how you're doing. Otherwise you don't have to talk, okay?"

Max's eyes glimmered with gratitude, or was it anguish? I read his T-shirt: ZOO YORK: BORN, BRED, DEAD.

When we hit the road, I saw the swarm of parents and realized we'd have to barge right through. Not the best PR, to parade an injured kid before the equivalent of Ironwood's stockholders, but I counted on Ruff Peterson's cardinal rules of camp counseling: #1) *The kid always comes first.* And #2) *No matter what happens, act like it's supposed to.*

The parents were mostly sunglassed thirty-somethings, trim in a StairMaster way. Who am I to condescend? On the whole they're fine people, do-gooders with the means to do much good. But with a wing-clipped boy in tow, I wasn't interested in their meddling.

Donning my business-as-usual smile, I forged a path into the human hurricane, while Max clung marsupial to me. At the eye of the storm stood Charlie Moss. Charlie was only five-feet-five, but still I could see him in the crowd, his frizzy red hair like a fishing bob. Red was how I had come to think of him: not just his hair or his capillaried nose, which appeared sunburned all year round; beyond the looks, he was smoldering, radiant.

Charlie was my age—his birthday a mere month after mine—but gave the impression of being more youthful and, as a result, accomplished beyond his years. When we were campers together, bosom bunkmates and tandem canoeing partners, counselors had lavished him with praise for the same achievements I completed without fanfare. And though I'd turned out more graceful and half a foot taller, it was hard to compete with Charlie's sheer glow. My muddled, indefinitely Slavic features were no match for his purebred Irish presence.

Arrival day was Charlie's tour de force. "Judy," I once heard him croon to a camper's mother—a woman he'd met maybe twice before. "Great to see you. Where's Marisa? What's she now, four?" And Judy, flabbergasted by this intimate touch, stammered, "Four and a half. We left her with a sitter." Later, back in Stonington or Mamaroneck or Wellesley, she'd tell her friends about this lovely camp where the director treated you like family. And so, year after year, they kept coming; enrollment was always overbooked by Christmas.

Charlie saw me, read through my calm veneer, excused himself. He steered me to the eddy of the road's edge.

"Problem?"

"Just a little boo-boo. Don't worry. We've got it covered, right Max?"

The kid only blinked, as if we'd rehearsed a system: once for *yes,* twice for *no.*

"Rutland?" Charlie asked—code for "How bad?" Rutland was the nearest hospital, a steep drive over Sherburne Pass.

"Oh, I think so. Apparently, there were sound effects."

Charlie tweaked his left earlobe as though fine-tuning a precision instrument. His winter job as an ambulance driver in Portland, Maine, made him expert in the calculations of triage. "If you go," he said, "who's helping campers find their cabins?"

"Simon's on it. He's got my clipboard. He'll do fine."

Charlie brightened, brought his hands together in a single

approving clap. "Good," he said. "Do what you need to do."
Then he gave a quick squeeze to Max's neck. "Hang in there,
kiddo. We'll be rootin' for you." With that, he marched back
into the clot of parents to resume his spectacular glad-handing.

And I—knowing nothing of the coming weeks' tumult, knowing nothing but the fact of an injured boy—sallied forth into the
minefield that was our future.

At the infirmary, Caroline swiveled in a cranked-up drafting
chair, sorting through a heap of medications. She would dispense
the meds at mealtimes through the summer—allergy serums,
pills to stretch attention spans—single-handedly wielding more
control over the camp dynamic than any weather pattern or
capture-the-flag competition.

"Knock knock," I called, prying open the screen door. "Got
one for you."

Caroline looked up, stone-faced, and deadpanned, "Nah,
he's too little, toss him back." But already she was on her feet,
her arm around Max, leading him to the examination table.
There was an almost electrical charge generated by her surety, a
hum that re-ionized the air.

"What's your name?" she asked, flicking on a halogen lamp
but directing its beam from the patient's eyes.

"Max," he said.

She raised an eyebrow. "As in: 'To the'?"

He chuckled, lips parting to show sterling latticework. Just as
quickly, a grimace hid the braces.

"Sorry," she said. "Hurts to laugh? I was trying to get some
endorphins flowing."

She palpated his forearm, shockingly bloated and meaty in
the gash of light. Max succumbed calmly to her handling. I'd
seen it before, how Caroline's presence anesthetized anxiety. The
only woman among Ironwood's hundred men and boys, she
imparted universal surrogate motherhood—ironic, considering
that in the outside world she was perceived as decidedly tom-
boyish (the only child of a father who wished for sons). At six

feet even, practically hipless, hair cropped beneath her time-worn Red Sox cap, Caroline confused men: Was she beautiful, or handsome?

She ceded Max's arm back to him. "Well," she said, "Mr. To The Max, winner of the First Klutz of the Summer award, I hereby pronounce you the owner of a broken wrist. What say we send you to the hospital for some X rays?"

Max shrugged—not sullen, just dazed.

"Broken anything before?" she asked.

He cocked his head. "Toes?" he tried.

"Nah, something real. See here?" Caroline thrust her own arm into the lamplight, displaying eyelet scars on either side of the wrist. "Baseball game in junior high. Slid headfirst into home—the winning run—but it jammed. Four titanium pins."

I cringed; a kid who'd just cracked his wrist shouldn't hear this. But Caroline had read him better than I had.

"I'll get *pins*?" he said.

Caroline bit an if-you're-lucky lip.

"Apocryphal," he said, "totally apocryphal," with full confidence in the nonsense phrase, and it was this odd, utterly convincing malapropism that stalled my engines, triggering the nosedive.

I suppose I could invent a less banal scenario, some witty or seductive remark he made. But isn't attraction always rooted in banality? Desire spits in the face of explanation.

Perhaps it was simply that now, hearing the terror vanished from Max's voice, I allowed my own fears to abate. Caroline was in control, the situation stabilized. I could finally study the boy who sat before me.

What snagged me about Max was the slang of his demeanor. Not jadedness, exactly, but an offslant edge to genuine sincerity—that pinch of salt that sweetens the fudge. You could see it in his posture, the teenage slump that verged on scoliotic. And in the way he wore his Brooks Brothers boxers, pulled three inches above his ratty jeans to take the piss out of their WASP propriety. His greasy baseball cap, and its slogan: BLAH BLAH BLAH. His was a calculated sloppiness, full of attention to the image of inattention.

When Caroline removed the cap to look at his scrabbled face, I saw that Max had a sneak-up-from-behind beauty. His flapper-length hair was as black as burned rubber, against which his skin shone uncannily pale: an unsunned, almost arctic shade.

He had started whimpering again.

"All right. Let me splint you up quick." She slipped a clear plastic sleeve around his arm, and with the twist of a valve it inflated. "Cool, huh? I hear they're all the rage in Paris this season."

She topped it off with a puff of breath. "Too tight?"

Max shook his head.

"Good. Then we're almost set. How about a little something to tide you over?"

"What is it?" he asked.

"Just aspirin, extra strength."

But I saw what she unshelved was Percocet. She turned to fill a glass of water for him. Before she could, he gulped the pill, dry.

"Yuck, how can you do that?" I asked.

He shrugged. "Practice?"

"With what?"

"Um, my mom's really into vitamins."

"Glad you brought that up," said Caroline. "Is your mother the one we should call?"

"No, don't worry about it."

Caroline shot me a glance. "Actually, Max, I *am* worried. It's my job."

He shrugged again (a gesture I soon would learn composed 90 percent of his vocabulary). "You could try, but my mom's in and out."

"Does she work?" asked Caroline.

"Yeah, she's an actress."

We oohed and aahed appropriately. We had no reason yet to disbelieve him.

"I'm sure she's got a cell phone then," said Caroline. "Or at least a car fax, right?"

"As if," Max said.

Now that he was talking more, I noticed his oddly scoured voice, what you'd expect from a pack-a-day smoker. From a kid his age, it straddled the line between cute and creepy.

"How about a regular phone," I suggested. "Where do you live?"

"Fifth between A and B."

I couldn't help laughing. "I guess that would be Manhattan?"

Hochmut is what Beulah Glick would have called Max's pridefulness—an Amish boy might be slapped for such a crime. Usually, it grated on me, too. One thing I relished about working at camp was the chance to strip city kids of their airs. In the woods, what was urban swagger worth? But Max's provincialism only added to his charm.

"Why don't you give me the number," said Caroline, "and I'll try."

Max dictated the digits stoically. I could see his eyes unfocusing, either from pain or from the Percocet kicking in.

"We should really get him going," I said. "Anything special I should tell the ER doctor?"

"Oh, thanks," said Caroline, "but I'm going to take him in myself. First casualty of the summer, I should be there."

I had counted on a van ride with Max. He was mine, I thought childishly. I found him! "What if something else happens here?" I lobbied. "You stay. I'm more expendable."

She looked at me quizzically. "No, Jeremy. This one's me." She grabbed the paper with Max's phone number and plucked a key ring from its hook. "Ready?"

Max scooched off the exam table and took a woozy half step, then paused.

"Come on, hon," she said. "The sooner we get there, the sooner you'll feel okay."

Max scrunched his nose. "Can I talk to Jeremy for a sec? Privately?"

Caroline glanced at me asquint, but I was equally surprised. "Sure," she said. "I'll, um, go start the van. Just come out whenever you're ready."

Max waited till her footsteps waned. When he spoke, his voice was stunted with embarrassment. "I'm all wet," he said, looking down.

I followed his eyes, but not his meaning.

"When I fell," he said. "I couldn't help it."

"Oh. Oh god, sure." Now I could smell it, a burnt-vinegar stink. There was a dark star on his jeans' left front pocket. "Let's see. What do you want me . . . I mean . . . ?"

I was the assistant director of a summer camp. I'd dealt with upchuck, impetigo, wetted beds. I'd once rescued a boy with mouth-to-mouth. But Max, this skinny mystery, rendered me clueless as a first-time baby-sitter.

"Can you just help me take stuff off?" he asked. "I'm not very good one-handed."

"Sure," I said. "Hop back up on the table."

Nervously I bent and untied his shoes. They were crimson Converse All Stars, sneakers I'd never felt cool enough to wear. I guessed them at size eleven or twelve, clumsy and auspicious: his destiny.

Next, I pointed to his low-slung jeans. He unhooked the belt, but fumbled with the button.

"This sucks," he said. "I feel like a fucking baby."

I decided not to tell him yet about the camp's no-cussing rule. "Let me," I said and, like a doctor checking for hernia, looked tactfully away when I placed my fingers.

He said, "I guess this fucks my drumming for a while."

"You play drums?"

"Yeah. My band's called Amateur Taxidermy. We play, like, millennial postgrunge."

I hadn't thought of grunge as something to be surpassed.

"Right-handed?" I asked, tugging down the pants.

"Of course. It's gotta be the one I break."

"Well, at least it's summer. You don't have to worry about homework."

"It's not homework I'm worried about," he said.

I skinned the jeans past his heels. "What then?"

Max moved his healthy hand to his crotch and jiggled it.

"Oh," I said. "Right." I tried to laugh.

"You have an extra pair?" he asked, meaning his boxers. "I don't want to put the jeans back on with nothing under."

"I doubt it," I said. "But I can check."

He snapped the underwear's elastic. "How about yours, then? Switcheroo?"

I saw his stingy half-cocked grin and was blindsided by the certainty of being teased. I should have told him no, or that I'd go get Caroline. What I said was, "They're tighty-whities. And they're way too big for you."

And what Max did was unleash the other half of his smile. "No prob," he said. "I wear everything big."

He hid behind the bathroom door to change. I could hear his dorky hop as he stepped from the shorts, then a muffled "shit" (him shinning himself on the toilet?). After a minute, his wishbone arm emerged through a gap, and at the end of it, his crumpled sog of boxers. I took them and handed him my briefs (fresh pair, thank god). I crammed his boxers into a Ziploc bag.

Max withdrew his hand into the privacy of his changing room. I paused a moment, fully exposed. What would I have said if Caroline returned, wondering what was keeping Max? How would I explain my nakedness? It felt as dangerous and liberating as a lie.

I stepped into my pants and zipped myself carefully inside, stashing the bag with Max's boxers in my pocket. He emerged seconds later, the stitched *Jockey* of my underwear visible through the open V of his fly.

"Still couldn't get the button," he said. "Or the sneaks."

I crouched before him to tuck the copper round into its slit, then stayed down to horn on his shoes. I tied them, doubled the knots, stood again.

"Thanks," he said, his blue eyes distant and watery. His smile had gone groggy, was now a pout.

"You feel all right?" I asked.

"Yeah. Everything's just kind of numb."

"You're not blacking out, are you? You're not going to forget me?"

He laughed girlishly, then grabbed his wrist and steadied it. "I'll remember," he said. "The question is, will I respect you in the morning?"

I walked him to Caroline's idling van, boosted him into the seat and strapped him in.

"Back in two shakes," said Caroline. "Try to limit further casualties, okay?"

As they pulled away, I would swear I saw Max wink at me in the side-view. Or maybe he'd finally let himself shed a tear. The tires spat dust, and I covered my mouth. There he was: piss and sneaker-sweat—unadulterated boyness—encrusted beneath my fingernails.

TWO

—◄○►—

Ironwood was the last and best gift my father gave me. He was a civil engineer, which, from what little I remember of him, seems almost poetically apt: He was civil, courteous, not unkind. He smiled when I brought his coffee or a crayoned birthday card. He never raised a fist. I think he loved me.

But my hunch is that he was better at fatherhood's theory than its practice. He understood the basic blueprint, but when it came to the nit and grit of building life with a boy, he would just as soon have hired a contractor.

We lived in Silver Spring, Maryland, and he'd landed the best job of his life, consulting on the D.C. Metro system. They were laying the Red Line deep beneath the suburbs. The Bethesda stop, it was rumored, would boast the longest escalator in the free world.

Dad let me visit once; I was eight. He found the smallest hard hat on the rack, tightened the headband past its last hole, and with duct tape secured it at my size. We rode an open elevator down into the shaft, each clank of gears razzing my nerves. I had expected bright lights and thrumming drills, an underground circus of machinery. But it was an off day, and the bulldozers hulked in hibernation. The huge expanse swallowed sound. Even my own breathing disappeared. There was the livening, fresh-blood smell of dug earth, and a residual metallic tang of diesel.

When the call came three months later, at four in the afternoon, I was home from school watching *Mighty Mouse*. In the kitchen my mother gasped, then banged her head against the wall. I knew there'd been an accident underground. When she confirmed it, saying my father hadn't felt any pain, that the toppling concrete killed him instantly, what I imagined was the quiet after the fall: my father, more asleep than dead, like those bulldozers I had seen, resting in the cool of upchurned soil.

The insurance money helped, but not enough. Mom took a job as secretary for a Pentagon lawyer. Then she enlisted, because the army would pay for schooling. Nights and weekends, she studied computer programming, earning a B.A. and a doubled salary. For her degree, she owed time to Uncle Sam. We moved from Maryland to Fort Dix, New Jersey. A stint in Ansbach, Germany, then stateside again to El Paso, Leavenworth . . .

I learned to pack my belongings in an afternoon. Waving good-bye grew as natural as shaking hands.

Regretting the instability of my upbringing, my mother sought a way to give me roots. Her first boss—the Pentagon lawyer—was the one who suggested summer camp. He had the perfect one in mind: Ironwood.

Ruff Peterson, the camp's founder, had been a buddy of his in the bad old days. They'd been early advisers in Vietnam, and then Ruff, disillusioned, quit in '66 and moved back to his family's Vermont farm. With windfall cash from selling untilled acreage, he bought some lakefront land near Killington.

Running a boys' camp had been Ruff's dream since his Dartmouth days. He started small, just him and two other counselors and a dozen boys in tents. Together they built the first cabin, then the next summer a barn-sized mess hall. Carpentry became part of the program, a lesson in hard work, self-reliance. Ironwood drew on the army's best themes—adventure, limit-pushing, camaraderie—but ditched the destructive elements. Ruff stressed respect, never denigration.

My mother decided it was worth a try. Fully supported now

on her own salary, she paid eight weeks' tuition with the last of Dad's insurance. It was the summer I turned eleven.

I'll never forget my first breath of Vermont. I'd flown to Boston, then boarded the camp-chartered bus: three drowsy hours gulping fake-pine air freshener. It was twilight when the coach huffed to a stop. We filed off, unloaded our trunks and duffels, still immersed in the bus's exhaust. Then a sweet, granite-tasting breeze diffused the diesel. I inhaled and immediately I belonged.

For almost two decades since, I've tried to pinpoint Vermont's secret summer blend. There's the smell of a thousand sugar maples burned in late-night fires, and a thousand more growing heavenward to replace them. There's the musk of skunks and nosy porcupines. But you can't single out the elements, or even put it down to just a smell, for in truth it's a synesthetic whole: the hullabaloo of spruce gum scraped off a tree and chewed; the azure sound of upbubbling springs; and the ever-present wake-up slap of green.

A day at Ironwood was a week was a lifetime. The counselors taught me to J-stroke a canoe in a headwind, how to tell time at night without a watch. We got purposely lost on the ridge top, then triangulated and found ourselves on the map. I built things: a woodshed, a dock. I poured concrete into Sono tube foundations for a bunkhouse that would stand for years.

In July we took a day trip to Deer's Leap and rappelled wildly down the sheer cliff. I had no fear. I was tethered to the granite monolith, and to a new sturdy bedrock of boys. Charlie, my just-made pal, harnessed up alongside me, and together, with impunity, we fell—the plunge a private tickle in our groins. That night, in our bunks, our heads nearly abutting, we made pledges we were sure we'd never break.

By summer's end, I could walk every trail with eyes closed, my bare feet trusting their new turf. I relaxed into the possibility of permanence. Shepherding me through it all was Ruff. Like his name he seemed at first abrasive, but when familiar, was a purr, a reassurance. Already past fifty, he retained a lank youthfulness that suggested the inconsequence of time. His magnesium crew-cut drew all eyes in a crowd, an ever-glinting flashbulb, spreading light.

Ruff was tall (*is* tall) by any standard—six feet something and a half—but to a sapling of a boy like me he was redwoodlike. His hands were as broad as Michigan ax blades. He could carve a tent peg, or replace a rivet on a pair of boots (as he did for me, when I thought I'd ruined my first pair) with such deft and casual manliness that growing up—which since my dad's death had seemed a daunting, pointless task—once again became a rousing prospect. Ruff was what I aspired to: all that flesh, under control.

When we arm-wrestled, he didn't, like other counselors, let me win, and I liked the security of being pinned. And when at night, sitting bunkside, he cupped my hand in his, I felt like Adam, shaped from dust to man.

I had never cried leaving anywhere; I'd never cared enough about a place. But that August, when I stepped onto the return charter bus, I was a mess of tears and phlegm. Ruff said we'd send postcards, talk on the phone. But I knew it wouldn't be enough.

During the summer, homesickness had baffled me. Other kids grouched and begged to phone their parents, beset by longings I couldn't comprehend. But that dreary fall and winter—counting calendar pages at what passed for my home—I understood the burn to be somewhere you're not. I was campsick, miserably so.

And though it's sometimes embarrassing to explain, and draws puzzled looks in the "grown-up" world, that's more or less how I've felt ever since. What others adjudge "real life" is for me a postponement of what my heart says is righteously real: summer with a hundred boys in Vermont.

Thanks to Ruff's "campership" fund, I spent four seasons at Ironwood, then weathered the terrible aimless gap from fifteen to eighteen, when I qualified for apprentice counselor. The next summer, after my freshman year at Middlebury (a college I chose for its Green Mountains location and its generous financial aid), I was hired as full counselor. Like a priest ministering his first Communion, at last I'd been released to my vocation.

The talent for camp counseling, like that for art or sport, can be coached but not truly taught. It's a gift: instinctual, absolute. Just as basketball greats have "eyes in the backs of their heads," the best counselors exert uncanny awareness—not peripheral sight so much as peripheral insight. I wondered if I had what it takes.

That first summer, Simon was the youngest boy in camp. He was in my Advanced Beginner swim class, but I couldn't, for the life of me, focus him. All he wanted was to writhe endlessly beneath the surface, a manic minnow, holding breath. He made us time him: forty seconds, fifty-five, a minute ten. Then he would burst forth, rigid and gasping, his sun-polished hair in his eyes. He could stay under longer than any other boy, but never did he stop to gloat or rest. He'd catch his breath, then down again he'd go.

Simon hardly spoke. Those lungs that exhibited such remarkable staying power could barely support a brief hello. But after a month of mornings in the lake—my hands on his hands, teaching strokes—Simon came eventually to trust me.

One day, as we toweled off after staying overtime so that Simon could attempt to break his record, I asked about the root of his obsession. Quietly he explained: If he trained himself to hold his breath for greater and greater spans, then, those evenings when his father came raging, and Simon hid underneath the bed, he'd stay noiseless long enough to go unfound.

On visiting day, Simon's parents arrived from Kennebunk at noon, but they couldn't find their son anywhere: not in his cabin, not the Lodge, not the road. When word came that the lake was the last place he'd been seen, a full-scale alert was raised. Ruff blasted the air horn to clear the waterfront. Rescue poles and a backboard were laid out. Counselors readied for a snorkel sweep.

I stood on the lakeshore, trying to calm the campers, but my mind was intractable with dread. How could I have condoned Simon's antics? I watched the boy's mother, hysterical with sobs; his father, fists holstered at his sides.

Of course. I ran, pulse galloping, to our cabin, and pulled Simon's trunk from underneath his bed. Nothing but dust mice and dirt. I did the same at all the other bunks. I searched on my hands and knees. No luck.

With a sore heart, I returned to Simon's bed, replaced his trunk. I was almost at the door when it came to me. I went back, hauled out the trunk and pried the lid. He was folded up in a human origami of fear, bloodless cheeks drawn, lips blue.

I lifted him onto the bed. Mouth-to-mouth worked in less than a minute. Simon coughed and then he cried in my arms. The next day I phoned a family social worker.

When Ruff retired three years ago, and the directorship went to Charlie instead of me, I briefly considered quitting. But only for a week, maybe two. Rejection couldn't keep me from the boys. I worked for *them,* I realized, not for Charlie.

I worked at Ironwood for a year more than a decade. I worked there every single year until now.

THREE

◄○►

I didn't plan to study the Amish. After Middlebury I enrolled in Harvard's Graduate School of Education. Teaching, I figured, wouldn't be that different from camp counseling. I'd still have summers off for Ironwood.

For a course on adolescent moral development, I was writing a paper about parochial education. My professor was bored with the usual suspects—yeshivas, Catholic day schools—and steered me instead toward the Amish. "Now, there's an interesting paradox," he said. "Their religion's opposed to college, even high school, but they've got their own education system. How do you teach kids *not* to value learning?" He put me on to a librarian at Widener: Somebody Miller; he could tell me all about it.

All I knew of the Amish was the movie *Witness,* Harrison Ford in a straw hat and suspenders. And hex signs. And that anyone who leaves the faith is shunned.

I found Miller's office in the cataloguing department. Books were stacked on every available surface, but the effect was more of reverence than neglect, as if each volume were too sacred to be disturbed. A framed diploma had been awarded to "Levi S. Miller," but the man introduced himself as Lee. He was thirty-ish, chap-lipped, thick-fingered.

"Amish schools," he said abruptly. "Sit for a while?"

I took notes as he unspooled a long thread of information: how until the 1960s most Amish attended public schools, but then the church fought for religious education, arguing all the way up to the U.S. Supreme Court, which in 1972 recognized a constitutional protection. . . .

I had stopped scribbling. I was transfixed by the man's strangely reconstituted-sounding voice, and by some other ineffable peculiarity. He had the off-kilter intensity of the sun during an eclipse: there but not there, both less and more than what's expected.

"How do you know so much about it?" I interrupted.

Lee looked at his hands and said, "I grew up Amish."

Now I heard the Germanic chuffing in his voice. "What did you do to get kicked out?" I asked.

"I wasn't," he said. "I was never in."

The Amish aren't baptized until their late teens, he explained. Only those who join, then break the rules are punished.

He wouldn't elaborate, but I met with him again the next week, and again the next, under the guise of learning about Amish education. Each time I tweezed more details of his story. He spoke of himself with secondhand detachment, as though recounting a forebear's biography.

He had grown up in Lancaster County, near a dip in the road that locals called "the Buck." He loved his parents and his nine brothers and sisters, but instead of tedding hay or cultivating corn, all he wanted was to stay inside and read. His family owned but two books besides the Bible: *Black Beauty* and *Little House on the Prairie*; he read them till he knew the words by heart.

The Amish forbid schooling past eighth grade. At sixteen, Levi—as he was still known—was hired out to an Amish turkey farmer. What got him through the days of tending to smelly poults was that he'd secretly subscribed to a correspondence course, using the mailbox of an "English" neighbor up the road. He studied literature, art history, ethics. He felt he had some greater destiny.

So when his father discovered his hidden course papers and told him he must quit or leave the house, Levi didn't have to think long. Having just earned his GED, he wrote to the president of

Valley Forge Christian College, who granted him a full scholarship. After that, library science school in Rhode Island. Then here to Harvard, surrounded by more books than he could read in ten lifetimes.

I asked Lee if he kept in touch with his family.

"I'll visit maybe every couple years. They treat me like a calf with no hind legs."

I couldn't stop thinking about him. He seemed so brave for having reinvented his world, like a sailor who, defying the ancient logic of a flat earth, aimed full speed ahead for the edge. He seemed brave and awesome, but also sad. What need could be so compelling as to make someone forfeit stability, belonging?

I told Lee I wanted to study ex-Amish folks like him—or, better yet, people who'd been shunned.

"If you really want to know what it means to leave," he said, "you'd better find out first what it is they're leaving. Go live Amish for a while."

I asked how that could ever be arranged.

"I'll introduce you to my cousins. They let a man stay with them once, a sociologist. They kind of liked it."

Which is how I came to meet the Yoders, Abner and Sadie and all their many kids. Despite an iffy start, my month-long visit to Lancaster County got extended to three months, then to six. I quit the Ed program and applied to the Divinity School. I became an expert in excommunication.

I arrived in Peach Bottom, Pennsylvania, on a Saturday in early September, the unmistakable hourglass-turn day when summer begins its seep to fall. Above contoured fields of corn and alfalfa, the sky appeared to be molting, gray swaths giving way to hearty blue.

The taxi dropped me at a homestead that looked like a drawing by an obsessive-compulsive artist. The house's zealously whitewashed façade was broken only by six dark green window shades, all pulled to precisely the same length. The weedless lawn might have been edged with a knife.

A man emerged from an outbuilding, wiping his fingers on his grubby gray trousers. The pants were zipperless—solid cloth where the fly usually goes—held up by thin leather suspenders. He wore a fraying straw hat and a shirt that had once been bright purple.

From beneath his hat brim the man peered cagily. "*Weah bischt du?*" he said.

"Excuse me. I'm looking for the Yoders?"

He combed his nearly foot-long beard with his fingers. "*Weah bischt du?*" he asked again.

I held my backpack's straps. "Maybe I'm in the wrong place. My name is Jeremy Stull and—"

"There you go! All I asked was who you are. You're going to have to learn some Dutch sooner or later. Might as well get started prompt, ain't?"

Abner introduced himself and we shook hands. I marveled at the thickness of his forearms.

I noticed children peeking elfishly from behind the corn crib, from the front porch steps, from the garden.

Abner rattled off a list of names it would take me days to learn. "That's Ezra, and Jakie, and Davey. And Dan, and Aaron, and Pickle Joe. The two girls and the little one are inside with Maem."

The boys looked like a trick of time-lapse photography, as if they were all the same boy at different stages. They were dressed identically, their hair all straw blond, their eyes a consistent cloudless blue. Only-child envy stirred within me.

The youngest boy toddled up and tugged curiously at my pants. He reached higher and ran his fingers along my zipper.

"Pickle Joe, *duh net,*" Abner admonished.

One of the older boys pulled the child away. "Do you know why he's called Pickle Joe?" he asked. "Because when he was inside Maem, all she ever wanted to eat was pickles!"

As if this were the dirtiest of jokes, everyone, including Abner, burst into giggles.

The Yoders, Lee Miller had told me, were "the plainest of the

Plain," part of a group who'd moved to southern Lancaster County to escape the touristy area around Bird-in-Hand. Away from all the worldly temptations, they were more likely to keep members in the church.

"Come along to the house once," Abner said, "and I'll introduce you to Maem."

I followed him into a linoleum-floored kitchen where a stout, snappy-eyed woman sat supervising two girls. She wore an unpatterned, burgundy dress covered by a long apron. The girls' dresses were smaller versions of the same, in blue and green. All three wore gauzy white head coverings.

"This is Jeremy," Abner said. "The boy from college." He pronounced it "cullitch," which sounded like a skin disease.

"I'm Sadie," said the mother. "These here are Lydia and Anne. Baby Sam's asleep in back."

Counting, I realized the Yoders had nine children—one more than an Ironwood cabin!

The girls appeared to be drilling inside an empty plastic tub, using a power drill that instead of being plugged into an outlet was connected to a rubber hose that led outside. I saw that they were drilling into a white foamy substance. Where the drill bit should have been twirled an eggbeater attachment.

Sadie explained, "It runs on compressed air, from a generator. We figured out where it works real good for churning butter."

"Well," Abner said, hitching his suspenders, "we've got another couple loads of hay to haul in yet. I guess you're welcome to rest a spell while we finish."

I could sense it was a test. I said I'd like to help.

"Okay-ah," he said, clearly pleased. Brown and Betty, his best team of Belgians, would be harnessed to pull the hay wagon. I should groom Brown. The boys would point him out.

They led me to the timber-frame barn, where the mottled light was both ethereal and coarse. Brute, digestive smells controlled the air. Ezra, at fifteen the oldest, was all business. He trod in steps just too wide for his legspan, as though the weight of impending manhood tugged him forward.

It was Jakie, the thirteen-year-old, who adopted me. His body, stuttering its way through the start of puberty, was a hodgepodge of mismatched components: stork-thin neck, downy cheeks still harboring baby fat, and hands as big as paperback mysteries. Goatishly, he kept butting his head into my side and snorting a private language through his nose, as if more comfortable with animal talk than human.

I'd known second-in-line kids like him before. Relieved of both the burden and the honor of being first, they tended to mooniness, caprice. At Ironwood, he'd have starred in the camper drama club, or carved funky sculptures in the crafts barn.

He butted me again and said, "This one." He pointed through the slats of a box stall to a massive chestnut-colored horse.

He climbed in and I timorously followed. I'd never ridden a horse; I'd never been this close. The animal's shoulder towered above me, a precipice of muscle.

"Here's a currycomb," Jakie said, handing me a tool with vicious-looking metal teeth. "I'll go fetch the bridle."

I could tell it hadn't occurred to him that a man my age might not know how to do this.

As I inched forward, Jakie said, "Wait. Look at me." Leaning back, he limboed underneath the horse's belly, then emerged with a daredevil smile.

All right, I thought, as he went off for the bridle. This can't really be so hard.

But horses, I would learn, like dogs, can sense fear. Brown shifted with regal entitlement, lifted one wrecking-ball hoof, swatted his tail. I tried to step aside but he blocked leftward. My fingers shook. I dropped the currycomb.

I looked for Jakie: not in sight. His brothers, too, had dispersed to their chores.

The comb sat in tangled straw below the horse's rear. Bend, I thought. Bend and pick it up. When I did, my nervous gulp brought chaff into my nose. I sneezed with all the force of an alarm.

Spooked, the horse stomped. Its hoof landed on my hand, my finger trapped between it and the comb.

I didn't even scream. I was in shock. As quickly as he'd stepped on me, Brown shifted away again and gave me a clear view of my finger. A good chunk of the tip was mashed to pulp.

Blood gushed at the furious pace of my pulse. Dark blood, the color of Sadie's dress. I'd just arrived. I didn't want to fuss. Maybe I would just see if they had Band-Aids, I decided. Were the Amish allowed to use Band-Aids?

Just then Jakie returned. When he saw the blood, his eyes brightened wildly. He led me in my haziness to Abner.

"Um," I said. "Do you maybe have something I could put on this cut?"

Abner glanced impassively at the finger, adjusted his hat's angle, and called for Sadie.

When she saw the wound, she laughed. "Was it Brown? Oh, that horse *is* a stomper!"

Did they realize my finger had just been crushed?

Sadie took me to the toolshed. She uncapped a cruddy jug of turpentine. "Give me your finger."

Turpentine? I was sure it would eat my finger off. I kept my hand at my side, shivering, short of breath. Then I thought: Am I going to trust her? Am I going to *be* with these people and try to understand them, or will I scurry back to Harvard and my books?

I held out my hand. I couldn't bring myself to look. Sadie poured a brown glub directly on the wound. I flinched, but there wasn't any pain. Immediately, all pain disappeared.

Now I was able to apply pressure. It took an hour, but finally the bleeding stopped. The nearest hospital was thirty-some miles to the north. The Yoders, being Amish, had no car.

Sadie said she knew how to make remedies. I thought about the turpentine. I stayed.

She applied beet and comfrey poultices, brewed pots and pots of plantain tea. (*"Sei ohre bledder,"* she called the plant, "pig's ear leaves.") She mixed a salve of meadowsweet and tobacco. And as the weeks passed and the skin regenerated—a tough new skin, without my fingerprint—I reveled in a kind of salutary blankness. I learned that yielding sometimes braces you.

There was so much I learned in Peach Bottom: how to disk with a team of mules, six abreast; how to tell a horse's age from its back teeth. I learned a spring wagon from a buggy from a *Hunskarich*. I learned words like smearcase and doubletree.

I wore the same clothes every day for a week, my underwear crisping with sweat, then bathed Saturday nights in water warmed atop a woodstove. Sadie would have fresh clothes ready, clothes she'd washed and hung in the sun to dry, so that they smelled clean and yellowly alive.

The sounds of Amish life became my sounds: the generator's wheeze as it gasped to life for milking; the gossip-hiss of kerosene lamps at dusk; the stark, exalted silence before each meal. The Yoders lived by a steadfast rhythm that was imposed and yet intrinsic all the same, a mother's heartbeat to the baby in the womb. Everything was both sacred and ordinary.

The children were unresentfully obedient. Each cared for the next cared for the next. (I watched nine-year-old Lydia changing Baby Sam's diapers.) Unlike the boys at Ironwood, whom we often had to bludgeon with activities, the Yoders kept themselves happily occupied. They took great glee in simple things: trying to toss a ball so it cleared the barn roof, watching for muskrats down by the slowpoke creek.

Sadie praised my way with the kids, so I tried to explain what Ironwood meant to me. She couldn't fathom how summer—for Amish the period of hardest work—could be frittered away with silly games. She wondered, too, why I'd spend so much time caring for others' children instead of having my own. I argued that I could influence nine hundred kids, not just nine, but the rinky-dink sound of "influence" gave me pause. Did camp mold kids as the Amish did? Should we?

I shared a bed with Jakie, in a room with Ezra, Dan, and

Davey, too. The room's air settled with a skintight coziness not unlike that in an Ironwood cabin. Late at night, Jakie often rolled and reached out for me, mumbling dreamy Dutch concerns into my neck. I'd roll him back but stroke his neck until he stopped.

We were bonded by our odysseys in alien surroundings: mine in Amish country, Jakie's in a growth-spurting body. He was more mature than most college kids I knew—he could milk the herd, drive a plow, guard his siblings—but at the same time so precariously naïve. (Once, when I mentioned a female friend of mine, he asked sincerely, "Have you bred your girlfriend yet?") After evening chores, we often climbed high inside the silo and pretended to get drunk on corn fumes. Our brotherhood was innocent intoxication.

Before my trip, a Harvard friend had criticized the Amish. "It's cruel. Depriving kids who have no choice." But the Yoders didn't strike me as deprived. They were poor in televisions, perhaps, and microwaves, but flush with assets I now sorely covet: kinship, purpose, support.

In October, two days before my planned departure, I asked if I could stay on for a while.

"Took you long enough!" Sadie said. "We hoped you'd ask."

I walked up the road to Gideon Lapp's, where, in an outhouse-like shed by a pond, sat a phone shared by six Amish families. I spun the rotary dial and made arrangements with my landlord, with the dean and registrar at Harvard. I called my mother, who was living in Arizona with her third boyfriend in as many years. Once she was satisfied that I didn't plan to convert, Mom seemed glad that I'd found a family, even if she wasn't part of it.

Abner never spoke of the ban. When I raised the subject once, his eyes darkened; he walked off to grease the fifth wheel on his wagon.

It was Sadie who would talk more openly. She had nursed me with her homemade liniments, and we were hitched by that inevitable lifeline that ties those in pain to those who don't avert their eyes. Evenings, as she sewed organdy *Kapps* for her daughters or mended seams on Abner's good *Mutze,* she'd explain the rationale for Amish shunning.

"It's like your finger," she said once when she saw me rubbing my scar. "If we hadn't treated that right away, it might've got infected and spread to your whole body. The *Ordnung*—our set of Amish rules—that's like a poultice to make the small wounds heal quick. If that don't work, you need medicine that's more *fressende,* that's got some bite. That's the ban. If your finger'd got gangrene, wouldn't you amputate to save the rest? Christ says you've got to cut off the hand if it offends the body."

"That's awfully harsh," I said. "Amputation?"

"Well, you get two chances to come right before you're banned. And even later, if you confess, you're *always* welcome back."

Meidung was strict, Sadie admitted, but also technical, limited. She couldn't ride in a car with someone under the ban, or eat at his table, or accept money from his hand. But if he handed money to a third person who then handed it to her, that was okay. Or he could lay the money on a table, and she could take it. Someone in the ban could even live in the same house as his family. If there were children who were not yet baptized church members, the banned could eat with them at a separate table.

When a shunned person was in dire need, the *Ordnung* dictated that members come to his aid. "Like Daed's cousin," Sadie said. "He was in the ban, but when his barn got hit by lightning we all helped him raise another. We just can't *accept* help from someone in the ban."

"Isn't it hard? Having to watch yourself all the time?"

"*Nee,*" she said. "In our way it's *easier* to be good—you know just where the lines are drawn."

Shortly after New Year's, the frisky mood in the Yoder house foundered. Abner and Sadie kept their bedroom door closed for a span of evenings. Hard Dutch whispers spoiled the peace.

I assumed that I'd overstayed my welcome. We'd been briefly hobbled by a misunderstanding in October, which I thought was successfully healed. But they must still have worried about my effect on the kids.

Saturday night, after I'd bathed and changed clothes, I took Abner aside and offered to leave. This had been a great experience, I told him. Unforgettable. But I could see I was causing too much strain.

Sadie was warming water on the stove. Abner beckoned her, and the three of us sat down.

"Maem, Jeremy thinks he's causing us our problems," Abner said.

"Oh, no! It's wonderful having you. To be honest, you're the one happy thing just now."

Sadie explained that her sister Beulah, who lived near Quarryville, was having trouble in her church district. Her husband Jonas had been put under a temporary ban, and Beulah herself was expected to avoid him.

"Her own husband?"

"Spiritual love comes before earthly love," Sadie said. "But it's the hardest test. That's why she's struggling."

The next day was an "off" Sunday. (The Amish attend church every other week.) Despite a savage chill, Sadie woke early to steep tea from vervain, chamomile, and catnip. The brew relieved stress. She'd bring it to her sister.

"Roll a coal away from the fire," she said, stoking the woodstove, "and soon enough it'll turn cold. The same happens to those who leave the church. I've got to help Beulah keep Christ's heat inside her."

When her tea was done Sadie wrapped the jug in a woolen shawl and shawled herself, too, for the long carriage ride. I could hear the wind outside, pummeling the leafless trees. Hoarfrost choked the light from windowpanes. And however dour and cruel I had once considered shunning, I couldn't help but think as Sadie left: Yes, keep Beulah warm, keep her inside.

FOUR

—◄O►—

First night at Ironwood was cookouts. Rather than subject kids to the hurly-burly dining hall—which rookie nerves would escalate to anarchy—we split into cabin groups and cooked outdoors. From the kitchen, each group fetched hot dogs (or, for vegetarians, tofu Not Dogs), marshmallows, juice, potato chips. Then they trooped to their cabins and built fires, relishing the quaint hobo charm.

As senior staff, Charlie and I roved the cabin area. Like anthropologists studying jungle tribes, we assessed camper personalities. One boy might squat on his haunches through the evening, resisting the decline to grubbiness; another might blackface himself with soot. You could learn startling amounts from a wiener roast. Who volunteered to gather birch bark for kindling? Who shared his stick? Who played with fire?

The cabins were named after Vermont mountains, from smaller local hills for the younger kids up to the high peaks for the fourteen-year-olds. Max was assigned to Mansfield, the tallest. I was saving it—saving him—for last.

Each cabin was a step into memory. Morgan Peak: my nights as an owl-spooked neophyte; Stratton: where I learned to splice a rope. At other camps, I'd heard, boys carved their names on bunk posts, claiming ownership by graffiti. But at Ironwood, my claim was *alive*. Ruff had told me it would be so. "You're part of something larger than yourself," he said, the day I became a counselor. "Sounds corny, but it's true. In the army, they used to tell us we weren't fighting for ourselves, or for our unit, or the whole dang infantry; we were fighting for every man who ever wore this uniform, and for every other man who someday might."

The Amish church provides a better analogy. *Gemee,* they call it, meaning congregation, fellowship—the timeless church that began with God's creation and that after the end of days will endure. It's each Amishman's duty, through right living and faith, to embody that true church on earth.

That's what Ruff meant: a holy stewardship. And if I felt ambivalence about Ruff's own stewardship, I buried it deep beneath my love.

I pinballed among the cabins, amassing my dinner piecemeal. A hot dog here, a Sierra Cup of bug juice there. By the time I'd visited Shrewsbury and Killington and Camel's Hump, I was sugar-rushed and bloated, short of breath.

It was fully dark now, the sky sulky and clotted with clouds. Two squirrels shrieked from rival mapletops. From the lake nudged a soft black breeze.

I homed in on Mansfield by the embers of its fire, and by the loonlike sound of laughs scuffing the lake. Mansfield was built on the water, where the lake pinched to a teardrop cove. Like all Ironwood cabins, it featured one open side—in this case the entire front. Wide wooden steps dropped to a deck on concrete pilings, providing full view of the inlet.

"I was an Abercrombie & Fitch model for their last catalogue," I heard as I ghost-stepped through the entrance. Recognizing Simon's flat Maine *a*'s, I paused to eavesdrop undetected.

"I ran the Boston Marathon in under three hours. And, um, let's see . . . oh, yeah, I'm completely unticklish."

"Number three," came an overweening voice. "Number three's the lie. Everyone's ticklish."

"That what he wants you to think, dorkus. Which means it's not. It's gotta be one or two."

"Yeah," a third boy said. "I mean, no offense, but I'm not sure you're, like, model material?"

"Which is it? Come on, Simon. Tell!"

I remember Ruff explaining the game on my own first night at camp, and the hush when I said, "My father got crushed to death." Years later, as a floundering novice counselor, I, too, began with Truth. Simon was my camper then, squeak-voiced and shivery, barely able to open his mouth. But I coaxed him into playing, and he shucked his stage fright, and now just look at him!

"All right," he said. "You guys are way too smart. I did finish the marathon, in two hours and fifty-eight minutes. And—as you'll find out the hard way if you test me—I'm truly not ticklish. I've never even ordered anything from A & F."

A flurry of *duh*s and *told you so*s.

"I'm sure," someone said. "Abercrombie & Fitch. More like Eversnobby & Bitch."

Simon glowered. "What did I say about cuss words?"

"Oops. I meant Eversnobby & *Snitch*."

Wait. Yes. Listen close. It was Max, bullshit detector set on high. His sass drew me closer, magnetlike.

"Jeremy!" Simon called. He was wearing his Williams College T-shirt, a naïve, exuberant shade of purple. His flyaway hair sprung alert. "Guys, have you met Jeremy? The assistant director?"

Two or three kids tendered polite hellos. Others shrugged and looked footward, which I took as a compliment: this was the standard greeting for their own.

"Telling some good ones?" I asked.

"Not good enough, apparently," Simon said.

The kids sprawled on the stairs and deck, their faces lit by a kerosene lantern. Three or four I recognized from previous summers, but the rest were new; I hadn't learned their names. On the bottom step sat Cornelio, Simon's co-counselor, a Peruvian mountaineer Charlie had hired to run our ropes course. His only English was rock-climbing terminology.

I pretended attention to all of them, but my eyes focused immediately on Max; I couldn't dodge the miracle of his presence.

He sat hunched against a railing post, knees to chest, his goofy outsized feet like a mistake of foreshortening. His BLAH BLAH BLAH cap was twisted rakishly.

"Jeremy," he said. "Check out this rigorous cast."

"Rigorous?"

"Kick-butt. The bomb."

He hoisted his arm like a trophy. Even in the kerosene lamp's dim glow, the cast shone a gaudy, highlighter-pen yellow.

"It's perfect," I said, claiming a spot beside him. "Now you won't even need a flashlight."

"I know. And the doc said it's totally unbreakable." He bonked the cast on the rough-cut planks.

"Ow," I said. "Doesn't that hurt?"

"Nope, I'm feeling zero pain. They make great 'aspirin' up here."

It wasn't just the cast, but Max himself who seemed to fluoresce. He had the same jester gleam as Jakie Yoder.

"People signing it?" I asked.

"Yeah, here. Plenty of room." He whipped a Magic Marker from his pocket, uncapped it with his teeth and forked it over.

I gripped his arm, surprised by its heft, and balanced it across my knee. The fiberglass was crowded with scribbles. "Skateboarding is not a crime!" Below that, a smiley-faced swine labeled "Pig," followed by hyperbolic boy-scrawl: "You're the coolest!" "Main Man Max." "Tough break for the toughest dude."

I hovered, stumped, recalling the stress of junior-high yearbook signing. You had to strike a balance between gushy and cool. There was the pressure of indelibility.

I glanced at Max's rangy frame, the whippet legs up to the snip of waist. Still peeking above his jeans were my Jockeys, now grimed with charcoal beyond memory of whiteness. "For Max," I wrote, pinching the letters to fit the free space near his wrist. "We can share everything. Jeremy." I went back to underline *everything,* but my hand slipped. The word got half crossed out.

"All right," Simon said. "Whose turn?"

"I think I was next," said a mousy camper. He had tar-colored hair and Groucho Marx eyebrows; he looked adorably fourteen going on forty.

"Okay. Hush up. Listen to Eli."

Aha! I thought, one of the Elis. This summer's roster showed four kids with that name, plus three Jonahs, three Jacobs, and a Noah. Their hippie parents, as they aged, had turned oddly biblical, making the camper list read like an Amish roll call. The boys' last names, though, betrayed their worldly, new-millennium loyalties. Jonah McGinty-Katz, Sol Rodriguez-Kennington. The great melting pot approached meltdown.

Eli touched the bridge of his nose as if pushing up invisible eyeglasses. "Okay. My grandfather is in a wax museum in Israel. That's number one."

"A wax museum?" interrupted Max.

"Yeah, where they have life-sized figures, but, like, made of wax?"

Max snorted. "That's a major claim to fame."

Other kids tittered, following his lead. There was an under-the-breath snicker about earwax.

"Hey," Simon warned. "Remember what I said about respect?" His voice cracked on the last syllable. But it worked. The cabin quieted.

"Number two," Eli said, "I'm an uncle. And three . . . um . . ."

The key, of course, was turning the lie to your advantage, in the same way that a smart job applicant, asked to confess a weakness, will say, "I work too hard" or "I'm bad at taking praise." The classic lie, heard in every camper game, was "I've never gone past second base with a girl"—which set up boasts of acrobatic conquests.

The best Eli could devise was, "This is my first time at summer camp."

For ten long seconds no one talked. What fun is there in chasing crippled prey?

Then a wiry redhead who sat on the deck rail, his butt

perilously cantilevered, spoke up. This was Dylan Shallot, a cat-faced fourth-year camper who tested my pacifist tendencies. "Let's see," he mocked, scratching his scalp cartoonishly. "I'm gonna take a wild guess here. I think you're lying about never having been to camp."

Eli frowned. The stitch between his woolly eyebrows deepened. "How'd you know?"

"Just a hunch. And maybe the fact that your T-shirt says Camp Chittenden!"

With horror, Eli looked down at his chest. A want-to-vanish look eclipsed his eyes.

A boy choir of derision sang out. "Right on his shirt!" "Sure fooled us!" "Retardo!"

Simon, who'd already played the heavy more times than a nineteen-year-old can stomach, didn't stop them. Cornelio sat mute, uncomprehending. I knew it was up to me.

But the reproach hadn't made it halfway up my throat when I heard, "Cool it. You're the ones who sound retarded. *Hee hee hee*. Like freakin' guinea pigs."

It was Max, a swooping superhero. Max, who moments earlier had teased Eli himself, but who now, seeing how badly skewed were the odds, stood up for the cowering underdog.

"Who made *you* king?" Dylan tried lamely, but the cabin silenced in deference to Max.

Eli's jaw, blubbery with quivering, firmed into a grateful smile. And Max, who could have gloated, instead gazed across the lake, as if refusing to rubberneck at a car crash.

"Max," Simon said, "since you've got the floor, why don't you go ahead with your turn?"

"He has to," said Eli. "He's the only one left."

It made sense that Max had finagled the anchor spot, so he could trump everyone else. With the index finger of his left hand he rubbed his fresh cast, as if summoning a genie from a lamp.

"Numero uno," he said. "I once skated ten blocks down the middle of Fifth Avenue."

He paused to let us picture the daredevilry. I envisioned applauding doormen, fuming cabbies.

"Two: My next-door neighbors are junkies."

"Wait," Eli asked, "what's a junkie?"

"God, do you know anything?" Dylan said, his squint-eyes thin as razor blades. "Junkies. You know, like homelessers."

I saw Max stifle a burp of laugh. "Actually, Dylan, a junkie is a heroin addict. Now can I finish?"

Dylan sniffed, imperious in defeat.

"Okay," Max said. "Watch the spinning wheel . . . round and round she goes; where she'll stop, nobody knows. Numerico trois: My best friend back home is gay."

The word zapped like an electric shock. Puzzlement pulsed through the group.

"That's it," Max said, his shrug belied by the nervy grin that curled his lips.

I was mystified by his final choice. And staggered. In the combustible, testosterone-fueled world of summer camp, every spark of homosexuality must be damped. Most boys intuit this. Even the schoolyard taunt of "faggot" is little used at camp, its utterance too inflammatory.

But here was Max, tossing a match.

The other boys hashed out a debate. Dylan argued that Max wouldn't make his last statement the lie, because that was the most expected gambit. But what about reverse psychology? asked Simon.

I studied Max for a reaction, but he remained poker-faced. He flicked errant bangs from his forehead, and they fell back, covering his eyes. He tried again—flick, fall; flick, fall—the gesture metronomic and mesmerizing.

Finally, a molasses-voiced Georgian named Toby surmised that statement number two was the lie. "If they're heroin addicts," he drawled, "wouldn't they keep it private? How would Max have seen them doing it?"

The logic was less than infallible, but the cabin was itchy to be done. "Number two," they ventured, and sought confirmation.

"Let me get this right," Max said. "You think it's a lie that my neighbors are junkies. Which means you think it's true that I skated down Fifth Avenue, and that Bryce, my best friend, is gay?"

His peers nodded. They were sticking by their choice.

Like a schoolteacher handing back an exam the class has bombed, Max shook his head with rueful condescension. "What a bunch of mastoids. You'd have to be freakin' crazy to skate down Fifth Avenue."

He laughed—a single haughty cackle—and a dumbfounded quiet overcame us. A poplar branch yawned in the wind. Below the deck, fish rose to the lake's dark surface with tiny burps that sounded our disbelief.

The kids questioned Max about his neighbors. As he told them of the squatters in the building next door who lounged on its needle-strewn roof, what I longed to ask was how he had met Bryce. Did he tease Bryce as he teased me? Were they in love?

After the hubbub subsided, I caught Max, turned away from the kerosene lamplight, dry-gulping a dose of painkiller; it had been six short hours since his fracture. I wanted to help the kid to his bunk and tuck him in, to release him from the need to entertain. I knew there must be a more private, dreamy yolk of Max concealed within that hardened shell. (A month before, I'd witnessed something in Lancaster County that made me see all boys as potentially double-faced. I squelched the memory of heavy metal, screeching tires.)

The other boys, though, were stoked. When Simon gave the order to clean their mess kits and brush their teeth, a collective whine of protest rose against him.

"All right, all right. What do you guys want to do?"

"Poker?" suggested Toby with good-old-boy gusto.

"Strip poker?" Dylan joked, but no one laughed.

Simon raised the wick on the sputtering Coleman lantern. "If you can't come up with anything better than cards, it's definitely time for bed."

"Maybe Jeremy has an idea," said Eli. "You know any ghost stories or something?"

I'd been keeping a purposely low profile, not wanting to step on Simon's toes (just as Ruff, though he must still have burned to visit camp, now stayed away all but one day each summer).

"I never had my turn at Truth," I said.

"Yes!" said Eli. "You have to. It's only fair."

"Let Jeremy go," came a salvo of support.

Simon flashed me a take-it-it's-all-yours look.

"Okay," I said, "give me a sec to think." I rubbed my palms together, miming the friction of my mind's engine in gear. It had been ten months since I'd basked in boys' attention. The thrill of performance hummed in my marrow.

"I once lived for six months without electricity" was my standard opener—a springboard for stories about the Amish. A variation was to say, "I had my finger crushed by a twelve-hundred-pound Belgian," and then coyly hide my hand until they guessed. Sometimes I used details from growing up an army brat, like having once steered an armored tank. Or I confessed show-and-tell talents I could legitimately back up: putting a necklace chain up my nose and pulling it out my mouth, playing "You Can't Always Get What You Want" on the harmonica.

I was weighing the options when I glimpsed Max doodling on his cast. He wasn't waiting for me, or anyone. All of a sudden my self-confidence dissolved to panic. Compared to his, my stories seemed wrung-out.

"Is he gonna go, or what?" Dylan mumbled.

I knew I had to say something, but my brain felt charleyhorsed. "Okay," I managed. "All right. Number one—"

A shave-and-a-haircut knock startled us. Some of the first-time boys, nerves frittered by the night, jumped up to protect themselves. Eli, in reflex, grabbed my knee.

It was only Charlie Moss. He stood at the cabin's entrance, hands behind his back as if hiding a rose bouquet.

"Ho ho ho," he called. "Have you been naughty or nice?"

And as he walked into the soft light, it struck me that there was indeed something Santa Claus-ish about him: the bellow-chested laugh, the endless charisma. Even as a kid his allure had been evident. The first day of our first summer, he stormed into our cabin, seeming to seek attention as a preemptive strike against ridicule. (He was odd-looking, florid-cheeked, munchkin-like.) It worked. The other newcomers and I immediately agreed to his plan of pooling all our contraband candy. "That way," Charlie explained, "if they find it, none of us get in trouble. If it's everyone's, then it's really like it's no one's!" Dutifully we produced our private stashes, which Charlie hid, then disbursed throughout the summer in equal lots. Only at camp's end did we learn that *he* had never ponied up. Arriving empty-handed, he'd charmed us into sharing.

That was Charlie at eleven, and more so now: selfishly selfless. His brashness fit snug with my restraint. Unlike the disposable army kids back home, Charlie was my first true friend. I allowed him to insinuate himself into an imagined future.

"Well?" he asked, his ho-ho-ho an echo in the trees. "Tell me honestly. Have you all behaved?"

"Better than perfect," Dylan said, squirming to peek behind Charlie. "Right, Simon?"

"If you kept your voice down, I'd be more inclined to agree."

Now came other toady testaments. "We're awesome!" "We're the best in camp!"

Charlie brought his hands into view and jiggled a mysterious paper bag. He smiled. "Well, Si? The verdict?"

"Oh, why not," Simon said (as if he could possibly have denied his boss). "They haven't brushed their teeth yet, anyway."

With a conspiratorial "Shhh," Charlie passed out Hershey's bars. The boys gobbled their bounty like rescued shipwreck victims, though they'd been away from home less than a day.

When he got to me, Charlie stopped. "Oh. Jeremy. Didn't realize you were here. I'm not sure I've got an extra. Do you mind?"

"Don't worry," I said. "I didn't want one."

Charlie knew I frowned on his sweet-toothing the kids; we'd had the old debate again this year.

The last boy Charlie came to was Max. "And to you," he said, "Max Connor of East Fifth Street, New York, New York; sacrificial lamb to the gods of liability insurance; I hereby bestow *two* medicinal chocolate bars."

Max went bulge-eyed. I, too, was caught off-guard; that afternoon Charlie had barely noticed him. But this was vintage Charlie. After the parents left, he must have boned up on Max's file.

Max, clearly humored by Charlie's routine, accepted the candy bars. He stored one under the tent-space of his knees, then fumbled to unwrap the other, one-handed.

"Here," Charlie said, "how thoughtless of me." He took back the chocolate, tore off the foil, and broke it into bite-sized rectangles.

"Thanks," said Max through an immediately chock-full mouth, the brown mush gunking his braces.

"You know," Charlie said, settling Indian-style between Max and me on the deck, "I broke my arm once, too. My first year in college. Want to hear?"

The campers inched closer. They would have jumped off a friggin' bridge if Charlie asked them.

"Spring break ski trip. My buddies and I drove all the way to Utah, forty-some hours straight, just piss stops and gas. It's late afternoon when we get there, but we head up to our campsite anyway, way way up in the backcountry, powder to our hips. Then it's dark, and it starts snowing hard. We can't see squat, but we've got to pitch our tents.

"My friend Mike goes off to take a piss and suddenly I hear him screaming. I run down to see what's up—you know, my EMT training. Next thing I know, *I'm* falling down, twenty, thirty feet? Flapping my arms like if I try hard I could fly."

Charlie flailed to dramatize the story; Max ducked to evade his threshing arms. In the shift, he inadvertently kicked his spare Hershey's bar. It plummeted from the deck to the ground.

"Hey, Max," I said. "Your candy bar."

He nodded but didn't really seem to hear. No one did.

"Max?" I tried again.

No response.

"I'll get it for you," I said.

As I slunk out and down below the cabin, I heard Charlie resume his tale. I couldn't make out the details, but imagined them well enough: avalanches and near-escapes and breathless derring-do, lions and tigers and bears. He'd probably made up 90 percent of it.

I ducked into the crawl space between the cabin and the hill. A startled bat winged inches from my head. Then another, and an angry third.

I made my way underneath the deck, gauging with gut sense where Max would be above. When I hit the spot, I bent down and found the Hershey's bar, which had landed only inches from the lake. It was slimed with algae, not worth rescuing.

I looked up again blindly to the deck. I rubbed my knuckles on the unplaned lumber, the way Max had rubbed his yellow cast. All that parted us was this hairsbreadth, splintery inch—as thinkable and as foolish as a wish.

FIVE

◄○►

Had there been campers like Max before? Probably. There must have been, but I hadn't seen them. Not that way.

Teenagers' bodies are instruments they're just learning to play—all trombone-slide, reed-squeak awkwardness. And just as one's affection for a junior-high orchestra has less to do with its musicality than its guilelessness, I was drawn to boys without exactly *wanting* them. My attraction was that of anyone who works with kids: a blood-thick, save-them-from-drowning passion. What schoolteacher isn't stirred in some part by desire? What soccer coach—what parent—isn't? To put up with the endless rigors of nurturing, you have to be at least a little smitten.

But sex? No. Definitely not with kids. To be honest, not with hardly anyone. There had been three or four women in college; a man, just once, furtively. In the jungle of desire, I played dead.

Campers tried to fix me up with their older sisters, and sometimes even with their single moms. I laughed their suggestions away. Like someone nearsighted who can only view his own face bespectacled, I couldn't see myself but through the lens of abstinence.

Sadie Yoder teased I'd be a bare-chinned old man (Amishmen grow beards only when married), but I didn't suffer any sense of lack. I was happily wed to Ironwood. Even in winter, camp centered me. Busy as I was with Harvard and trips to Lancaster, I corresponded with scores of campers. I cooked dinner when they passed through Cambridge, treated them to Celtics games

49

and ice cream. When kids sought advice about pimple control or proms, I was the one to whom they turned.

I couldn't imagine deriving as much satisfaction from a single mate as from a swarm of devoted, clinging boys. Their love is so urgent and unencumbered. They haven't yet learned the shame of asking for it.

And then Max.

It wasn't lust, exactly, not at first (my body slow as ever on the uptake), but a much purer—and more terrifying—captivation. I might have missed him, as I'd surely overlooked previous boys, if my blinders hadn't so recently been stripped.

In late May, I'd driven to Pennsylvania for my final research trip of the school year. I spent Saturday in Elizabethtown, at the Young Center for the Study of Anabaptist and Pietist Groups, poring through archives, taking notes. That night I stayed at a B & B in Smoketown, then met Sunday with an ex-Amishwoman named Emma Riehl. (Emma, who drove a red Mustang to her JCPenney job, was what I think of as kid-in-a-candy-shop ex-Amish; I always wonder, when I meet these former faithful: Do their heaps of new conveniences make them content at last, or is ownership a poor substitute for belonging?)

Our interview finished earlier than expected, so I decided to visit the Yoders in Peach Bottom. I hadn't seen them in fully a year. Twice I'd planned to stop by, but the first time Sadie was in labor with her tenth child, and the next they'd gone to a funeral in Ohio. This was my last chance to see them before camp. I missed them, and missed who I was when I was with them.

On the way back I thought I'd pass through Quarryville, in hopes of running into Beulah Glick. In the three years since our Plain & Fancy breakfast, I'd heard from Beulah half a dozen times. Her husband, she wrote, rebelled even more once he was shunned, buying a phone, a VCR, a microwave; Beulah kept her old wood cookstove. She joined a Mennonite church, but Jonas refused to come along. Resentment festered. And loneliness, always the loneliness. Some mornings, she found herself cooking snitz pies by the dozen, as though readying to host a quilting frolic; then at noon, when no one came, she threw them out.

I longed to write back, to offer comfort. Beulah said not to; Jonas wouldn't stand for another man "meddling." Obviously, then, I couldn't visit, either. But I could drive into one-horse Quarryville, stop in at shops and grocery stores, tempting fate to toss us together.

This was my equivocating balance: loyal both to the shunner and the shunned. I couldn't tell Sadie about Beulah, or vice versa. Neither sister knew that I knew the other.

I headed south on Route 272. The first rain in weeks had sprinkled overnight; in the fields new corn swaggered, jaunty. Roadside stands brimmed with early strawberries. In a hunch that Sadie might have baked a fresh pie, I stopped at a Turkey Hill Minit Market for some ice cream.

I bought a gallon of vanilla and came out just as a jacked-up 4x4 burned to a stop. Two teenagers, a boy and girl, jittered in the cab to a wham of Guns N' Roses that shook the truck's frame. They looked like mall rats gone rabid: tawdry anger.

In the truck bed, another couple popped a Budweiser can, the girl's laughter frizzy as she sipped. She had the wide, freebie eyes of a girl scared to be dumped, and maraschino lipstick, slightly smeared. Her beau—in a Phillies cap and a greasy jeans jacket— claimed the beer from her and downed a sloppy chug. She lapped the errant dribbles from his fingers.

"Nice boys don't play rock and roll," screeched the radio.

The guy hopped out and unhooked the gas hose. His hand on the nozzle was immense. As he turned to pump, his profile looked familiar. Could he have been an Ironwood alum? I flipped a mental yearbook of past campers. Or maybe he was the kid brother of that counselor—what was his name?—the one whose parents moved to Lancaster.

The girlfriend now also climbed out. In an amorously feral maneuver, the boy doffed his cap and head-butted her shoulder. Then he snorted and kissed her hard and deep.

I looked closer. My throat stung. It was Jakie. I hid my face and hurried to the car.

I knew about *rumschpringa,* the "running around" period for Amish youth before baptism. They join a "gang" of Amish friends for Sunday "hoedowns." Some shingle their hair, install radios in their buggies. I'd heard of Amish teens driving cars.

But Jakie? Sweet softhearted Jakie? With his tongue down this "English" girl's throat?

The last time I'd seen him, two months shy of sixteen, he seemed just the same old tender boy—loopy, sure, but categorically Amish. We played Dutch Blitz and Dare Base with his siblings. How could he have turned so quickly from that to this?

As I studied him more, though, through my dusty windshield, I could see the Amishness still about him. His pants: suspendered Amish broadfalls. And his posture: deferential, unprotected. I wondered how long he could be both things at once, and when, like his aunt Beulah, he'd have to choose.

Jakie capped the tank and paid for the gas. Then he helped his girl into the truck bed. She lit a cigarette and sucked a gaudy drag, then pulled Jakie close to "shotgun," recycling the smoke into his mouth.

Jakie blinked with a stunned look of glee as he swallowed. I swallowed, too. How would it feel?

The driver cranked the heavy metal two notches louder, then honked and squealed out onto the road. The engine's backfire made me flinch.

I couldn't bring myself to drive on to Peach Bottom. What would I say to Sadie and Abner? I'd lost my energy for finding Beulah, too. I pointed the car north and retreated.

In Lancaster I noticed the gluey ice cream, puddling on the passenger floorboard. I pulled over and ditched it in a Dumpster. Did every boy have a secret self inside? Did I?

SIX

In the morning we woke to blue-lip chill; a rainless cold front had stealthed past after the cookouts. This was my favorite summer weather—liquid air, goose-bumpy breeze—as if the earth thumbed its nose at global warming.

In my counseling days, I'd have leapt from my bunk. "Get up!" I'd call to the kids as I bobbed push-ups. "If you're not up when I hit ten, *you'll* give me ten." It was militaristic but not at all unfair, because I never asked for more than I did myself. *Always lead from the front,* Ruff had taught us. *You have to earn your right to be stern.*

But now, as assistant director, I slept alone. My army-surplus tent was pitched in a no-man's-land above the infirmary. I found T-shirt and pants and sluggishly dressed in my sleeping bag's warm luxury.

Once clothed, I hiked a private path to the Lodge. The just-risen sun shot down through beads of dew, prisming light among the trees. The sky gleamed the kind of bionic, stainless blue that makes people believe there's a heaven. And in that brisk lambency I found myself gaining clarity about the day before. I always discounted opening day to staffers: all norms were waived, all bets off. Now I just had to believe my rhetoric. After a year of single life in the city, inundation with boys excited but terrified me. Max, I decided, was only a lightning rod I had raised to redirect that terror. He was a kid—cute, alluring, whip-smart—but still, just a kid after all.

Breakfast's bustle helped confirm my perspective. A dozen disasters-in-the-making caught my eye: a slick of spilled OJ, a brewing brawl. With insectlike, multifocused vision I watched the wonderful disarray that was camp and remembered that I could handle it. I had to. Who had time for nerve attacks?

Ken Krueger, the head cook, flustered up to me with basket-case eyes. The bread man, he said, had screwed up Ken's order and delivered only two stinking loaves. How could he make sandwiches for lunch? One look around provided inspiration. Use leftover pancakes from breakfast, I proposed. Tell the kids it's tradition. Eureka!

Teddy Trimble, a baby-faced apprentice counselor, brought a hyperventilating twelve-year-old before me. The boy explained that this morning, on opening his trunk, expecting work boots, swimsuit, et cetera, he found halter tops and a bagful of barrettes. I deduced that the trunk belonged to his little sister, who'd started soccer camp in New Hampshire yesterday. A call to that camp's director, another to UPS, and the kid ran back, grinning, to his Wheaties.

That was the wisdom they paid me for: the King Solomon of summer camp.

In the far corner where the older boys sat, I saw Max and his Mansfield compatriots. Already they looked like a unit. All but Eli wore the same clothes as the previous night, rumpled and sooty, smeared with mud. Toby shoveled cereal into improbably rodent cheeks. On a banana's mock telephone, Dylan yakked.

Max presided at the head of the table, spoon-conducting this silly symphony. But from this distance I felt only an avuncular, surface warmth, not the deep-tissue incineration I'd feared.

The Lodge was a drafty barnlike structure with a high ceiling that amplified sound. Lighting was provided by three "chandeliers"—antique wagon wheels, adorned with low-watt bulbs. On the walls hung rattletrap mementos: rust-riddled sap buckets unearthed from nearby woods; "misery whips" (big-toothed, two-man crosscut saws). There were laminated maps of the region, stickpinned at sites of interest. An IRONWOOD banner, the old-money green of Ruff's beloved Dartmouth. And on the mantel of the stately granite hearth, a portrait of the patriarch himself.

When the tables were cleared, the campers—mouths no longer occupied by food—devoted themselves fully to noisemaking. The decibel level surged to bughouse proportions. Charlie, mounting the stage in front of the fireplace, attempted to quiet the masses. Rather than shout or wave, he stood still.

At first, no one noticed. Some boys arm-wrestled on the oatmealy tables. Others drumrolled knuckles, stomped feet.

Through it all, Charlie maintained his pose: stiff, silent, imperturbable. His steady-state presence neutralized the energy. One table of boys saw him and abashed themselves to quiet. Then the next table saw the first and shut their mouths. More and more, till no one dared to cough.

When it was so quiet that I could hear, through the adjacent kitchen's wall, the walk-in refrigerator's hum, Charlie made a show of checking his watch. "Thirty-seven seconds," he said. "Not bad. But from now on, anything more than fifteen, I'll be annoyed. Should we make a deal? I won't waste your time standing here unless I have something important to say. Please don't waste mine, making me wait. Agreed?"

A hundred boys nodded their heads as one.

"Good. Now a few other basics."

Charlie explained the grounds on which a camper could be sent home: fighting, stealing, destroying property. He laid out the laws about weekly rotating chores, scheduling, fire procedures, mail. Then his voice shifted, plumbing the lower depth of his octave, and I knew it was time for the tree speech.

"Yesterday," he began, "we were in a hundred different homes, leading a hundred lives. Now we're here, all together. Some of us have been before; others are new. But I like to say that we all belong to Ironwood, and Ironwood belongs to all of us. Like anything that belongs to you, you have to take care of it. That means taking care of one another.

"Think about trees. Each has its own roots and trunk. But it's also part of something bigger: the forest. The trees shelter each other. The leaves from one fall to the ground beneath another, and turn into mulch to help it grow.

"Remember, our camp's named for a tree. The technical name is hop hornbeam, but the locals call it ironwood. It's not the biggest. Maples are bigger. Ash, oak, spruce. Actually, ironwoods are scrappy. But it's just about the strongest tree there is. They use it for ax handles and baseball bats.

"And you know why it's so strong? Because when a storm comes up, does an ironwood resist with all its might? No, it bends. It knows that as long as its roots are secure, then when the storm's passed, it'll spring up tall again.

"That's how I hope we can be here. We don't always have to fight for our way. We should never be afraid to bend a bit."

This was Ironwood's *Gelassenheit*—a willingness to yield—but unlike the Amish version, our creed went unenforced. We had no punishment, no castaways.

"Lastly," Charlie said, "I want you to know that you can always talk to me, about anything, no matter what."

He paused, peering out across the boys, and I'm sure each felt that Charlie looked only at him. He lifted his jaw, canted it just so—the exact expression worn by Ruff in his portrait.

I reeled with a hot, familiar anger. *I* wanted to be the one addressing the boys with this time-honored introduction. Who believed it—who *lived* it—more than I?

But Ruff's gaze pierced my bubble of entitlement. (The portrait had been unveiled when Ruff retired, the very day of Charlie's induction as director.) The artist had captured Ruff's enigma perfectly. He seemed at once to be looking directly in your eyes, and also past you into some unknowable distance. Did his scant smile signal judgment or support?

Charlie led a rendition of the camp song, pointing to a poster board on which the words were Magic Markered. His boostering tenor held up all the rest: *Roots firm in the ground, Ironwood. Toughest tree around, Ironwood. . . .*

"All right," he said when the song was done. "Just one more

bit of business and we'll get on with the day. You've all met Caroline. She's got some health matters to discuss."

Caroline bounded coltishly onto the stage. She wore her father's vintage U.S. Navy shirt (their name—McManus—sewn on the pocket), and her Red Sox hat at a gangsta-rapper angle. Her cheeks were catalytically flushed.

"To continue Charlie's tree metaphor," she said, "you guys ever heard of Dutch elm disease?"

A half-dozen scattered hands were raised.

"Yup," she said, "it's a really nasty fungus. Came into this country a few years ago, starting with one little tree, and then, like that"—she snapped—"almost every elm got sick and died."

I could see where she was going, and it tickled me. Not having been raised at Ironwood as we had, Caroline cultured an irreverence for Charlie's Moses-on-Sinai act.

"As Charlie said, people are like trees. And living in close quarters, we're susceptible. I don't want some Dutch ironwood disease to kill us all."

She bared imaginary fangs, gnarled her fingers into claws, and the campers guffawed at her mock horror. But the need for health control was no joke. Last summer, impetigo had hopscotched among the cabins, and by season's end a stomach bug ran rampant. The American Camping Association threatened to revoke accreditation.

"Here's another way of putting it," Caroline said. "You've all heard 'One rotten apple spoils the basket'? Okay, Ken, can you bring me the basket?"

Ken Krueger appeared with a tub of Granny Smiths.

"Great. Thanks. All right, let's say . . . how about Dylan comes down with a chest cold." She lobbed an apple to wide-eyed Dylan Shallot. "You got sick last year, didn't you Dylan?"

He conceded as much with a shrug.

"Right. Now shake hands with the two people on either side of you. That's how easily sickness can spread, just by touching."

Dylan followed her orders, and Caroline promptly flung apples to the new victims.

"Now the three of you, do it again: shake hands with two more people near you."

They did so, and Caroline tossed six apples.

Another round brought the number of apple holders to nearly thirty. Two more quick cycles and every camper was tainted.

Caroline held up her basket; only one forlorn-looking fruit remained. "See how fast it spreads? That's why we've got to be extra careful. The most important thing is to keep your hands clean. There are three sinks in the washroom down below and I'll always keep them stocked with soap. And not that we don't trust you, but I'm going to ask for volunteer hand-checkers at every meal. They're going to inspect your hands, and if they're not pink and wet and clean, you're going to be turned away. It's pretty simple: no washy, no eaty. Let's all try saying that together."

She cupped her ear with vaudeville exaggeration, but the response was mostly insolent snuffs.

"Can't hear you," she said. "Try again."

This time, with only one or two dissenters, the group bleated, "No washy, no eaty."

"Very good. Thanks for your indulgence. And now, on the way to first activity, enjoy your last unclean culinary experience of the summer. Ready? Gentlemen, eat your apples!"

Amid a crunching dissonance, the boys herded out.

It was a crackerjack performance, and I congratulated myself for recruiting Caroline. I'd spotted her four years ago at Harvard, when I arrived early one afternoon for my Moral Reasoning course and found the classroom occupied. This willowy woman in an umpire's mask adjudicated a rowdy student competition: who, in the shortest time, using only his mouth, could ensheath a banana in a condom? When she saw me, she dismissed the gathering. But I was curious and quizzed her as she cleaned up. She was studying to be a nurse practitioner, it turned out, and meanwhile trained peer health educators.

I told her about camp, and to call me when she was certified. Two years later, almost to the day, she did. Ironwood gained a nurse; I gained a pal.

Caroline and I were drinking buddies without the need for drink. We shared an affinity for the underdog, mine expressed through allegiance to certain boys at camp, hers as a caregiver, but even more as a Red Sox fan. Her devotion to the perennially near-miss team involved a codependency of hope *(there's always one more strike)* and hopelessness *(the world's unjust; good guys lose)*—a superiority complex based on falling short. This was a hair-shirt legacy from her father, who'd grown up in clannish South Boston. (Fathers were another mutual preoccupation: mine gone, and thus impossible to make proud; hers still living, but impossible to please.)

As Caroline swatted the last apple chomper out the door, I applauded her virtuoso gimmick. "I'm in awe," I said. "If they gave Oscars for camp counseling . . ."

She shrugged it off. "Just an old trick of Dad's."

"You never told me your dad was a camp nurse."

"Oh har har, a nurse, that's just like him. Nah, I think he saw it first in the navy, on his sub. Then he adapted it for his Amway pitch, to motivate salespeople."

"Well, it works. I'm totally motivated. I've got a feeling this is going to be the perfect summer."

Caroline rubbed her chin. "Too late for perfect. That kid. Max."

His name short-circuited my gaiety. "What about him?"

"Don't know, exactly. I tried to call his mother, but the number he gave was disconnected. I figured maybe I'd got it wrong, I'd check his health form, try again. But apparently he doesn't have a form."

"Sure he does. We wouldn't have let him in without one."

"It's not in my files. You mind checking Charlie's?"

"No problem," I said, despite my hurried heart.

Caroline thanked me and made her way to the door, citing parental phone calls to return. At the threshold, she dipped her hand into her basket.

"Forgot," she called. "You didn't get one. Here—"

SEVEN

—◀o▶—

Charlie Moss lived in what we lovingly called the Dump, the tumbledown cabin that Ruff constructed in Ironwood's debut summer. Rooms had been added, torn off, rebuilt. Asphalt shingles covered one wall, cedar shakes patched another, and the rest wore only rain-curled tar paper.

In spite of its decrepitude, the shack commanded the reverence of a reliquary. Campers, barred from entering, spun myths of what transpired within. Even counselors approached reluctantly, as if they hadn't earned the right.

The Dump was also Charlie's office (as once it had been Ruff's). He'd marked it his own by hanging, above the bed, the special ax he'd been awarded as a camper. (My own ax I kept at home in Cambridge.) Sometime in the eighties the Dump had been rigged with electricity; now, on a makeshift desk—a junkyard door spanning two sawhorses—Charlie's PowerBook incongruously hummed. There was a slouching gooseneck lamp, a phone and its blinking message machine. In the corner stood a three-drawered gray steel cabinet containing Ironwood's files.

As director, Charlie reviewed every camper application. I made a point not to, except for those of identified "problem" kids. I liked meeting boys at face value, un-prejudged. But Max's face was a mask I had to peel.

I babied the door shut behind me, switched on the lamp. Pulling open the cabinet's top drawer, I experienced the unspoken titillation known to every ilk of professionally sanctioned snooper. I thumbed through the manila folders and found "Connor" in the alphabetical sequence. But the typed tab read "Connor, Nicholas." There was no file for a Max. I checked the neighboring folders to see if perhaps it had been misdocketed; I searched the *M*'s in case dyslexia was the culprit. Still nothing.

I opened the file for Nicholas:

Name: Max Connor
Age on June 1: 14
Height: 5'5"
Weight: 97 pounds

The form was filled out with what could have been a carpenter's pencil, so smudgy and ponderous were the markings. Some letters were small and tight, others—*p*'s and *l*'s—protruded out of proportion. As I read, I could hear Max's croupy voice.

Have you ever slept away from home before?
Lots of times with my bud Bryce. Does Tompkins Sq. count? (we don't really sleep but we stay all night)

Why do you want to come to camp this summer?
Cause NYC smells completely bogus!! (no really cause Pop and Giz are being nice)

What do you think you can contribute to Ironwood?
Not much now, but if I get rich later (when Amateur Taxidermy goes platinum?) I could send a couple thou

Do you have any questions about the camp program?
Any half pipes in VT? Anywhere to skate?

Oh, Max.

Most kids, even those revealed as cheeky once camp has begun, are cowed by the application's officialdom. Not Max. He wanted us to understand that he saw behind the curtain and that he knew exactly who the wizard was.

Part two was the parents' questionnaire. Here the questions were meatier: "How does your child interact with other children?" "Has he undergone a major change such as a move, a divorce, or illness that is impacting on his life?" "Is there anything else we should know?"

Some parents penned hagiographies, as if petitioning the Nobel committee. Addenda were not unheard of: Xeroxed report cards, soft-focus photographs. Others were more circumspect, responding with monosyllabic confidence.

On Max's form, under the question about interacting with other children, someone had written in perfect Palmer script, "Nicholas gets on fine, unless provoked."

The name discrepancy still unsettled me. It wasn't abnormal for a boy to go by a nickname, but if he did, especially if the alias was so different from the given name, that fact was usually noted by the parent. In Max's materials, there was no acknowledgment, as if one of the selves were a spy or an imposter.

Where parents were supposed to discuss "any major change" in the boy's home life, the respondent had written, "Well, I suppose you should," then crossed it out and added, "Pls. see letter, attached."

The letter had been unstapled from the cover sheet. A tawny stain marred the paper's bottom edge, the frown of half a coffee mug's circumference.

Dear good camp folks,

My name is Sylvia Connor and I'm Nicky's grandmother. If you hear him talking about Giz, that's me (not sure where it came from). His grandfather Jim, my husband, he calls him Pop. We're the ones who found Ironwood for Nicky and who are sending him there this summer, if God willing you'll accept him. The camp was recommended by our friends the Laskys (Neil Lasky used to work with Jim at Maxwell House) who've got a summer cabin up near Ludlow and have heard about Ruff Peterson for years.

Since Nicky's father, our dear son Max, died two years ago, it's been hard on Nicky would be an understatement. We haven't been able to see the boy since the funeral, so it's tough to compare exactly, but from what I can gather he's running kind of wild. There's been problems at school, truancy and insubordination, I'm not sure what all. He broke a kid's nose. He "ran away" (says it was just going to the beach for a few days). But he's a good boy when you get right down to it. Smart, too, if he'd ever let it show.

His mother, well, I try not to speak ill of anyone, but I guess to be kind you'd call her a "case." She seemed full of promise when Max married her, lots of pizzazz and hoping to be a big movie star. But that didn't quite work out, and it's been mostly waitressing and God help me I don't want to know what else. And since Max died, you can't hardly blame her, she's had a pretty rough run of it. Two times that I know of she's been to rehab. Welfare, which they're trying to cut her off of. When we call the apartment there's hardly ever an answer. Sometimes the line's disconnected or the number's changed.

I'm sorry for it, but to be honest, she's not blood and there's only so much we can do. But Nicky, he is our blood, and that's why we're trying to step in here. We don't have much money, but enough to cover the summer for him if we batten down the hatches. He really needs some good friends right about now. We're hoping you can help him.

The thing about his dad dying. Well, truth told, our Max took his own life. Nicky's the one who found him. Can you imagine how a boy must feel?

We live out in Hawaii now, the big island. Jim had his stroke almost four years back, and I'm pretty much at my limit caring for him. We spent one lifetime raising Max, and got our hearts broke hard when he left us. We're too old now to have another kid. It might sound selfish but I'm being honest. So we're sending this form and we can

send a check when you give us word. We don't know
what else in God's name we can do.
Yours sincerely,
Sylvia Connor

I turned the letter over and hid it facedown in the file, as if
that could undo its revelations. All I could think was how I'd
asked, when Simon first brought him to me, if Max's "parents"
had driven him to camp. I gagged on a familiar earthen smell.

And can you blame me then for imagining that I could help
him? That while I couldn't give him back his father, or provide a
mother who would mother him, I might offer him special under-
standing? This was my hubris, my well-intended hope.

I held up Max's part of the application again, rereading
his scrawled responses. With my newly gained knowledge, he
seemed funnier and braver and sadder all at once. I focused on
the line about sleeping over with Bryce. What did they do when
Max stayed over? Was he really just a friend, or something more?
I pictured Bryce as someone older—maybe my age—a neighbor
turned surrogate dad.

But no, that was succumbing to armchair psychology. The
world was surely more complex than that. The only man I'd
been with was a freckled stranger who winked in the Widener
men's room, then waved me into a stall, kneeled, swallowed, and
walked away. In my carrel afterward—filthy-feeling and nervous, as if just *thinking* could still get me caught—I wrestled
with explanations for why I'd done it. Had the man reminded
me of my father? Was he the age my dad had been when he died?
The answers were negative—not the slightest resemblance—
which eased me but left me wondering.

I turned the page over in case I'd missed something. When I
did, I saw that Max had pressed with triplicate force, leaving a
relief of his cocky answers in reverse. I imagined the stipplings
as a set of Braille instructions. If only I knew how to read them.

EIGHT

—◄◦►—

Summer camp is theater—a two-month run with no intermission—and, like any performance, requires great effort to come off as effortless. There were the usual opening-week panics: forgotten flashlights, misplaced footlocker keys. Some campers complained of hunger; others refused to eat. The bed wetters needed help washing their sheets.

Afternoons brought swim tests and boating instruction. As one of the few non-waterfront staffers certified in advanced lifesaving, I was called upon to spell the weary counselors. I also ran the first-aid intensive, which campers took to qualify for overnight hikes. Because his wrist would ground him for at least a month, Max declined to sign up for the course.

When I saw him, he always flashed a cryptic, sidewise smirk that made it seem he had read the file on *me*. He evinced the usual teenage missed-note gawkishness, but some notes, I felt certain, he flubbed on purpose. He bent tones like a snake charmer; I was bewitched.

I longed to probe for clues to his knowingness, but inevitably, when I ran into him, I was rushing. The unfortunate truth of camp's opening week is that the older kids get shunted to the side. Days went by without my finding time to speak with him. We would pass on the road, exchange our three-second enigmatic looks, then off I'd march to the next scraped knee or swamped canoe. His eyes were like mirrored sunglasses: he could see out, but I couldn't see in.

Max wasn't the only one I had trouble connecting with. I'd

promised Simon I would help him organize an "issues night" when kids could discuss their worst fears (he wanted to help boys who felt trapped as he once had), but I missed both the times we arranged for meetings. I barely found a minute to nab Caroline and give her Max's grandmother's number.

Caroline was more overtaxed than I was. By day three, she warded over a past-capacity infirmary; mystery illnesses had stricken a dozen campers. It was homesickness, same as every year. But we indulged the kids, letting them come on their own to the realization that the cure was not rest, but activity.

At the first full staff meeting, a week into camp, Jim Talbot asked to add to the agenda. "Lumber abuse," dictated Ironwood's longtime maintenance man (pronouncing it *lum-bah,* with a tinge of exotic danger). A lanky salt from a family of Maine lobstermen, Jim had a face that you could tell, despite its current tautness, would shrivel like a dried-apple doll. Everything about him, from the highwater Dickies he always wore to the pencil implanted behind his ear, toed the line of frugal practicality.

Jim oversaw Ironwood's lumber supply. Campers were allowed to appropriate wood for "reasonable" projects without asking his permission. For the most part, the honor system worked; kids added bunk shelves, fixed rickety cabin stairs. But tonight Jim had a terse complaint: Some boy had snatched a couple sheets of plywood, not to mention a goodly length of two-by-four—lumber set aside for this summer's building project, a spruce-log shelter up the old logging road. Worst of all, the boy was using the wood for a skateboarding ramp.

I fought a grin: Max, of course. Who else?

"Couldn't even saw it," Jim scoffed. "Broken arm, I guess. So he had other kids working for him. Ordering them around like a crew boss. I told him if he wanted to skateboard, might as well have stayed in the city."

A debate ensued about the appropriateness of Max's project and the meaning of the "Ironwood way." Bill McIndoe—a stumpy pug of a first-year counselor who, like Simon, had once been my camper—couldn't see anything wrong with Max's plan. "Isn't that exactly what we tell them to do? Be creative, take the initiative?"

"Not skateboarding," Jim objected, the word spat out like curdled food. "Hiking, swimming. Natural things."

Then what about the baseball diamond? Bill pointed out. Shouldn't it have remained a hay field? But baseball's the national pastime, came the rebuttal.

Round and round, the argument chased its tail.

Charlie, flexing his directorial muscle, finally strong-armed the men to silence. "Now, what do we know about this kid? Simon, Cornelio—you're his counselors?"

"Yeah," Simon said. "He seems, you know, all right. He's a trouper about his broken wrist, at least."

Cornelio nodded. "Max make me laugh," he managed.

"Okay," said Charlie. "Anyone else?"

A long pause. Tap of pens against idle notebooks, shuffle of feet on the floor.

Finally Doug Rose, the head of campcraft, mentioned that Max had mouthed off yesterday when Doug was teaching knots. Doug was in his sixth summer at camp. He had a fiancée in Baltimore, a newly minted social-work degree, and an SUV that he kept immaculate, as though expecting his two-point-three kids to materialize at any moment. We called him Doug Rose-Colored Glasses. But his view of Max was decidedly darker.

"I was showing the kids how to tie a bowline on a bight," he said, "and Max was all 'Yeah, bite *this,* man.' When I told him to cool it, he got pissy. Next thing I know he's tied a noose and he's hanging himself."

"Wasn't he maybe just kidding?" said Teddy Trimble. His apprentice counselor's walk-on-eggshells voice cracked. "Actually, I thought Max was sort of funny."

"To each his own," Doug said. "Ask me, that kid finds trouble like flies find you know what."

Why didn't I speak on Max's behalf? My voice here would carry decisive weight. But my fondness for him was a noose looped around my own neck; once named, it might tighten, strangle me.

Charlie yawned ostentatiously, as if to indicate impatience with slow learners. "I'm glad that something like this has come up so soon," he said. "You first-year counselors, especially, should pay attention. See, the problem is that nobody has a sense of this kid. You have to remember, he's not a problem, he's a *person*."

I found myself nodding, reminded of what a good counselor Charlie was.

"Now, I just happen," he said, "to have a rapport with Max. I like him and I think he likes me. So I'll go ahead and have a talk with him."

I didn't hear much past "rapport." What rapport? Just because Charlie had given Max two Hershey's bars? Or had they palled around in the intervening week, when I was too busy to notice?

Caroline, who'd sat on the meeting's fringe, preoccupied with ordering supplies, now spoke up belatedly. "Oh shoot, wait, this is Max? Max Connor? I'd meant to bring him up anyway."

Max's wrist was giving him trouble, she explained. The pain wouldn't quit; at night he couldn't sleep. She'd scheduled a follow-up exam for tomorrow. "But I just realized I can't take him," she said. "It's my day off. Maybe you can, Charlie? Kill two birds with one stone?"

But Charlie said he'd be tied up all day with ACA paperwork. He'd have to have his talk with Max later.

"Then I still need a volunteer to go to Rutland."

I might have been a novice auction bidder, so hasty was the hand I raised.

"Jeremy?" said Caroline. "Aren't you off tomorrow, too?"

"Yeah, but I was going into Rutland anyway," I lied. The truth was, I hated days off and rarely took them.

"You sure?"

"If the kid's hurting, he's got to see someone."

"Fine. I'll tell Max to meet you at Van 2 after breakfast."

When the meeting ended I left the Lodge and walked, past the familiar shadow of a quaking aspen, up the path to Lookout Latrine. On the air wafted a caramelized, desserty redolence. It was warmer tonight outside than in.

Humble outhouses were perched throughout camp; every few summers, when their holes filled, we moved them. But Lookout Latrine was permanent. A composting three-seater, it presided above the Lodge to handle all the mealtime calls to nature. I pushed through its saloon-style doors to find Charlie asquat on the first seat.

"Hey," he said brightly, pulling in his feet so I could pass.

I brushed away sawdust, took down my shorts, and sat.

"Not bad for week one," Charlie said.

"No," I said. "I thought it went smooth."

"Some of the new guys are a little starry-eyed. Were we that naïve at nineteen?"

"Sometimes I wish we still were."

I remember how odd it seemed, when I was new to Ironwood, that people could shit together, let alone while chewing the fat. For my first weeks I avoided Lookout Latrine; when I had to go during meals, I trekked to a distant downhill privy. Then one suppertime, my stomach and a bad curry conspired against me. I was lucky to make it as far as Lookout. Just at the loudest moment, Charlie appeared.

"Nine-point-six from the British judge. Eight-point-two from the Russians—you were robbed!"

I laughed nervously, which loosed another torrent.

"Better," he said. "But the technical difficulty was low. Most routines now have doubles and triples." He whipped down his pants, lowered himself, and with astonishing control tooted three farts.

"You're crazy," I said, but his utter lack of shame cancelled my own embarrassment. In the gap between his legs I could see his bare parts and I wanted him, suddenly, to look at mine. I let go another surge.

"That's it," he said, patting my thigh. Goose bumps erupted on my skin. "Friends who shit together, fit together."

And so we did. He was my hide-nothing friend.

But our attempts at friendship beyond camp proved disappointing. We lived too far apart for easy visits, so made do exchanging contentless postcards. Later, in college, we hiked together—Katahdin, the Presidential Range—but without camp's imposed intimacy we weren't sure how to relate.

When Charlie moved to Maine after Princeton, and I began grad school at Harvard, he drove down one winter weekend. At first, it was all hugs and reminiscence. Just seeing him freshened the city air. But after two hours, silence constricted us. We decided to see a movie: car chases, guns.

In the theater bathroom, just before the film's start, I claimed the urinal next to Charlie's. "Remember peeing off the top of Deer's Leap?" I said. "When we didn't know Ruff was standing at the bottom?"

I laughed, but Charlie's face stayed tight. "Keep your voice down," he hissed. "We're in public."

After that, we confined our friendship to the summer. It's not that we drifted apart; at camp the next year, we were thick as thieves. Like a bathing suit tucked away through the long winter months that fits perfectly again the next June, our bond, we discovered, was seasonal.

This disconnection between my lives was troubling. My camp friendships, like Charlie's, didn't translate into the "civilized" world, but neither could I find replacement friendships at home. I would meet someone promising—another student, someone my age—but sipping occasional coffee at Au Bon Pain was not like eating-sleeping-crying for two months. The flame never fired hot enough to solder the joint.

So I studied, e-mailed my favorite campers. I went alone to late-night films. I waited for summer to come again.

The exception was Caroline. After her first camp stint, when we both returned to Cambridge, we made dates at least once a week. We took Vermontish strolls in Mt. Auburn Cemetery, ate dim sum across the river in Chinatown. She took me to a Red Sox–Yankees game at Fenway Park, the nave of her emotional architecture. Sitting in the grandstand, beneath pennants marking all the championships that the Sox had played for but not won, we spoke of dreams and disappointments. I told her about Beulah and the other ex-Amish whose isolation pained me; she drew parallels to the AIDS hospice where she cared for the dying and disowned. For the first time outside of camp, a connection pulled tighter. Our friendship was perennial, evergreen.

But the next fall she moved to Indiana for a job as head nurse at a prep school for boys. (She claimed she hadn't sought out another all-male institution; it was merely the best offer she'd received.) We chatted online and on the phone, but week by week the closeness dissipated. I was sentenced, again, to solitude.

"You don't think something's up?" Charlie was saying.

The dark hemmed in close to the latrine, almost textured. From the Lodge rose a faint hum of plumbing.

"With Caroline?" I said. "Seems normal to me."

"Not distracted? Tonight she barely said a word."

"Just swamped. First-week hypochondria."

"My bet?" Charlie said. "She's hot for someone."

"Oh, come on."

Charlie had a penchant for romantic drama. His own dating history was a star-crossed saga of relationships that burned bright, then imploded. A few summers ago, his then-current girlfriend had visited camp for a weekend. She was Tunisian and didn't speak much English, but still managed to boss Charlie around. After she left he was tyrannical for days.

"I'm serious," Charlie said. "Caroline's in heat. She's got that whole glazy-eyed thing going."

"Okay, you're right," I said facetiously. "She's got a burn for Jim Talbot. He's definitely her current MMILF."

"Her MILF?"

It was counselor braggadocio to speak of MILFs: Moms I'd Like to Fuck.

"Not MILF," I said, "MMILF—maintenance man she'd like to fuck."

Charlie's laugh lasted only a polite moment. "Bill McIndoe," he said with gossipy triumph. "I saw her looking at him when he was arguing about the skateboard ramp."

"Doubt it," I said. I knew Caroline liked her men lean and shortstoppish. "Anyway, big deal. What if?"

"He's a first-year counselor. He's nineteen!"

"Yeah, and she's what, twenty-six?"

A wind teased up the slope and into the latrine. The doors on their rusty hinges whined.

"It's not right," he said. "Affairs between staff members."

"They're adults. Not like a counselor and a camper."

"No," he said. "No, of course not." He quickly finished and hauled up his pants. "Enough intrigue. Pleasure doing business." He tromped out and down the hill.

In the morning, I strung up Max's boxers like a white flag from the van antenna. I'd woken early to find the underwear—still stiff with his accident—and clean them in the washroom sink. The ploy worked. Max spotted them and goofed a grin, his braces spangly and generous with sunlight.

"Thanks," he said, unmasting the pennant. "Yours are in my laundry bag. Or somewhere."

"No sweat. I've got plenty."

"You sure?"

"Yeah, yours to keep, a souvenir."

"Cool," he said. "You're the 'nads, Jeremy."

Climbing into the van from our respective sides, we might have been newly assigned partner cops. There was a genuine but slightly forced camaraderie.

Max was bareheaded today, no sniggering baseball cap—his version of dressed up for the doctor? But the rest of his attire was standard: scuffed All Stars, hangdog jeans. TOY MACHINE, read the logo on his overlarge T-shirt, in letters spanning two tattooed fists.

"Buckle up," I said.

He rolled his eyes but complied. His left-handed proficiency had improved.

I knocked on the dashboard as if it were good-luck wood. "Ready?"

"One sec." He spread the boxers on the dash to finish drying. They effused a newly laundered, fresh-start scent. "All right," he said. "Let's make like bananas."

I pulled onto the road, where campers dawdled like Calcutta cows.

"Doofuses," Max sneered. "In New York—bam!—they'd all be mowed down."

"This isn't New York," I reminded him.

We cleared the last lingerers and the maple-shaded lane was ours. Still, I kept to the camp's ten-mile-per-hour limit. I was ever-conscious of setting a good example.

Beside me Max jittered in his seat, drumming some interior tune on his thigh.

"Nervous?" I asked.

I heard nothing, but guessed his response a shrug.

"You like camp so far?"

Still nothing.

I sank with the worry that I'd lost him. Was it my New York comment? Was my driving too priggish? Gravel sputtered beneath the tires.

"Well, you lucked out on counselors," I said. "I just met Cornelio, but Simon I've known forever. I was *his* counselor when he was just a pip-squeak."

Max air-guitared the span of his seat belt. He might have had on headphones piping raucous tunes to his brain. But then, as if someone had killed the music, he turned to me. "I like Simon," he said, "but he's, I don't know, too iffy. He's afraid to really yell at kids."

Now I was the speechless one. It was out of bounds for a

camper to critique his counselor so directly. But Max's evaluation was dead-on. I was adjusting to his conversational style: the trancelike unreachability ruptured by bursts of wit or insight.

He bent forward and inspected the dash console. "Apocryphal! A radio." He grabbed the on/off knob and looked at me with dare in his eyes.

"Go ahead, if you can find a station."

"Really?" he said. "Hot diggety."

Since Ironwood's cabins lacked electricity, our only music was homemade with guitars and my earnest harmonica. For kids like Max, whose folksy quotient hovered near zero, the moratorium on recorded tunes was torture.

As he scanned through static and occasional wheezings of melody, I turned west onto Route 4. Now that we'd hit blacktop, we had about twenty minutes of driving time. How could I wriggle out from the straitjacket of small talk? At the very least, I needed to raise the issue of his skateboard ramp. If things went well, I hoped to plumb more important topics. His home life. His father. Bryce.

Studying him as he worked the radio, I saw, in the dappled windshield light, the hint of mustache shadowing his upper lip. The summer I was Max's age, Ruff had kept me up one night for the gift of Barbasol and a razor. He slathered his jaw with foam, then watched as I copied his actions. After shaving his own face, he started in on mine, modeling the correct angle and force. "No going back now," he said, as with each stroke he swiped away the awkwardness of growing up.

Max had finally tuned in a station strong enough to surmount the area's steep geography. We caught the last bars of a pulsing "Duke of Earl" leading right into "Book of Love."

"I hadn't pegged you for an oldies fan," I said.

Max waggled a thumbs-up. "Oldies but goldies, Mom always says."

I wanted to ask about his mother. Before I could, Max rolled his window down, stuck his head out, and bellowed: "Oh I wonder wonder who, ba doop boop who. . . Who wrote the book of love?"

He retracted his head. "Man, just smell it!"

I obliged, rolling down my own window to guzzle the streaming high-test air. There was a sweet, gazpacho-like mix of summer foliage, and the sneezy hint of fresh-mown hay. "You can't tell me you get this in Manhattan," I said.

"Nope. This definitely beats piss and rotten trash." He poked his head out again and howled at the sky.

I marveled at his ability, despite the maturity life had forced on him, to be such an unmitigated *kid*.

The van tackled an engine-straining uphill, then crested onto the flat of a glacial valley. No matter how often I drove this stretch, it floored me: a textbook, U-shaped basin, as though a giant ice-cream scoop had cut a swath of land. The weather had held the entire week, an almost unheard-of span of zincky, transparent skies. Today the valley was preternaturally vivid. Along the ridge, each single spruce appeared separate and dimensional, a stand of benedictory totem poles.

We drove on, Max an easy, humming presence beside me. The wind from the open window mussed his hair.

"So, Max?" I asked.

"So, Jeremy?" he answered in perfect mimicry.

"There's something we have to talk about."

"Uh-huh." It might have been just an under-the-breath accompaniment to the radio.

"It's no biggo. Really. Just this skateboard thing." I kept my eyes on the road, but I could feel him withdraw, a hermit crab pulling in its legs. "Listen, don't get freaked, all right? Jim Talbot's a good guy, but he's kind of old-fashioned. He just doesn't get skateboarding."

I paused to sneak a glance at Max. His chin was jutted in devil-may-care defiance. He was drumming his kneecap with his index fingers.

"We talked about it at staff meeting," I continued—then,

appealing to his outlaw ego, added, "You'll be proud to know you're officially a 'problem camper.' But it's basically blown over. If you can just lay low for a while? I mean, personally? I think it's cool. It's creative. But maybe you can finish it with used wood? That way you stay out of Jim Talbot's hair?"

I realized I was saying everything in question marks, the gingerly inflections you might use to calm a criminal. We'd climbed almost to the top of Sherburne Pass, the high point of Route 4, after which came the steady downhill to Rutland. Steep earth boxed us in on either side: Killington to the left, Deer's Leap to the right. From the van issued sounds of overwork: a nervous, metallic gnash; shudder of gears.

"Max?" I said. "Did you hear me?"

He adjusted the radio's knob. "Yup."

"And?"

He yawned mammothly, then the yawn devolved into a belch. When his jaw was relocated, he sighed. "I don't see why Jim had to be such a dick about it. But who cares, we're not even building the ramp."

"What do you mean, you're not building it?"

"It wasn't really working, so we're gonna just make a grindrail instead. Anyway, Eli's bunk was falling apart. So we fixed it with some of the wood and brought the rest back to the pile. Okay? You don't have to pussyfoot around."

"Well," I said. "I guess that solves it."

Max shrugged and went back to his drumming.

The resolution left me pleased but off-kilter. I had the sense of having been deprived of something.

On the radio, the track shifted to the Chordettes, crooning their classic "Lollipop."

"Killer!" said Max. "This one's the bomb!"

He upped the volume and sang along, switching heedlessly between bass and falsetto.

"Come on!" He pinched the loose skin at my elbow. "Get ready. Do the thing. Do the thing."

He fishhooked his index finger deep into his cheek, then plucked it for the chorus's cork-pop sound.

"You missed it," he chided when he saw my hands still on the wheel. "Bryce and I always do this part together. It's much better with, like, two guys in harmony."

He cocked an ear to the radio, waiting. His whopping All Stars jigged on the van floor.

"Okay," he said as the chorus approached again, "here she comes."

"I can't," I protested. "I'm driving."

But as the pistons whined and we topped Sherburne Pass, my right hand was yanked from the wheel. Max forced my finger into my shock-widened mouth.

"Oh, lolli-lolli," sang the Chordettes, and what could I do but relent? I curled my finger, then torqued it past my cheek's stretching point. Max did his own cheek with his gimpish right hand. The two of us, in unison: *pop!*

NINE

—◄○►—

Max's appointment was in the hospital clinic. To get there from our parking spot we had to pass Emergency, and my gut queased with sympathetic panic. But as we entered the overlit building, Max's verve allayed my unease. He slide-tested the floor—determined it ice-smooth—then speed skated, arms pumping, down the hall.

"Careful," I said. "You want to break the other one?"

"Relax, dude," he answered, sliding faster.

Yes, I thought. Relax. Let our buddyness rule the day. The heat of his grip lingered on my wrist.

Max insisted on signing in for himself, practicing his left-handed penmanship. Then we took seats in the waiting room, in hard plastic chairs the Crayola pink of false cheer. A coffee-stained table was strewn with old *Newsweek*s. Hallmark posters graced the bright walls: an upside-down tree sloth mouthing the words "Hang in there!"; three fluff-ball kittens, captioned "You're *purr*-fect the way you are!"

I rolled my eyes, and Max rolled his back: conspirators in superiority. Around us waited a ragtag group of patients. A turtle-skinned woman sucked life from a tank. A father ignored his snotty son. I thumbed through a rumpled magazine, reading accounts of world crises long ago resolved and reviews of books by now in remainder bins. I tried to get comfortable, but the tiny, unyielding seats were hemorrhoidal.

"These chairs," I said. "Where'd they get them, a kindergarten tag sale?"

Max shrugged. The chairs were fine by him.

"Well, with your skinny butt, what difference does it make?" The words spilled out before I considered them.

Max was unfazed. He poked my thigh with his good hand. "As if you're fat! You're totally buff. I'd kill to have legs like that."

The compliment sent fire down my spine. Just as quickly, Max doused the flame.

"But why," he asked, "are your shorts so freakin' short?"

I tugged self-consciously at my Woolrich camping trunks, Boy Scout drab with brass-colored snaps. They were the only kind I'd bought for fifteen years. "I thought that was the point," I said. "Isn't that why they're called 'shorts'?"

"Yeah, 'shorts,' not 'nothings.'"

I couldn't judge his balance of kidding and contempt. "Why don't *you* wear shorts at all?" I said. I flicked a finger at his hip-tumble jeans—the same pants he'd worn all week. "And why do you let them hang down like that, six sizes too big, like maybe you'll fatten up all of a sudden and won't have time to buy a new pair?"

"Whatever," he said, sliding into his trademark slouch. He looked to the nurse's desk, to the wall clock, back to the nurse. Impatience pulsed at the corners of his jaw. "Do you think they'll, like, give me some more pills?" he asked. He cradled his arm like a swaddled infant.

"I thought you were doing better. Skating down the hall and everything."

"It hurts, all right? Why doesn't anyone ever believe me?" Max glared. He shuffled through a dozen magazines.

I'd begun to think of his mood as a bubble I was charged with keeping aloft. A gentle puff and he was launched into buoyancy, all grace and kaleidoscopic luster. But any sudden, invisible downdraft could send me scrambling.

"Speaking of painkillers," I said. "Want to know the best I ever had?"

"Sure," he said, in a way that could have meant no as much as yes.

"Turpentine."

"Turpentine?" The bubble caught a current, flitted higher. "Ballsy," he said. "Do you drink it or just huff it?"

"God, neither. Are you crazy?"

"What then?"

"It's a long story. You want to hear it all?"

"Sure," he said. This time the word was resolute.

"Okay. You know who the Amish are?"

"Um, I think. Like Kirstie Alley in *For Richer or Poorer*? Wearing those weirdo costumes all the time?"

"That's a lousy movie, but yeah. They're Christians who believe in being separate from the world. So they won't get hooked up to electricity, or own cars, only horses and buggies. They wear those 'weirdo costumes,' and get the exact same haircuts—everything as plain as possible—so that they stick out from the rest of the world, but within the group *no one* sticks out."

"Yuck," said Max with a flip of his raven bangs.

"Well, that's what most English people think—'English' is what they call non-Amish. That's 'cause we're brought up believing the most important thing is to 'find yourself.' With the Amish it's the opposite. They work just as hard at losing themselves. Instead of aspiring to be famous, or 'fulfilled,' their goal is to be humble and obedient—whatever it takes for the community to function."

"So there's no such thing as an Amish rock star?"

"Uh, that would be a no."

"Screw that," Max said, crashing a make-believe cymbal. "Sounds like life imprisonment."

"Yes and no. I mean, obviously, there's a ton of restrictions. But in a weird way, that can be a freedom."

I pictured the Yoders and their cloudless-sky eyes, a clarity I'd assumed at first to indicate absence, but in time came to see as brimful self-possession—just as the silence at their supper table was one of the richest, most holistic sounds I've heard.

"Do you see how it could be kind of appealing?" I said. "If most of the choices are made for you—how to dress, how to act, all that—then you can focus on much more important things."

"But what if your 'important things' aren't what the group thinks is important?"

"Aha! Great minds think alike! See, what I do—when camp's not in session—is study the Amish, or actually, the ones who stop being Amish. If they put themselves above the group, or try to have something beyond what the group allows, then they're excommunicated and shunned. It's called *Meidung*. Basically, you get cut off from all your family and friends. They're not allowed to eat with you, or do business with you. Think about it: if your whole life has been in this tight, conformist community, getting shunned means that everything is destroyed. That's why it's so effective. Most Amish who break the rules, once they see how nasty it is being shunned, repent and come back. But there's always some who just can't conform. They're the ones who fascinate me. How do they handle living in the outside world, where they don't have all those restrictions? Do they find the freedom they were looking for, or just a different set of traps?"

I might have told Max about Beulah Glick. Her latest letter had been especially bleak. Raising Benny without help from her mother and sisters caused more stress and strain than she could handle. Maybe that explained her recent miscarriage. Meanwhile, her resentment of Jonas grew. "You know how cider gets all gassy when it turns? And puffs its plastic jug into a bomb? That's us. That's Jonas and my's life."

I thought also then of Jakie Yoder. Was he still dressing English, running wild? Had he figured out which self was truly his?

The snotty toddler tripped and began to wail. Everyone in the waiting room grimaced.

"Did I miss something?" Max asked. "Where does turpentine come in?"

"Right," I said. "I was getting there. For part of my field re-search, I went and lived with an Amish family. In Pennsylvania, this tiny town called Peach Bottom."

I told him the story of my first day with the Yoders: the mam-moth horse, the currycomb, the sneeze. When I got to the tur-pentine, he winced. His gaze skittered down to my hands.

"No way," he said. "I can't believe you let her."

"Me neither. But I guess my trust paid off."

"So that was it? I mean, that, like, cured it?"

"Well, no, it was still a really bad wound. But Sadie cooked up all these homemade remedies, and after a while the skin just grew back."

Max stared again at my raw-looking finger. "Dang, that's ro-bust. I don't have any scars. Just some road rash on my knee that went away."

"You've got a lifetime to accumulate damage. You should be happy enough for now to stay intact."

Max sucked a fingertip into his mouth, then plinked at the harp string of his braces. "Hey, you know what's cool?"

"No," I said. "Tell me what's cool."

"You got your injury on your first day with those people, just like I broke my wrist the first day of camp. We're, like, bonded by our wounds."

"Guess so," I said.

For a long minute, Max was quiet. Like a student puzzling a brainteaser, he bit his tongue. "So," he finally asked, "can you feel stuff in that finger?"

I held it out straight, then tapped the end as though testing a microphone. "Yeah, in a weird way. Sometimes there's pain. Mostly, though, it's like when your arm's asleep. You know you're touching it, but you don't really feel the actual sensations, just sort of the *memory* of touching?"

Max nodded, as if he knew just what I meant. Then he asked quietly, "Can I feel it?"

I wasn't ashamed of the injury. I'd often bragged of it in the game of Truth. But that was all bluster and war-story posturing, nothing so baldly intimate.

"I'll be careful," he promised.

"I know," I said. "Of course you will."

He took my hand, uncurling the battered finger. Disgust and curiosity mingled in his gaze. I let him rub—his caress a kind of mutual meditation—and through the callus I felt not just the memory of touch, but for once, for a moment, touch itself.

"Nicholas Connor?" called a nurse, consulting her clipboard chart. There was no trace of nurture or solicitude in her voice. She might have been announcing, "Connor, table for two."

Max inspected his hands, all concentration, as though aware for the first time of their miraculous design.

"Nicholas?" the nurse called again, this time looking directly at him. All the other patients looked, too.

"Nick?"

Finally, he startled and bolted up. "Um, yeah. Right here. I mean, I'm ready." Hitching his jeans to near-respectability, he shambled past the nosy onlookers.

"Max?" I asked. "Want me to come with you?"

"No," he snapped, without looking back.

After he disappeared down the hall, I hovered in the peculiar autism of waiting, unable to read or strike up conversation, overwhelmed by sensory input: the hiss of lifesaving oxygen; the sickly toddler's diaper smell; and the sheepish, soothing tickle in my finger.

Fifteen minutes later Max stormed into the room. Red patches like hives mottled the skin below his eyes, which were narrowed into icy, vengeful slits.

"Let's go," he said.

"You're set with the paperwork?"

"Let's just get out of here." Without waiting, Max bulled through the crowd. He nearly toppled the wrinkled woman's oxygen.

I chased him down the corridor, his sneakers screeching on the tiles; I slipped and almost tumbled before I caught him.

"That faggot," he said. He didn't slow his stride.

"Hey—language! Just tell me what the doctor said."

"He said pain's natural. Just deal with it. Take Motrin. How the fuck does *he* know? I should break *his* fucking wrist."

"But that's good! He said you're healing normally?" I reached for his shoulder, then thought better of it and retracted.

He missed the obvious "Pull" sign at the exit. "Shit," he yelled, punishing the door with a kick. Then he mastered it and we were in the parking lot. Compared with the clinic's fake lighting, the outside world blazed painfully bright, a vast tarmac griddle flamed to high. Ahead of me, Max looked overexposed.

Then he stopped, and his shape regained its depth. I looked up to see what had halted him. Outside Emergency, an ambulance had rolled in. EMTs withdrew a gurney from the vehicle's open doors, its angular insect legs unfolding. In staccato flashes like strobe-lit horror movie effects, I saw: white sheet, ooze of blood, awful eyes. Then the sliding glass doors swallowed them.

In the van, Max was silent. I drove through Rutland, back onto Route 4. We passed a doughnut shop where I usually stopped for post-doctor treats, but this time the mood was all wrong.

A score of sentences formed in my mind, made it halfway to my larynx, petered out. "Max," began some of the thoughts. "Nicholas," began others. "I want to tell you . . . ," but I didn't know what. The quiet hung heavy, funereal.

"Listen," I finally said, as we passed Rutland High, on whose grounds summer-school students looked captive. "I'll talk to Caroline, okay? Maybe she can call a different doctor. Or maybe she has some extra Percocet."

Max turned away and rested his temple on the window that he hadn't bothered this time to roll down. He rocked, his skull thudding on the glass, and I knew his pain was more than that in his wrist.

I drove on, eastward, retracing our morning route, my hands

restive on the steering wheel. I tried the radio, still tuned to oldies. Ritchie Valens pined for his long-lost Donna: "Since she left me, it's never been the same . . ."

Max stabbed the scan button to banish the cloying voice. Static . . . static . . . classical . . . static. He gave up and clicked the power off.

We'd begun our ascent of the mountain. The noonday sun shimmered on the road. Up the road climbed, as far as sight and farther, a path to places past imagining. "Dream," I heard my father's voice urge in memory. "Dream rainbows. Dream pots of gold." It's what he said each night, tucking me in.

And then it was my own voice, addressing Max: "You know, I hear my father sometimes? Saying stuff to me? Sometimes small stuff, like 'Look both ways' when I'm crossing a road, or what to order in a restaurant. But usually more important things. Things he really said, or things I wish he had."

I didn't dare look at Max, but paused and listened. He was mouth-breathing; he'd stopped banging his head.

"He died when I was a kid. There was an accident. I was only eight, which means now I've lived more than twice as long without him.

"I remember when he died, the thing that pissed me off most was that we'd been in the middle of an argument. That morning, before he went to work, we were fighting about whose turn it was with the garbage. We had a rotation system to help my mom. And he claimed it was my turn, but I knew it was his. I *knew* it. He was the dad, though, so he got his way. Then at school I remembered something he'd said the day before when I was hauling out the trash—something about how I waddled when I was carrying it—and he wouldn't be able to deny it. I was going to tell him as soon as he got home that night, and make him apologize and promise to take three turns in a row. I had a whole speech memorized.

"But he never came home. We got the call from the foreman that afternoon. And then everything was crazy, our house full of strangers. And for the rest of the time I was growing up, I had to take out the garbage by myself. Every time. I hated doing it, and I hated my dad for it, too, and I felt guilty as hell for being mad.

"It probably sounds dumb: taking out the trash. But is it dumber than anything else you could say? 'He didn't love me enough'? Or 'He loved me too much'? Or 'I never even had the chance to know him'?"

I stopped then. I breathed. I breathed out.

Then I looked to Max, whose head still rested against the window. The safety belt cut under his chin, and I wondered if, in an accident, it would save or strangle him.

We'd reached the top of Sherburne Pass. At the Inn at the Long Trail, two backpackers waited to cross the highway, survival gear burdening their shoulders.

"What it comes down to?" I said. "For me? Is not being able to say anything to my dad ever again. Not being able to ask him questions. Or to call him up and tell him I need help. Or that I'm happy."

I blinked to diffuse what might have become a tear. In my tightened throat, rapid blood-beats ached.

As we eased over the last rise, I glanced at Max, sulked into the vinyl seat. But for his steady stare, I might have thought him asleep, so even were his breaths, so still his body. His anemic skin was translucent, with mother-of-pearl shadings: capillary pink, vein violet. It spurred a fantasy that later, when things worsened, I'd return to: being able to unzip Max's skin and reach inside, to rearrange his wires, defuse his bomb.

"How come you didn't say anything?" he asked. He continued to stare at the road, his frail features mannequin-still.

"About what?"

"At the doctor's. When the nurse called me Nicholas."

My shrug hinted at apology. "I figured you'd tell me when you were ready."

"But you knew?"

"Your grandmother sent a letter. It's in your file."

I wondered if this would anger him back to silence. Every teenager is a conspiracy theorist, on the lookout for adult collusion, and in Max's case, there was ample cause for suspicion. But as we shuttled through the glacier-hollowed valley, the van buffeted by blasts of wind, I felt the space between us cinch closer. The air around Max mellowed—it's the only way I can describe it—as the aura above a bath softens with steam.

"The only people I've ever told," he said, "I mean really told?—were the police." His voice was small and almost spectral, the whisper of a seashell against an ear.

"My dad was the best. He was, like, the one who held things together? I mean Mom, she's great and all, but sometimes she, you know, gets carried away. Even back then—before."

He looked at me, obviously hoping he didn't have to explain.

"But Dad was solid. He had this pretty cool job at the aquarium in Brooklyn, helping design their exhibits or whatever. I used to take the F train out there to meet him sometimes in summer, and if I was early I'd go over to Coney Island and watch people riding the Cyclone. I loved how when they got off they looked sick and blissed-out all at once."

He paused, drifting in remembrance. He could have been describing his own face.

"Anyways, I knew everything wasn't perfect, but Dad never seemed depressed. Not in front of me. He was talking about a trip to Hawaii to see Pop and Giz. He had some scheme about borrowing frequent flyer miles.

"Even Mom, I don't think she got him down that much. Nights she didn't come home, or came home, whatever, messed up, he just put her to bed and didn't talk about it.

"It was one of those nights. So Dad and me made it guys' time. We made Spam sandwiches in the Snakmaster, and Tater Tots, and popped cans of Miller Lite. Don't worry, he only let me drink, like, half a beer.

"We had the Beach Boys on and we were singing along all girly. Then I had the idea to surf, so we stripped down to our boxers and stood on the folded-up ironing board, pretending. We were having a total blast.

"And when the tape ended I was catching my breath, and

Dad grabbed me and gave me this big kiss, right on the lips. He said 'I love you.' He was really good about that, not like some dads. He said 'I love you' and positive stuff all the time. And so he kisses me, and then nabs me around the throat with his big hands and just squeezes and squeezes and I start to get a little freaked. But just when I can't breathe anymore he lets go and kisses me again, on the forehead. 'You're the best thing that ever happened to me,' he says. 'Don't you ever forget that. The best.'

"And then he gave me twenty bucks and told me to go out and have some fun, no curfew. Splurge, he said. Pringles, ice cream, whatever. Maybe bring some goodies to the homelessers in Tompkins Square Park. It was something we sometimes did.

"So I put my clothes back on and went out, still humming stupid 'Little Old Lady from Pasadena,' and I bought like three pints of Chunky Monkey. But then I realized I didn't have spoons. How would the homelessers eat it without spoons?

"I head back up to our apartment and I don't know why, just to be goofy, 'cause we'd been having so much fun, I decide to walk in juggling the ice cream. So I've got them in the air, and I'm saying, 'Hey check me out, not bad!' when I miss and one of the pints hits the floor. And something splashes on my leg. Something warm.

"There was red everywhere. Red. Almost black. He was lying on the ironing board. All curled up like a baby, you know, with his thumb in his mouth. Except it wasn't his thumb. It was a gun."

Max let out something like a sob. Spit and disbelief rattled in his windpipe.

In seconds, I had the van in the breakdown lane, hazards flashing. "Oh, Jesus," I said. "Oh, Max."

"Behind his head it was like . . . like if you squashed a doughnut. If you just squashed it. My dad."

I reached for him but was hindered by the safety belt; I could only cup my hand around his neck.

"You don't have to say any more," I started, when a crescendo of honks interrupted.

It was an Ironwood truck. I dropped my hand.

"You all right?" Jim Talbot called. He was returning—I judged by the rolls of tar paper—from a trip to Goodro Lumber. He leaned across his passenger seat, peering inside. I saw him note the sun-bleached boxers on the dash.

"We're okay," I said. I waved him on.

"Sure?"

"Yeah, we're fine. No big deal."

Jim took one more gander, waved back, and drove away.

When his truck disappeared around a curve, I unlatched my safety belt. I leaned over and undid Max's, too. "Come here," I said. "Come over here."

At first he didn't move. He was still trapped in his story's loop. "They wouldn't let me ride in the ambulance. They wouldn't let me. They just took him away."

I replaced my hand on his skinny neck, where I could feel a pulse, tentative and necessary.

"Asshole," he said. "Why'd he do it?"

He slumped into the space between us, and I caught him, and held him, and hugged.

"Why?" he asked, his voice muffled by my shoulder.

What could I tell him? That there's no accounting for what any of us wants? That love could be the reason just as surely as the lack of love?

Max was motionless, pure deadweight, his body as heavy as that of someone paralyzed. I felt an odd satisfaction propping him up, my empathy mixed with the triumph of having broken through to him.

I clutched him tighter, this ragged bruise of a boy, and without wanting to, wanting desperately not to, I imagined kissing his trembly lips.

Then I imagined more than a kiss.

Immediately I tried to erase the thought, but my groin churned with an obscene thrill of blood. I stiffened, unable to pull away.

Max cried openly now, high-pitched whimpers. Every sound

sent titillation through my chest. My body was suddenly as un-familiar as the one cradled in my arms.

"Max," I said, the way I'd always wanted my father to baby me. "Max . . . Max."

The van started to shudder as a truck approached in the traf-fic lane—a flatbed piled with poles of spruce. Its displaced air slammed us, invisible yet overpowering, shaking the van like a flimsy balsa model.

Keys rattled in the ignition. Exhaust blasted through the vents. And as the truck hurtled into the grimy distance, we clung to each other, helpless in the aftershock.

TEN

Given all that happened—and all that could have—I guess it's lucky I was pulled away from Max the next two days. At the time, it seemed a punishment.

Each year we sent a group overnight to Mount Moosilauke, the first major peak of the Whites. The mountain was maintained by the Dartmouth Outing Club, of which Ruff was a lifetime member. Years ago he'd initiated an annual exchange, whereby the boys lent their muscle for a day of trail upkeep in return for a stay at Dartmouth's Ravine Lodge.

Bill McIndoe was set to lead this year's trip, but the afternoon before departure—while Max and I returned from Rutland—he learned that his grandmother had died, and he caught the next flight to Miami. Doug Rose, as head of campcraft, asked if I could fill in. Teddy Trimble, he said, would come along and assist.

(Crippled Max couldn't join the expedition. It's not safe to swing an ax with one hand.)

After breakfast we loaded the van with grass whips and mattocks, and by eight o'clock we hit the road. We breezed along Route 4, almost traffic-less at that hour, then crossed the Connecticut River to thread north through New Hampshire. "Knee-high by the Fourth of July" was the proverbial goal for corn, but with only a day to go, this year's crop would be lucky to reach mid-calf. The passing farms stretched thirsty and threadbare, fields and barns blurring nauseously. Or maybe it was just my astigmatic mood.

The boys were peskily loudmouthed—"Ninety-nine Bottles";
catcalls at passing cars—but I let Teddy play disciplinarian. For
my part, I barely noticed their antics. Through the racket I heard
only Max's pitiable voice, the heartsick recollection of his sobs. I
was suffering an almost chemical need for him, a hypoglycemic
panic for his skin. It terrified me.

Then the kids broke into a new tune, a rowdy Ironwood standard: "I wanna be a dog, I wanna wag my tail, / Chase cars and
knock over garbage cans, / bite the man who brings the mail." I
held the steering wheel, trying to keep myself grounded in the
present. I gripped it even tighter. No use.

I'd been in Peach Bottom just more than a month. My crushed
finger was tender with new skin.

It was the Sunday of *Ordnungsgemee,* the special all-day
church service two weeks before communion. (The Amish hold
communion twice a year, in fall and spring.) Only baptized members are allowed at the affair, so children would be baby-sat at
Gid Lapp's. But at breakfast Sadie announced that because I was
here, the Yoder children could stay at home.

Like city kids greeting a snow-day proclamation, the Yoders
hooted and banged their spoons. *"Welle mie-ah fische geh!"*
they shouted. *"Welle mie-ah fische geh!"*—which by now I knew,
given the frequency of the plea, meant that they wanted to go
fishing. Pickle Joe—too young to understand the logistics, but
old enough to catch the germ of excitement—capered across the
living room.

When the dishes were cleared, Abner and Sadie set off in their
carriage, looking like the stern Amish I'd imagined before meeting them. Sadie had stayed up late with me the previous night,
explaining the import of *Ordnungsgemee.* It was a time, she
said, for self-examination and purging of self-will. The bishop
would review questionable practices, because for communion to
be received, the entire fellowship must be united. Just as grapes
were pressed for holy communion wine, and grains of wheat
crushed to make the bread they'd share, so must each church

member yield to the whole. One by one, they'd be asked to affirm the *Ordnung*. "There's no way to hide when they ask you," she said. "If you say 'I'm agreed,' you'd better be."

October wasn't the best time for fishing. Nor, to my knowledge, did the Yoders' creek hold much life beyond the odd salamander. But the kids' excitement didn't depend on catching fish. They were keyed up by the change from their everyday routine. The adventure would be its own happy end.

We found an empty margarine tub and headed for the garden to dig worms. As I sifted the dew-heavy soil, I recalled an afternoon at Ironwood, building a mud city with the youngest boys. Absentmindedly I whistled the camp song.

"Jeremy, *shick dich*!" Jakie barked.

He'd been teaching me rudimentary Dutch, starting with the phrases he heard most often, like "behave."

"Me? What'd I do wrong this time?"

"*Duh net*! No whistling on Sundays!"

"Why?"

"The chickens will all die."

I tossed a handful of dirt at his chest. "That's crazy. You don't really believe that?"

"*Ya*. That's what Daed always says."

His siblings all nodded confirmation.

Overcome by my own snow-day impulsiveness, I jumped up. "Let's do a test," I challenged.

And so I found myself crouched in the chicken coop, surrounded by puckering Amish kids—a pied piper of debunkment. We whistled competing melodies, surely dissonant enough to slay a flock of hens. But after three minutes, when we stopped, the birds were fine.

"See?" I said. "Still clucking, happy as clams."

Pickle Joe and Jakie danced a gleeful do-si-do. Anne and Lydia patty-caked their hands. Only firstborn Ezra appeared nervous, sizing up the sky as if expecting rain.

"Relax," I said. "I could even play my harmonica today and I bet they wouldn't die."

"You have a harmonica?" Dan and Jakie called at once.

When I said yes they implored me to fetch it.

I kept my old Hohner Marine Band in my backpack, for amusing campers during rainy days and hikes. So far at the Yoders I hadn't brought it out, worried that it might be unwelcome. But the children's curiosity was so ardent, so convincing; I'm a sucker for showing kids new things. With their parents gone, what harm could it do?

I played "This Land Is Your Land." I played "Home on the Range." You'd have thought I was Mozart. The kids marveled at every squawk and moan, and each in turn demanded a chance to try: Jakie uproariously snorting through the reeds, Lydia and Davey improvising tunes. Even Ezra, after admiring the pearwood body and brass plates, approximated a half-decent scale.

Our fishing plans were abandoned in favor of a hootenanny. Dan dumped the worms from the margarine tub and refilled it with corn kernels: a maraca. Pickle Joe and Aaron banged on milk cans. I taught the girls to make blade-of-grass whistles.

So there I was: a counselor at Camp Yoder.

Until now I'd felt beyond incompetent in Peach Bottom. My first day, I'd screwed up a ten-year-old's chore, laming my finger to useless. I spoke their language less proficiently than a toddler. Everything that normally marked me as special—my hyperarticulateness, my Harvard ID—was discounted, even disparaged, in this world. But charming kids is a boundary-crossing talent.

We broke for lunch—peanut butter and popcorn—then resumed our jamboree on the lawn. I taught them the daffy, unimpeachable tunes that were always hits with Ironwood's youngest kids: "Don't Put Your Finger in Your Nose," "Mail Myself to You." I sang "Playmate, come out and play with me, and bring your dollies three, climb up my apple tree." To my astonishment, they finished the verse in Dutch: *"Greisch nunna mei Reiah Fass, shlide nunna mei Kellah Dei-ah, unn mie-ah sinn gute Freind, fer immer meh."*

Their hands-down favorite was "I Wanna Be a Dog." As they sang about wanting to flirt with French poodles and pee on telephone poles, the kids frisked with canine earnestness, panting and rolling in the grass. Jakie gamboled up and licked me on the cheek.

At afternoon's end, as the air gained an undertone of chill, Sadie and Abner returned from church. Sadie, looking grave, trudged straight into the house, while Abner unhitched his frothing horse.

"Daed," Jakie shouted when Abner reemerged from the barn. "Daed. You're not going to believe!"

"Really?" he said with weary indulgence. "How many did you catch? *Eens?*" He held up a finger.

The children shook their heads.

Abner added a second finger. *"Zwee? Zwee Fisch?"*

"Nee," said Jakie. "We didn't go fishing. We learned songs."

"Songs?" Abner said.

"Ya!"

The kids clustered around me, clamoring for a performance.

"Maybe later," I said. "Your dad just got home."

"No. Now," said Jakie.

"Now!" said Lydia.

They gathered choirlike, an insistent semicircle. Pickle Joe jumped on me, piggyback.

"Okay," I said. "Maybe just one. But quick." I wanted Abner to witness how much the kids adored me; I wanted him to see how good I was.

I was counting them off to start when Lydia interrupted. "No. With the harmonica. With the harmonica."

Succumbing to her passion, I pulled it out. With every fawning breath in my lungs, I wailed accompaniment while the kids clapped and boisterously sang. "I wanna be a dog, wanna drool on the ground, / Scratch fleas and ticks and run after sticks, / I just wanna be a hound."

We were about to start another verse when Abner said, *"Genunk.* That's enough."

Jakie was still frolicking in his puppy dog routine. Pickle Joe was attempting to whistle.

The second time, Abner's voice cracked with fury. "*Genunk*! Ezra, Jakie, Lydia. All of you. I believe you have some choring to do."

Silence.

The kids, like beaten pets, scrammed.

I, too, turned away, but Abner called me.

"Jeremy. While you're living here, I have to ask you to respect us."

"I do," I said. "Of course I do. I just thought a couple of songs—"

"Musical instruments are not our way." There was a barb in his tone I hadn't heard before. "I won't have the children learning such things. You'll put it away, or I think you'll have to leave." He stalked with hard-line footsteps to the house.

I braced myself with the steering wheel's austere rubber curve. I stared at the mundane passing dairy land. At the tops of their teenage lungs, the campers sang.

I could feel Max's presence next to me. Like a snowflake, our embrace had been nearly devoid of weight, but implied all the crush of avalanche.

Sick at myself, and shaky, I pulled to the shoulder. Weakly, I called, "Piss break."

The campers lined up along the highway ditch and played crossed swords with their arcing urine streams. They joshed and giggled and squealed. I stayed in the driver's seat, haunted. Their squeals sounded too much like cries for help.

The Moosilauke Ravine Lodge was every boy's Lincoln Log fantasy writ large. Monster lengths of spruce—as thick as fifty-five-gallon drums—were stacked with rough-hewn artfulness, creosoted a masculine, rustic brown. (Ironwood's own spruce shelter was still slated for construction, if ever I could get the project started—but it would be humbler, a hundredth the size of this.)

We were greeted by a man whose overlong features—top-shelf

arms, puddle-jumper legs—suggested irrepressible striving. His Dartmouth Woodsmen's Team T-shirt showed a pine tree toppling. But he was ten years too old to be in college.

"How's camp?" he said as he strode toward us. Despite his clodhopper boots he moved with streamlined precision, as though testing his own aerodynamic design. "You all know Petey Wooster? In Morgan Peak cabin? That's my son. I'm Jay Wooster."

Now I recognized the bottomless blue eyes, unchanged from the fifteen-year-old Jay's. My first summer at Ironwood, he'd been the oldest, strongest boy—Ruff's pet camper, idolized by all. What on earth was he doing here?

"I'm Jeremy Stull," I said. "You wouldn't remember me."

"Jeremy, sure. Ruff talks about you a lot."

"You're still in touch?"

"I teach at the Mountain School in Vershire, a couple towns from him. My Petey's named after him, from Peterson."

I vaguely recalled Ruff's boasting of this, once.

"Now that I'm an Ironwood parent," Jay said, "I thought I should get more involved. I do volunteer trail work here—I'm an Outing Club alum—so when I heard you guys were coming, I signed up."

He explained that a devastating late-spring ice storm had felled hundreds of trees on the mountain. A student crew had cleared the worst of the blowdowns, but the Snapper Trail, an old ski run, was still a mess.

"Ready to be human bulldozers?" he asked the boys.

They responded with loud, demonic vrooms.

Jay furnished axes and bow saws and peaveys to supplement the tools we had brought. We filled canteens, tightened boot laces, and were off.

Stoked by a bona fide mission, the campers goose-stepped with self-important flair. All but Eli, Max's weakling cabinmate. He scuffed in front of me, the last boy in line, one foot straight and the other pigeon-toed. If he blundered today, as he had playing Truth, there would be no SuperMax to protect him.

The trail steepened, maple giving way to beech, then fir. A pewter sky poked in patches through the forest, and as we rose, it lowered in proportion: shirred clouds just beyond reach. I wondered if it might finally rain.

After another mile, Jay delegated the point position to Teddy Trimble. He moved back and filled me in on his story. Following in Ruff's footsteps, he'd gone to Dartmouth and joined the Outing Club. "Just like Ironwood," he said, "except co-ed!" On a backcountry ski trip, he fell in love with the leader, a telemark instructor named Sue. After six months, at nineteen, they were married. (That's why he'd never returned to Ironwood.) In a year Petey was born; two years after him, a daughter arrived, Carrie.

"She's nine now," Jay said. "So you'd better start a sister camp soon!"

He asked then about me. There didn't seem like much to say. We were just four years apart, both custom-designed by Ruff, but Jay had turned out so much sturdier.

We turned a crook into utter complication, the foliage of downed trees riotous. Split-open trunks tangled lurid, exposed, as disconcerting as broken bones.

"This is ground zero," Jay said. "Some guys can chop and saw, others can drag brush. Then in a while we can switch."

The boys fanned out, claiming their turf.

"Make sure you've got enough space," Teddy reminded them. "Your safety circle should be at least how much?"

"Five feet," they sang in unison.

Jay gave the heave-ho command. Bow saws growled with the sound of hungry dogs. Wood chips sprayed like sparks.

I hiked from camper to camper, lending tips and encouragement. Abe Rottnek, a sweet albino kid who'd been a favorite of mine last year, struggled to limb a length of trunk. I showed him how, if you swing upward, from the stump toward the leaves, branches pop off with single swipes. "Limb toward the limbs," I made him repeat, just as Ruff, fifteen years ago, had drilled me.

The kids stuck on log-dragging duty soon found themselves also dragging. Jay suggested singing as a surefire spirit-lifter. The boys lit into "I Wanna Be a Dog."

"Not that again," I said. "Please, something else."

"I'll teach a work song," Jay said. "A sea shanty."

Soon the forest echoed with "Haul Away, Joe"—which, despite its nautical origins, worked just fine for this landlubber lugging.

> *Louis was the king of France before the revolution*
> *(Way, haul away, we'll haul away, Joe)*
> *Then he got his head chopped off, which spoiled his*
>   *constitution*
> *(Way, haul away, we'll haul away, Joe)*

Jay surveyed the trail reopening through the woods. "Great job," he said. "Finish the logs you're working on, and then we'll have a snack."

The choppers and sawyers double-timed. Sawdust spat from deepening kerfs; *whoop whoop* and a balsam dropped in two. After a minute, only one boy remained working: pencil-armed Eli, who wasn't chopping his log so much as clubbing it. I could see the ax dulling with every stroke.

I overcompensated with the heartiness of my coaching. "That's it. Keep your knees bent. There you go."

But Eli was tiring; each swing misfired worse than the last. The other campers shivered in their sweat-soaked T-shirts, body heat wicking away in gusts.

Teddy bit his lip; his eyes asked me silently to intervene. I waved him off and turned back to Eli.

"Almost there. Four more good ones and you'll have it. One. Two. Three. Four!"

The log barely registered his nibbles.

One boy sniggered. I turned to silence him with a glare, but frustration surged in me as well. That the human body could fail so miserably was galling.

"Eli," I finally said, more brusquely than I'd meant. "Why don't you hand me the ax?"

Meekly, he relinquished the tool. Ruff had a mantra: *What a boy starts, a boy should finish.* But philosophy would wait for another day. The group was starving, borderline hypothermic.

Like a baseball player in the batter's box, I swept the ground with my boot. I checked my safety circle, asked two boys to give me room. Then I hitched my pants, flexed my thighs, and swung.

Whump. The blade bit with satisfying force. There was the burn on my palms from the varnished handle's friction, the un-ambiguity of arms-to-ax-to-wood. I swung again, harder, on the money. Then two chops on the other side of the notch. All my malaise—the confusion of my desire for Max—surrendered to one overriding wish: to hit the log as hard as possible.

One more home-run swing and I'd have it. I whipped up my arms and let fly.

Within a millisecond of the *whump*'s absence I knew I'd missed. There was a worthless metallic ping, an instant of cen-trifugal weightlessness, and then the horrible thud against my boot.

"Ow!" I screamed. "Shit! Fuck fuck fuck!"

I crumpled and grabbed for my left foot, still yelling to ward off the pain. Then I realized there wasn't any pain. The blade, slowed just enough by its glancing off the log, had sliced laces and tongue and sweaty rag-wool sock, but stopped just short of my skin.

"Oh god," I said. "Oh Jesus." My body shook.

The boys stepped back as if suddenly aware that I might be dangerous. Teddy, too, was dumbstruck, still practically a boy himself. But Jay rushed forward, first-aid kit in hand, and knelt to inspect for wounds.

"I'm okay," I told him. "It didn't. It stopped." I fingered the lewd-looking cut leather.

Despite my protests, Jay took charge. In the first-aid kit he located a roll of adhesive tape. He bound my boot mortifyingly tight. "There," he said. "Not pretty, but it should hold."

He gathered the group and insisted they don wool and poly-pro. Then we passed a bag of trail mix, and as the boys stole peeks at my foot, I overate in antidote to disgrace, my pinesap fingers souring the gorp.

Jay tried to save face for me with a story. "It's ironic," he said, "since we were just singing sea shanties. This makes me think of how in the old days, when a new ship had to be built, all the adzemen—you guys know what an adze is, kind of like an ax on its side, for hewing planks and beams?—well, all the adzemen who needed work would line up in front of the hire-boss, and you know how they'd apply?"

"With their résumés?" Abe Rottnek guessed.

"Not likely, since most of them were illiterate. No, what they'd do is, they'd roll up their pant cuffs, and the ones with the most scars on their calves would get the job. See, even the very best guys were bound to have accidents—it's just how dangerous these tools are—so scars were a sign of experience."

It was a good story, maybe even true. And as the boys milked Jay for details, I forgave myself this one mistake. *Everyone* misses some of the time.

Then it occurred to me that by Jay's accounting, I would have been denied. I'd missed the log and missed my foot as well.

Scarless me: always almost, never quite.

We finished our snack and started work again. The choppers now sawed, the sawyers dragged wood. I halfheartedly super-vised. The next verse of the old shanty stung:

When I was a little boy, so my mother told me
(Way, haul away, we'll haul away, Joe)
that if I did not kiss the girls my lips would grow all moldy
(Way, haul away, we'll haul away, Joe)

At four-thirty Jay pronounced us done so we'd have time left to bag the summit. Shouldering our tools, we clambered over the re-maining blowdowns. The Snapper Trail led into an old carriage road that moseyed along the ridgeline's slope. Eli hiked in front so he'd be the first at something; I lagged sluggishly behind.

From previous trips I knew the bald peak to afford a glorious 360-degree view. To the west you could see the Green Mountains' smooth musculature, and sometimes the delicate Adirondacks. But today fog stole any perspective. I could see Abe Rottnek and a smudge of boy beside him; a cairn marking the summit we'd have missed. The only vista was a murky veil of gray.

We made the Ravine Lodge just in time for dinner. Muddy and unshowered, we gorged on lasagna—replacing what seemed a week's calories. The Dartmouth guests smiled wanly at our skankiness and turned away.

After cream-soaked gingerbread for dessert, we gathered on blankets before the hearth, where a fire licked up the stony throat. Jay dimmed the lights—pendulous wagon-wheel contraptions like the ones at Ironwood—and began the infamous Doc Benton story. I'd heard the tale before: Mad doctor seeks eternal youth, haunts the mountain. I knew the gimmicks—the timing of hidden crew members' yells, the contrived crash of kitchen pots—but in the firelight, wind seething through the old spruce roof beams, I could still reliably be spooked.

Jay had come almost to the first big scare, when Doc Benton throws a girl down the ravine. I braced myself. Eli and one other boy had started dozing, the rest were poised anxiously alert. Abe Rottnek, to my left, gnawed his pinkie.

"... and threw her down the mountain screaming," Jay whispered, his calm delivery shattered by a rash of shrieks from the balcony. The dirty trick set off a chain reaction. The dozers woke with howls in their throats. Even I, who'd known it was coming, lost my breath. Abe grabbed me, burrowing as if to crawl inside my skin, his thin white arms scraggy with goose bumps.

Here I was again: a boy curled cashewlike into me, his breath timed with my own chest's rise and fall. How many dozens of hours had I sat like this? With Simon, Bill McIndoe, so many more. Now, after Max, it was different. It should have relieved me that I didn't burn, too, for Abe. But consciously *not* feeling a desire concedes that desire. Would every boy now be a possibility?

While Jay droned about caretakers in the haunted summit house, I slipped from under Abe's weight. "Back in a minute," I lied, and crept out to the porch.

The couch I sank into smelled of rain and shucked corn. The night had cleared to show the Milky Way's weave: stars clumped so densely that they looked all of a piece, the way cell upon cell forms our skin. But I knew the stars actually burned light-years apart, and sped more so with every passing second—a fleeing, untouchable universe.

The next scream didn't even cause my neck to tense: someone else's terror, distant catastrophe. If Abe panicked, he could grab Teddy, or himself. Then, closer, a different sound. Muffled crying.

I followed it to the kitchen's screen door. Inside towered stockpots, baking trays, cookie sheets; like a Christmas star, a whisk topped the stack. I recognized the setup for the story's final trick. Jay would hint at ghost sightings right here in the lodge, inexplicable kitchen accidents. At that moment, a student crew member, stowed away in the room, would yank a pan and crash the construction.

Again I heard a stifled, quiet moan. I scanned the room: fridge, sinks, double stove. Then I saw the half-lit shapes of two students, one linebacker-sized, the other pigtailed. Awkwardly they chased each other around a cooking island. The woman had something square and brown in her hand. She lunged across the countertop and swung.

When her hand reached his face, he didn't flinch, but started chewing. Her weapon, I realized, was gingerbread. She stuffed another chunk of the dessert down his gullet, then held her hand playfully on his mouth. He moaned again—the sound that initially had drawn me to them—not a cry, but held-back giggling.

The guy reached behind him, found the pan of gingerbread,

and smeared a pawful on the woman's cheek. They spun in their goofy, contentious lovers' dance, hands in each other's mouths, unyielding.

My own hand drifted to my lips, where yesterday Max had force-fed me. I tasted the salt of my own skin.

The crew members finally truced and collapsed into a kiss. Inches away, glimmering in the flicker of pilot lights, the pot-and-pan tower mutely swayed.

ELEVEN

——◄◦►——

We awoke to a chorus of "Yankee Doodle Dandy." Jay tooted the bugle of his fist. "Breakfast!"

Red, white, and blue food-colored pancakes were served, plus a pan of eggs starred and striped with ketchup. The gingerbread lovers I'd watched the night before were waiters today and heaped our plates with seconds. When they thought no one saw, they traded glances.

By lunchtime, students overtook the Ravine Lodge, preparing for evening hikes up the mountain. It was traditional on Independence Day to ascend the granite peak for its god's-eye view of fireworks. Outing Clubbers toted knapsacks stuffed with alpine picnic fixings; frat boys might haul a keg of beer. From the summit, Jay said, it appeared as though the sky were a pond filled with rainbow-spitting fish.

But Ironwood had its own Fourth of July traditions. We thanked Jay and piled into the van.

"Say hi to Petey," he called. "See you on visiting day!"

I steered us down the washboard road to the highway.

The missile monument in Warren, the town's oddball claim to fame, for once looked appropriate: jingoistically American and erect. In Orford, a parade idled before its go-ahead: spiffed-up Model T's, a candied-apple fire engine. We passed trailer homes festooned with frilly bunting.

The boys were jazzed. They recounted homemade celebrations, illegal cherry bombs and bottle-rocket mishaps. "Ninety-nine bottle rockets on the wall," improvised Abe Rottnek, "ninety-nine bottle rockets. Shoot one high, lose your eye, ninety-eight bottle rockets on the wall."

The campers crooned another laughing verse. Even tone-deaf Eli sang along, and I, too, added my voice. Since I'd witnessed the amorous crew members, I'd been buoyed by the possibilities of connection. I wasn't sure what relationship Max and I could safely forge, but as we sped to camp, I was hopeful there could be *something*.

I stopped at the Bass outlet in West Lebanon to buy a cheap replacement pair of boots. To reward the kids' patience I gave them each three dollars to go across the street to McDonald's. Hungry teens are so easy to win over. The boys high-fived and anointed me "wicked cool." I swelled with a pride verging on patriotic.

We were welcomed home with a crotchety salute by Jim Talbot. He stood at the camp bell, looking dispirited in a stovepipe hat and cotton beard. A clutch of campers strutted haughtily around him, mocking his Uncle Sam costume.

"Look!" said Teddy. "Look what they made him do!"

The boys added hoots to the ruckus.

I had to give Jim credit: a die-hard Ironwooder. For as long as I could remember, we'd deemed July Fourth a Day of Revolution. Whatever the kids said should go, went. One year they said underwear should be worn outside of clothes; another, they gobbled ice cream for breakfast. Like the medieval church's Day of Misrule, the fun was underpinned by pragmatism: by condoning this temporary, controlled insurrection, we hoped to deter serious acting out.

"Having fun yet?" I called to Jim.

He pointed his finger accusingly. "I want you."

Jim had seen me and Max in the breakdown lane, touching. Did he think he'd seen more? Did he suspect?

"I want you," he repeated, with the same prim inflection, and I realized he was speaking in character. They'd restricted him to Uncle Sam's one line.

Before they could force me into similar degradation, I hustled to my tent to unpack. I was eager to clean up and find Max.

The canvas was weighted with humidity. A wet-dog smell emanated from inside. I guessed—with a decade's fine-tuned experience—that we'd have the summer's first rain by sunrise. But the sky would hold, I was certain, for tonight. Leaving the flap agape to air out the tent, I grabbed clean clothes and hiked up to the showers.

I finished dressing as the dinner bell rang. At the dining room's entrance, Dylan Shallot stopped me with the tollbooth gate of his arm.

"Hand check," he said officiously.

I showed him my palms.

"Nope. No good. Can't come in."

"But I just showered. I haven't touched a thing."

"I know," he said. "That's the problem. Too clean. Today, you need dirty hands to eat."

Caroline appeared behind him. "What could I do? There's a revolution raging. Don't worry, soil's actually pretty clean."

I retreated down the stairs to the lawn. Squatting foolishly, I stained my hands with grass and mud.

"Better?" I asked, back at the door.

Dylan turned my hands this way and that—a palmist deciding how candidly to predict the future. "All right. But next time, no funny business."

Inside the Lodge, I greeted Caroline with an elbow hug, keeping my dirty hands away. "What craziness have the beasts wrought this time?"

"Nothing too bad," she said. "They made all the counselors take swim tests and sweep their cabins. We had a scene this morning, though. The troops showed up blabbing about 'life, liberty, and the pursuit of happiness,' by which they think Jefferson meant Tylenol with codeine."

"You didn't."

Caroline swatted me with her own muddied hand. "No! I gave 'em Coke syrup instead—I always keep it stocked for stomachaches. They got all giddy, pouring it in their canteens. They even convinced themselves that they liked it."

"You're a born diplomat," I told her.

"Hey, you taught me everything I know."

The dining hall was disarrayed with half-full cups of juice, strewn clothes, the staff table overturned. At Mansfield's normal spot stood only an empty bench.

"Seen Max?" I asked.

"Apple orchard, I bet. Charlie took their cabin down to help him set the launchers. Thank god. He was getting on my nerves."

"Max?"

"No, Charlie. Came up to me at lunch with this creepy look, and said something like was I lonely with Bill McIndoe gone to Miami."

I chortled. "He's convinced you're having a secret fling."

"Bill? He's nice, but that squished little body!"

"That's what I told Charlie."

Caroline traced loops around her ear. "Why's he so weird with me sometimes? Like a jealous husband. When I was new, I thought he wanted to get in my pants, like he supposedly did with the last nurse. But he's never even made the slightest move."

"He *is* jealous," I said, "but not about other counselors. It's the boys. They like you too much."

"Well, excuse me for doing my job."

"Forget it. Just keep doing what you do. And in the meantime, enjoy Bill McIndoe."

"Shut up!" She twisted a noogy on the top of my head. "Or I'll tell Charlie it's *you* and Bill."

I squirmed away, my skull smarting, stupefied. Why would she say that? Just a joke?

"Getting back to Max," she said. "Have you noticed anything odd?"

Odd wasn't all I'd noticed. "What do you mean?"

"This morning? I was at my desk, filling out the daily log, and suddenly I heard Charlie go, 'Stay calm. I won't hurt you. Just take off your blouse, real slow.' I whipped around and it was Max, not Charlie. His imitation was completely spot-on. But for a second I didn't know if he was kidding. Then he laughed and said, 'Don't worry, this revolution business is dumb.' He walked away."

Max's crabwise flirtation sounded all too familiar. "You know fourteen," I said. "Hormones, hormones. And he's a ham. He loves to goof around."

"But there's something more," Caroline said. "You know those ads during *Saturday Night Live*—how you're never sure if they're real or still part of the show? Don't get me wrong, I think he's a doll. But that's the thing. Is he *trying* to make me think that?"

"He's just a kid. He's young and confused, is all."

"Well, I can see why. I finally talked to his grandmother."

"And?"

"And, first of all, when I said I was calling about Max, she burst into tears. Finally she said I must mean Nicholas. I'd totally forgotten the name thing."

"Was she upset when you told her about his wrist?"

"She just said she hoped the camp's insurance would pay for it."

Poor Max. Everyone wanted him to be someone else's problem.

"Still no contact with the mother?" I asked.

"Nah. Grandma says don't expect anything much."

"And his wrist?"

"Hasn't complained to me lately. Guess the pain's gone away."

"Good," I said. "Good, at least there's that."

A cadre of ten-year-olds in camouflage stomped up and commanded us to sit down right now!

"What," Caroline asked, "on the floor?"

"Yes," said a boy masked by a triangle of bandanna. "You're lucky we're even feeding you."

Ken Krueger, the cook, appeared behind the kid, his thumbs manacled with twist ties. "If you're smart," he said darkly, "you won't struggle."

Acquiescing to the prepubescent guerrillas, we slumped to the floor. Already, it was squalid with gobs of peanut butter, a banana slice awaiting liquefaction. How could they have dirtied it so in just a day?

"Snazzy," said Caroline, pointing to my boots. Against the filthy floor, the new leather gleamed.

"Emergency purchase. Put an ax through the old ones."

"You what?!" She leaned closer to examine my instep. She had a nurse's need for symptoms, evidence.

"Long story," I said.

"But you're all right?"

"Yeah, fine." I knocked on the floor, which underneath its current grime was still wood.

The rebels returned then with "dinner": fluffernutter/ chocolate syrup/raisin sandwiches, to be munched with hands behind our backs. They dangled the food before my face.

At the lake's end, the farmers who'd once suffered this valley had left behind a scrabbled hillside orchard. Macoun mostly, interspersed with Cortland. These days the apples grew carbuncled, wormy, but we kept the trees in Yankee optimism. A blighted stand at the knoll's crest, however, had been cleared to prevent the spread of disease. The resulting bald spot, with its unobstructed view, was where we gathered yearly to watch fireworks.

I skirted the hill's twisty path. Wet with dew, rye tickled my fingers. Years of apples, composted naturally in the soil, basted the area with a cidery, fermented smell.

I heard Charlie's voice—"That's it. Tamp it tight"—and, turning the last bend, I saw him: hands on his hips, glowering. Half a dozen boys with shovels toiled below him, backlit by the setting sun. Toby, Dylan, Eli . . . not Max.

I swallowed a chalky sting of wanting, and called out in my gung ho counselor voice, "Hey! How's the pyrotechnics squad?"

"Hey," they called back, each at a slightly different time, a machine-gunning volley: "Hey-hey-hey."

"You guys psyched? Gonna be a killer show?"

"This is *cool*," said Toby, his Georgia drawl adding an extra syllable. "We can fire, like, five rounds at once!"

He showed off the mortars they'd sunk into the ground, steel pipes like the fingers of a giant, buried alive.

Eli rattled off the specs of shells. "These here are your basic Chinese six-inchers. You got your cap there, covering the blackmatch."

I pretended not to know the details, allowing him the pleasure of newfound expertise.

"Check out their names," Toby added. "Brocade Chrysanthemum. Silver Tiger Tail. Flash Salute—that's just noise, no sparkles."

"That's some pretty serious firepower," I said. "You're not planning a coup, are you? Don't take this revolution thing too far."

"We're not playing any games," Charlie said. "I already explained what a responsibility this is, which is why Mansfield gets to do it. These are explosives. All normal rules apply."

"Yes, sir!" barked Toby.

"Aye aye," Dylan chimed.

"You've certainly established who's in control," I said. Then, trying to sound casual: "Max around?"

Charlie stamped some dirt, shifting a mortar's angle. "Around here somewhere," he said. "Why?"

"I just had a message. I guess I can tell him later."

Charlie squinted as though the sun were not behind him, but in his eyes. "He couldn't really help here, with his arm. I told him he could wander off awhile."

"Oh, okay. Do you need any help?" I was hoping he'd say no, that he had everything covered, and I could go searching for Max.

"Actually, yeah, we need to build a fence. I don't want anyone within fifty feet."

I masked disappointment with practicality. "You have baler's twine or something?"

Charlie pointed to a tawny skein. Next to it: a sledgehammer, wooden stakes. "Take a helper. Let's see . . . Eli?"

Go figure: the king of klutziness. But I decided to welcome this chance for repentance. Be patient, I thought. Be patient.

We finished our barrier just as a throng of boys armied up the hill. I posted Eli at the fenceline and hollered for reinforcements. Jim Talbot and Doug Rose helped herd the kids to the clearing. Like picky dogs, campers circled their roosts.

After ten minutes, everyone was settled. Eli gave Charlie the message: fire when ready.

I paused to catch my breath and calm myself. With every second, the dusky sky darkened. A strangely warm, glutinous haze drifted from the lake. Turning back, I resumed my hunt for Max.

I'd looked for him already in the horde: flash of hair, dark as night; skinny body, shoulders slumped—a dozen campers could have been him, but weren't. Now I weaved through the clusters more methodically. A ten-year-old stopped me to babble about his day, all the things he'd made his counselor do. I didn't hear him. I was searching, thinking: Where?

A magnesium burst of light strobed the orchard to high noon. A second later: *kak-kak-kak,* like bullet fire.

I looked up, knowing a hundred pairs of eyes were looking with me, to the unblossoming of a Blue Peony with Golden Pistils. A pollen of colored light dusted the sky, as if to fertilize the apple trees.

"Ohhhh," cooed the crowd. There was energetic applause. From below the hill, a collective gusty "Yes!"

The flowerburst was followed by another, then a third. Violet streaked the sky, a second sunset. Sperms of light squiggled to that telltale fireworks sound, the audible equivalent of a corkscrew. ("Whistles and Fish," Toby had called it.)

The splendor made me all the more desperate to be with Max. I backtracked, avoiding sky-eyed campers. When each blazing shell for an instant chromed the night, my pupils snapshot images of boys. But none of them was Max. Then blackout.

Maybe he'd found his way back to Charlie. Even with his bad arm, couldn't he load a mortar? Couldn't he pull the cap, launch a shell?

I ducked under baler's twine into the orchard. My eyes were useless. I stumbled, righted myself, dodged scratching arthritic limbs. I raised my hands like a hostage in a stickup.

Gradually, the shapes of Charlie and the boys revealed themselves, lit by emergency flares.

"Two at once," said Charlie. "Mortar one, ready to fire?"

"Ready," said a boy—not Max.

"Mortar four?"

"Ready." Not him either.

"On the signal. Three, two, one, *launch*."

A nervous sizzle, then the detonation. From this close, it should have been more chemistry than art, but the sense of miracle was even greater. How did these metal hunks beget such vibrancy?

Charlie ordered the boys to load the next two rounds. I stepped forward, wanting to catch him in the lull. When I said his name his whole body flinched.

"Jesus! Jeremy. What the heck?"

"Didn't mean to scare you. I'm just still looking for Max."

In the flare-light, Charlie's face glowed jack-o'-lantern orange, as though something flamed beneath the skin. Lacy flecks of cinder dulled his hair.

"For Pete's sake," he said, "I can't deal with that right now. We're firing. Get the heck out of here."

"I was just worried, because—"

"Forget it, you can't stand there." Charlie turned to the boys. "Ready on mortar two?"

I moved quickly, shunted by his brusqueness, heading toward the lake, toward solitude. Compounding my loneliness was genuine anxiety; it had been hours since anyone had seen Max. At camp, that was a significant absence. If he wasn't in his cabin when the fireworks concluded, we'd have to organize a search brigade.

In the smokey distance loomed the shoreline, which, before I could see, I heard: the water's rhythmic romancing of the land. As a kid, I'd sought refuge by this shore. Because we moved so often, following the army's reassignments, I had learned an early distrust of landscape. I never knew, when I woke and peered out my bedroom window, which terrain would greet my sleepy eyes. Tumbleweed Texas? Leavenworth's waving wheat? But water was always water: mellow, mirrorlike, an equalizer. A Kansas lake looked like one in Germany; the same ocean caressed every continent.

I shuffled toward the easy lapping sound, squinting so the next blast wouldn't wreck my vision. When it came, the lake flickered like a busy switchboard, a reflection of attention-demanding lights. Something else demanded my attention. Something closer, a glint of silver on the shore. At first I thought it was a symptom of momentary flash-blindness, but within the streak a darker shadow moved.

I distinguished the broad frown of an almost upside-down canoe. Underneath huddled a boy. My boy. Max.

He wore an extra-large Zildjian Drums sweatshirt, tugged skirtlike over his bent knees. The sleeves hung puckered and empty, as though an accident had sheared off his arms.

"I looked everywhere," I said. "Worried sick."

Max leaned back against a thwart. He might have been defending the canoe.

I knelt beside him. "This isn't some Fourth of July stunt? That rebellion business is supposed to end at sundown."

Max stayed mute. His body chattered in fidgety discomfort, each tic pinging against the metal hull. His gaze was directionless, unfocused.

"Max? You okay? How's your wrist?"

The last word roused him. Some wire had reconnected.

"I knew it," he said. His lips parted into a slipshod grin. There was a dreamy, drunken quality to his expression.

"You knew what?"

"If I waited. If I just waited long enough, you'd come find me."

"Here I am," I said, playing along, and took the chance to pat his knee. Quickly, I forced my hand back to my lap. "Why aren't you helping with the fireworks? Or at least watching? And where'd you get this canoe?"

"No really, I knew," he said. "I was pissed at first. Your taking off. But then I thought, it's not his fault. He'll come back. He'll find me."

A salvo erupted overhead. Max's eyes turned spacily upward, but I kept staring at his face. Moment to moment, he seemed a different kid: now silent, now chatty, now gone. The only constant was what he did to me.

"Want to canoe?" he asked chipperly, as if it were a sunny afternoon.

"Max, I don't think it's the right time."

"I just thought it would be, you know, more private."

"Private?"

A skyrocket zoomed above us, but instead of the usual shattering radiance there was only a thud, and more darkness. From the hilltop came a disappointed groan.

"I paddled all the way from the waterfront, you know."

"You serious? One-armed? You couldn't have."

"Yup." With a furtive twitch, he flipped bangs from his eyes. "Took over an hour, but I did it."

"Why didn't you ask someone to help?"

"I just, you know, wanted to be alone. On the lake, it's like nobody can touch you."

Yes, I wanted to say; yes, I know. But eventually you have to return to shore.

"So?" he asked again, shivering. "Can we?"

Boating after dark violated camp rules; I'd already been gone too long from the boys. But how could I deny Max the calm water's solace? How could I deny him anything?

"We have to be quiet," I said. "And not tell anyone."

"Apocryphal," he said. "You're the king of kings."

He tried to get his arms back in the sweatshirt, but the cast got stuck inside the sleeve. When I helped him, he flopped at my mercy. He didn't say anything about pain. But within his relaxation lurked a curious tightness, the loose-but-stiff weight of sleeping limbs.

Stealthily we slid the canoe down the bank. Max took the bow, I took the stern. When I pushed us off, I was surprised by the water's easy parting. The surface appeared solid, butter-smooth.

I paddled with swift, determinate strokes when the fireworks granted auditory cover. The velvet night swaddled us in its folds. That protection—warm within the cold, safe within the wet—took me back to another time on the water. The Grand Circuit swim. I was fourteen.

Every summer the fittest boys attempted the Grand Circuit, a grueling four-mile perimeter swim of the lake. No one since Jay Wooster, three years earlier, had made it, and only five kids in the camp's history. All season, I'd worked up my endurance. I'd managed half-miles, full miles, two; now it was time for the test. Four campers joined me in the challenge (not Charlie, who was nauseous and stayed in bed). Ruff rowed beside us in a dinghy stocked with water, sleeping bags, thermoses of soup.

We swam and swam and swam. Breaststroke, elementary backstroke, side. The afternoon was cool, briskly September-like, an orange nip of crispness in the air. The lake stretched to blue infinity.

By halfway, all the others had dropped out. Ruff asked if I was ready to stop, too. I told him no. Definitely not. No way.

Another mile, another cove, a cramp in my abdomen. But when Ruff asked again, I still said no. I wouldn't quit yet. I swam.

The sun sank behind the ridge, and a petulant wind was stirred. My ears whistled with the sound of cold. My thoughts felt mangled. Does cold have a sound?

"You don't have to do this," Ruff said.

I barely nodded, conserving energy. I was soaked, yet my tongue throbbed with thirst. I dipped my head and took two meager strokes.

"You don't have to prove anything," Ruff said. "I couldn't be prouder of you than I am."

His words sifted through the water like poetry in a foreign language: elegant nonsense.

I swam.

By the time Ruff towed me to shore, I was blue. The rattling of my teeth was all I heard. I had made it to within a quarter mile.

Ruff married two sleeping bags and tucked me inside, then stripped and crawled in beside me. He held me in his staunch, warming arms. He breathed on my neck. I wasn't swimming.

Soon I drifted off to the lilt of his assurance: "You did great, I'm really proud of you. You did great. You're safe now. I'm so proud."

What seemed like hours later, when I woke and looked at him, I saw that his eyes were blurred with tears.

After fifty yards I stowed the paddle and let us glide. Our rock-a-bye cradle went adrift.

I dangled an arm in the amniotic water. I lost track of what was lake, what air. This, I imagined, would be the feel of kissing Max. He was a rawboned, floaty silhouette.

"Private enough for you?" I whispered.

He whispered back, "Yeah. It's ace. Perfecto."

Against the boat, wavelets made quiet gulping sounds. An ellipsis of bubbles marked everything unsaid.

"Shoot," said Max. He twisted in his seat.

"What?"

"I have to piss. Pretty bad."

"We're not that far. I can head back to shore."

"No. I'll do it here. Hold her steady."

Before I had time to dissuade him, or to cite the no-standing-in-boats rule, he was on his feet, wobbling recklessly.

"Whoa," he called, then chastised himself. "Shh!"

"Careful," I said, wishing I could brace him. He was at the bow, too far, beyond reach.

"It's like pissing in the back of a Greyhound," he said. "You can't hardly hold on to yourself."

He stood a long time, silently coaxing. Each pissless second raised the bar of embarrassment. Finally, he half turned and asked with scratchy breath, "Could you, um, you know, make some noise?"

"Noise?"

"Yeah, like, swoosh your hand in the water?"

His voice choked and I recognized broken Nicholas, the tremulous boy beneath the boy.

I whirlpooled my fingers in the calm lake water; the distraction finally allowed him to go. There were two spurts to start—I couldn't see them, but heard the splash—then a piddle, a spout, a stream. Like a blind man's, my other senses sharpened to compensate. I thought I could smell his urine: sweet-and-sour.

Abruptly, the stream ceased. The canoe jarred as Max shifted his weight to get the zipper. He muttered, complained of numbness in his fingers. He tried again, got nowhere, gave up.

His clumsy turn almost tipped us over. I counterbalanced, spreading my knees to the gunwales; rivets pressed painfully in my flesh. "Watch it," I said. "What are you doing?"

He completed his tipsy pirouette, then crawled over the thwarts toward the stern. When he settled himself, he was facing me, close, hunkered down; his man-sized feet abutted mine.

"That's better," he said. He breathed deep. Then, as though his lungs harbored magic launching power, he exhaled and a mortar split the sky. For a sensational instant, his face blazed.

"Max," I said. I wanted to tell him how beautiful he was, more beautiful than the sequined show above. I wanted to talk about risk and fate. An ax almost chopped off my foot, I might have said. We're always *this close* to tragedy, and to love.

He spoke first. "Thanks a lot for coming out here." He'd reverted to a tentative, purly voice.

"Sure, I'm glad to. This is . . . fun."

Go ahead, I thought. Do something. Now. I remembered Ruff, after the Grand Circuit: his breath on my neck, his heat.

Max looked at me. Not exactly at me—at my chest, maybe lower. "Jeremy?" he said. "Can I talk to you?"

"Of course. Aren't we talking now?"

"You're the only person. Well, Bryce too. I wrote him a letter. But here, you're the only one I want to tell."

"You can tell me anything, Max. You know that." I tried to sound like a counselor, calm. My pulse trilled a ragtime in my veins.

"If I tell you, promise not to tell anyone?"

"Sure," I said.

"Not anyone at all?"

I promised.

I knew what he planned to say. He was beating me to the punch of confession: his attraction to boys, to men, to *me*.

"There's something . . ." he began, then drifted off.

My hand somehow landed on his knee. "It's okay. Take your time. I know it's hard."

My palm rode his kneecap as it jittered manically, each bounce of the bone shifting his jeans. At the baggy crotch his still-unzipped fly winked at me; it took everything I had not to look. Was he wearing my underwear, the pair he'd kept?

My fingers snuck an inch closer, two. If I reached inside I could obviate awkward words. I could spare both of us embarrassment.

The signal traveled down from my brain to my arm, then my hand, aiming for my scar-tip finger—a terrifying, liberating jolt. After all this time, the circuit would be grounded.

"It was Charlie," Max said. "He messed with me."

There might have been a detonation of fireworks just then. Or the blast might have happened in my skull. I yanked my hand from Max's thigh and hid it in my crotch, then behind me, incriminating evidence.

"What are you—" I stuttered. "What do you mean?"

He wouldn't look at me. His knee had stopped jittering and

he was now completely still, pulled into himself, arms and legs drawn tight. There was practically nothing of him left.

"Max. Tell me what you're saying."

Sweat spread in my underarms, my crotch; it clammed the fingers that had just nearly groped him.

Max turned his head away, toward the shore. I could see the moist glimmer of his eyes.

"Max?"

He only breathed.

"Max? What did Charlie do?"

In memory I heard Charlie, then Ruff, doing something; darkness kept my teenage eyes from seeing. Envy. Dizzy stars. Loneliness.

"You know," Max said.

"No, I don't." My tone was way too sharp. "I don't know, Max. I don't know anything."

"Charlie," he said.

"Right. Charlie what?"

"He made me, you know, do stuff."

"What kind of stuff?" After all these years, I was still wondering.

A frizz of light opened in the darkness: a dandelion puff, a ring of fire. Reflecting it, the lake was seething, molten.

"You don't have to be ashamed," I said. "But you have to give me some kind of idea."

"Don't make me say it, Jeremy."

"Then show me. Don't say anything. Just show."

With his head still turned away, his body brittle in its crouch, Max moved his good hand below his waist. For the quickest of instants he jiggled it. It was the same gesture, exactly, he'd made the first day, as I helped him shuck his pee-stained pants.

"When did this happen?" I demanded.

"Yesterday. After lunch. You weren't around."

"Where?"

"The infirmary."

Hands shaking from what I might have done—what I'd come

within a blink of doing—the feeling that spiked was jealousy. The infirmary was ours.

"Was Caroline there?"

"No," Max said. "Afternoon off."

"Okay. So what were you doing there?"

He sniffled. I was worried I'd made him cry.

"I was looking for, you know, that stuff." He chewed his lip. "Those allergy pills. Antisomethings."

"Antihistamines?"

"Yeah."

"And Charlie was there?"

Max shook his head. "He came in after."

"Anyone else? Did anybody see?"

"I don't think so."

"And he made you . . ." I couldn't bring myself to say it.

"Yes, okay? Yes. Don't you believe me?"

Above the orchard, another shell exploded. Then another. The finale was approaching.

"Yes," I said, "of course I do. I'm just—" I wanted to believe, and also didn't want to. "Listen, it's a serious accusation. Can you tell me any more details?"

Max faced me again. Now he did begin to cry. I wanted to reach for him and hold him, as in the van. But there would always now be a gap between us. The gap of what I'd almost done, and Charlie had.

A murderous clap split the air. Then a bright gash on the wrong side of the sky. This was the real thing. Thunder and lightning. A front.

An updraft broadsided the canoe, spun it like a weathervane. The boat would be a magnet for lightning.

"Got to head in," I said, reaching for the paddle.

"Wait," said Max. "You're not going to tell? You promised."

"That's not your worry. Let me decide that."

He grabbed the shaft to stop my paddling. "You can't! I don't want people to know."

The struggle tipped us close to the water. Another two inches and we'd swamp.

"Stop it," I said. "We've got to get to shore."

I battled a fierce headwind to stroke through rising chop. Spent fireworks ashed upon us, then rain. (There had been rain that long-lost night, too.)

The canoe shuttled closer to the shore. I heard shouts from the orchard, instructions, a countdown, then a tantrum of fire-cracking pops. But the sky remained dark, unconsummated. The mortars must have dudded in the downpour.

Max turtled himself into his sweatshirt. His eyes were dismal with tears.

And as raindrops pelted us—implacable, bulletlike—I imagined all the spangles unreleased: Firefly Comet, Golden Orchid, Peacock Tail.

TWELVE

—◄○►—

Embalmed by memory, Max's disclosure seems not so much a single shocking moment as it does the fruit and the seed of *all* moments: what every heartbeat until that instant led me to, and what's guided every clumsy heartbeat since. But the truth is, things could have turned out differently.

These days I suffer acute awareness of consequence. When I leave my carrel to wander the halls of Widener, I see an undergrad, Harvard cap turned backward. He's studying a thick statistics text. His pencil drops, rolls beneath his chair. If I pick it up, might this lead to conversation, lifelong friendship? Or will he think: Who's this guy, some sort of queer?

Demolition experts hired to raze a skyscraper have to gauge the perfect sequence for their blasts. The correct order brings the harmless sigh of implosion; a single glitch wreaks catastrophe. In their aid, the detonators have equations, computer models, and so, nowadays, rarely fail. I had only yearning, intuition.

I pass the student, unhelping, unhelped.

I lost Max as soon as we docked. Before I could drag the boat a safe length up the shore, he was out and away into the dark.

The rain came in shards like shattered bits of sky. But the storm itself offered some relief: a challenge that would surely be surmounted. Rain-ruined paths could be patched or replaced; what happened to a ruined boy?

Halfway up the orchard I hit mayhem: muddy campers, wielding frantic flashlight beams. The younger ones, howling, latched

123

on like drowning victims. Their hands revolted me, reminders of my own. I wanted to pull away, to give warning: *I* might pose more danger than the storm. But their need was a call I had to answer. I gathered them and paired each camper with a buddy, then herded them toward their dry cabins.

In a hundred yards we stumbled into Charlie. I thought at first to accost him, to clutch him by the throat. What had he done? (What had *I* wanted to do?) But I saw that he, too, was guiding boys to their bunks, and I had to postpone my accusations. In times of crisis, Charlie was a beacon of safety. Campers gravitated to his rock-calm. So did I.

By the time each boy was toweled and tucked into his bed, my skin had the consistency of rotten fruit. My new boots, which I hadn't had time to Sno-Seal, were ponderous, pulpy swells of mud. All I wanted was my sleeping bag.

The trail to my tent was now a flume. I sidestepped it, bushwhacking, driven. Soon I could see something was off. The tent like a fatally wounded beast keeled forward, its right corner sagging liquidly. My own fault: I'd left the flap open. Rain sogged the canvas till it staved of its own weight, allowing more rain to blow in. My sleeping bag was a sack of wormy lumps.

Was this punishment? But as usual, I'd done nothing, not quite. So, then, not punishment: a warning. To act—and hold back—more carefully.

With "reasonable cause to believe" that Max had been abused, I had to inform Child Protective Services; the law gave me twenty-four hours. How often in staff trainings had I stressed this? Not complying was abetting a crime. But this was trickier than our training scenarios.

I wanted to ask Caroline's advice. But telling her was basically telling CPS; surely she, once informed, wouldn't stall.

Nothing could be done, in any case, at this hour. I shed my boots and slipped into my sodden sleeping bag. I swiveled to my right side, to my stomach. Sleep taunted me from its great distance.

I tried my back, but that way I could see the leaking roof. I slugged deep in the bag. I remembered.

It was the last week of our last camper summer. Charlie and I were hellbent on becoming "Lifesavers," a wilderness first-aid rating Ruff invented. We had passed basic first aid, then advanced, then CPR. Ruff devised the new rank just for us.

A Lifesaver should be able to withstand the deep woods with little more than a Swiss Army knife. After all, Ruff said, if *you* can't survive adversity, how will you care for other victims? An aphorism: *Save yourself to save the rest.*

Identification of edible plants was required: Queen Anne's lace, Jerusalem artichoke. Orienteering using only stars and sky. Weaving cordage. Lighting fire without a match. There were other, hard-to-define qualifications, the kind that can't be checked off a list. How does a fourteen-year-old "accomplish" *responsibility*? *Character*? These were code words for "Does Ruff really like you?"

Almost daily he stole us away for tutorials. We missed meals so often that the cook gave us the key to the walk-in fridge; when we needed snacks, we helped ourselves. We asked for canteens, water filters, compasses, and they were all duly requisitioned.

Soon we were camp celebrities, shrouded in rumor and intrigue. It was whispered that the Lifesaver's last requirement would be to trap, skin, and eat an animal. The youngest boys begged to know the truth: Would we have to chew skunk or porcupine? Charlie and I, milking every moment of our fame, shrugged and flashed enigmatic smiles. The truth was, we knew no more than they did.

After four summers, our friendship was solid as stone—part of our lives' topography. In long afternoons of backcountry hiking, noting coon tracks and patches of jewelweed, we talked of home and family. I told Charlie how scared I was of forgetting my dad, how with each passing year his features dimmed. Charlie told me how he sometimes wished that his father *were* dead; then his mom might stop drinking so much. At day's end, when we could, we went swimming together, an illicit dip out of counselors' view. In the darkness, I could barely see his form, but I felt that it held something of mine. Once, we met underwater in a hug and came up laughing. His body was a page I longed to turn.

Late on a Sunday afternoon, with four days of camp to go, Ruff plucked us from our cabin activity. He ordered us to pack knapsacks with clothes and sleeping bags and to meet him at the docks ASAP. Charlie and I didn't speak as we hightailed it to the waterfront, but I knew our minds whirled with the same thought: This was the last test; we were going to skin an animal; this meant we were sure to be Lifesavers.

Ruff waited by the canoe rack. He handed us each a small plastic bag of food—hot dogs, instant oatmeal envelopes—and shouldered his own backpack.

"To the Point," he said. "It's not far. Follow me."

The Point was a polyp-like, quarter-mile moraine that poked from the lake's opposite shore. "Glacial excrement," Ruff called the formation, a waste heap left by retreating ice. Its ground was different, mattressed with spruce mulch, the soil fecal-smelling and peaty. By the water's edge, like twitchy, shamefaced adolescents, fir trees blistered with sap.

We hiked single file. In the lead, Ruff swatted kamikaze deer flies and dispensed terse naturalist commentary. "Moose," he said, toeing a pile of turds. Later, knocking a hemlock riddled with perforations: "Yellow-bellied sapsucker. Recent." Silently, I logged the gift of every fact.

At land's end stood a crude lean-to. Spruce boughs formed the low roof; the floor was a sheet of ⅜-inch plywood.

"Cool," said Charlie. "Where'd this come from?"

"Built it a while back," Ruff said. "A couple summers before you came."

"No way. It's been here this whole time?"

Ruff squinted gravely at us both. "You don't need to tell anyone about it."

God, no. Of course not. We never would.

Looking back, it strikes me as funny and disturbing that Ruff could make so much of so little. The Point was a twenty-minute walk from the waterfront, unguarded by fence or booby traps. But Ruff deemed it off-limits, so it was. That was the marvel of his rule, and its tyranny. He could jack the stakes of the ordinary to teeth-chattering heights. Everything mattered. Everything honed an edge.

We dropped our packs in the secret shelter, which appeared big enough to sleep only two.

"Dinner before dark?" Ruff challenged.

I wondered how we could catch, skin, and roast an animal in the scant daylight that remained; then I remembered the bags of food we'd brought.

We gathered squaw wood and lit a modest fire, whittled sticks to skewer hot dogs. Ruff's franks turned out brown and succulent, Charlie's and mine carcinogenically black. It didn't matter; excitement was all I tasted.

Dusk dropped its scrim over the valley. A breeze nibbled from the cooling lake.

"You know," Ruff said, doling Hershey's Special Darks, "I don't bring just anyone out here. But it's not a reward. It's an investment." A pine knot popped in the fire. "You're my best kids. You'll come back as counselors?"

Just as soon as the rules allowed, we pledged.

"Good. I was hoping you'd say that. Then eventually I'll retire, and one of you will be in charge."

Inconceivable! Without Ruff, wouldn't the cabin foundations all crumble, the sparkling lake drain away?

"Then *you*'ll bring campers out here," he continued. "It's hard to imagine, I know. You don't think you'll ever be a fogey. But getting older doesn't have to mean getting *old*. A real man is still partly a boy."

The puzzle perplexed me: Which part became man? Which stayed boy? I pictured two liquids, forcibly emulsified, always at risk of separating.

I thought, too, of my father. I owned a photo album spanning his life, pasted up by my mom after he died. But the shots depicting him as a child were alien. How did that boy connect to the man I'd known?

My own body was recently mutinous, threatening a similar disconnection. Hair sprouted from my armpits; my nipples were tender swellings. I was becoming someone I didn't recognize.

Ruff snapped his hot-dog stick in two. "Where you are now is the best of both worlds. But you're growing up fast, so be careful. If you lose the boy, you might never get him back."

Soon the sky was leached of all light, and night unfurled its artistry, the stars so crisp and transcendently clear as to seem a schoolchild's rendition. There were the Dippers, cartoonishly obvious; the Milky Way's gaudy, careless smudge.

Ruff showed us Hercules and Cepheus and Draco. I wasn't very good at constellations. I would find Draco's head, then follow star to star, trying to identify his tail. But the tail stretched endlessly across the hemisphere; my eye was too convincible.

Ruff said tonight we'd see meteors. The Perseids.

"Why are they called that?" I asked.

"They shoot across Perseus. Up over there."

We lay on our backs on the cool, mossy slope below the shelter, arms crossed cadaverlike. Hushed and unmoving we awaited the meteors, as though they were easily spooked.

Charlie saw one first. "There," he whispered. But Ruff and I had already missed it.

Soon another flared, streaking across Andromeda. We all saw it and sucked in our breath.

Then another. And another. Three at once.

Like a rain of light, I thought, or perhaps said aloud, because Charlie said, "When it rains, it pours." It was true, just like the old Morton's motto: God was salting his glorious creation. There was an ordained perfection to the scene: the meteors, the alchemical touch of breeze. We were joined in awe of things bigger than ourselves.

Then Ruff said we should think about bed. I had *been* thinking about it, hoping that Charlie and I might share the snuggly shelter.

"One of you can sleep with me in the lean-to," Ruff said. "And the other—" he shrugged, motioned upward. "At least it's not supposed to rain."

Charlie and I exchanged glances. I thought about proposing that we both sleep outside, leaving the shelter to Ruff. We could join our sleeping bags, combine our heat.

We stepped up the bank toward the campsite. The smell of charred meat hung thick, libidinal. In the fire pit, only embers remained.

"What we'll do," Ruff said, "is flip for it." He dug into his pocket for a quarter. "Okay, Jeremy, you call it."

I picked tails. Ruff flicked the coin into the darkness, the silver catching starlight as it spun: blink blink—a mini-meteor.

Ruff snatched the coin and brought it near his face. A quick consoling wink at me. "Heads."

"Let me see."

"Here," he said, but he dropped it. "Oh well, I guess you'll have to trust me."

I didn't want them to see my fallen face. I unrolled my sleeping bag on a rootless patch of ground, pried off my boots, and crawled inside.

Ruff and Charlie settled in the shelter. "Not bad," said Charlie. Ruff echoed, "Not bad at all."

All evening, I'd fantasized about Charlie. Now I realized how much I also longed for Ruff. Barely a week had passed since my Grand Circuit swim, the warmth of his blond-tangled arms.

He and Charlie both forgot to say good night.

I don't know how long I dozed, and when I woke, I wasn't sure what had roused me. The stars had wheeled a quarter turn, upending Hercules. The Big Dipper wantonly spilled space.

It was cooler now by ten degrees. The air smelled burnt and blackly resinous, and also—enticingly—of chocolate. The duplex where my mom and I had lived in Germany emanated a similar sugared scent. I would sit on the stoop, wondering what the neighbors had cooked.

From the shelter, I heard a shift of fabric. A clunk against plywood. A groan.

"You're freezing," I heard. "Let me rub your back."

A minute later: "Turn over, I'll do your front."

It was Ruff's voice, and he didn't attempt to hide it. Had the shelter fooled his sense of decorum?

"Nice?" came a whisper. "You like that?"

Charlie answered with a happy purr.

For a minute, maybe more, they didn't talk. I wished I was with them, between them, inside. I wished I was far away, back home.

I spied a meteor, then a second, faintly striping. An owl hooted somewhere on the ridge. There was the sad, thirsty licking of the lake.

Then more human noise: a giggle, a double "shhh."

Charlie's voice, thin and wavery, made a sound like begging. "Oh," or "ow," or something in between.

I hated him and wished that I *was* him. I hated what had stiffened in my own hand.

"What's that?" Charlie said a bit too loudly.

"Don't move. Just stay still," admonished Ruff.

"But it tickles."

"I said don't move."

A tussle. The swish of something. Plastic?

"See?" said Ruff.

"It's too dark. What is it?"

"A Ziploc. Now it's got you locked inside."

"God, that's weird," said Charlie.

"It's our secret. So beautiful. You're beautiful."

I knew then that Ruff's quarter-flipping hadn't mattered; he had chosen Charlie long before that.

Eventually, I must have fallen back to sleep. When I woke again, the sky was now perilously dark, raindrops nettling my face (or were they tears?). A dense chilling fog, unbreathable. The cloudless evening had deceived us all.

In the morning, I struggled with my wet sleeping bag, trying to stuff it in its sack.

"Help you with that?" Ruff asked.

"No," I said. "I've got it on my own."

I didn't want to accept Ruff's help ever again. I didn't want anything from him.

But three days later, at the awards banquet, Ruff gave me and Charlie axes with "Lifesaver" stippled on the heads. I cried with genuine gratitude. I wasn't strong enough to turn my back on Ruff's approval. I needed it. I needed him. Still do.

And Charlie? He'd cheated me and saved me all at once; how could I ever blame or forgive him?

Back in camp, the kids all asked what animal we'd caught. To them we were heroes, pioneers. Our mystique gave their aspirations meaning.

I couldn't tell the truth, nor could I lie. "Sorry," I said. "It's a Lifesavers' secret."

I extracted myself from the sleeping bag, donned dry socks and sneakers, a poncho. My first thought was to find Max at his cabin. I wouldn't necessarily even wake him. I'd just look upon the question mark of his curled, sleeping form to know that he was still whole, surviving. If caught, though, how would I explain? A midnight trek down the hill for . . . what?

Instead, I trudged groggily to the Lodge. A honeyed mug of tea became my goal.

The rain, to my surprise, had stopped, except for windblown drizzle from the trees. The front had left a hover of tundra-smelling air that hinted at vast expanses, escape. But who knew what next storm might bluster through? Even the stars shone uncertain. They faltered like candles against some cosmic draft, yellow to vein-blue to white.

I entered the Lodge with cat-burglar steps. In the hearth, the embers of an evening fire lingered with just enough glow to throw shadows. The wagon-wheel chandeliers cast astonished o's on the ceiling.

I padded to the kitchen, where the pilot lights bestowed another degree of sight. I filled a pot and set it on to boil. Then back to the dining hall, to the fire.

Silently, in the gloom, I sat. There was the granite of the hearth beneath me, as solid and rough-edged as truth. The floor, oiled by a thousand barefoot boys (I knew each board like my own knucklebones). And the air—everywhere, the air. For so long this had been my anchored home. But what exactly was I anchored to? The firelight played tricks on Ruff's portrait.

The flame was in need of attention, so I stood and went for the cordwood stack. But the wedges I found were too big; I feared smothering the tender coals. Neither was there kindling in the box. Which cabin was assigned that chore?

I felt my way to the camper mail station, seeking scrap paper to jump-start the fire. I knocked over a cup holding a dozen ballpoint pens; they scuttled away like light-startled roaches. Locating finally some Ironwood stationery, I began twisting a pile of mini-wicks. (Ruff's long-ago instruction of fire-starting technique remained clear as a memorized alphabet.)

As I crumpled the letterhead, something Max had said came back to me. I was the only person to whom he'd tell his secret, *except*. Except, he'd already written Bryce.

I should have been glad to think Max had another ally, should have welcomed this sharing of the burden. Instead, I bristled. Why did Bryce make me so anxious? Because I didn't know him. Because here I was, weighing Max's needs against mine against the law, but for all I knew Bryce would screw up everything. He was a wild card. A risk. A monkey wrench.

All right, I'll admit it: I was jealous.

Before I quite knew what I was doing, I hauled the mailbox to the hearth and dumped it over. Letters were collected at breakfast every day; if Max had mailed it that afternoon, it should be here.

I sorted through postcards addressed to "Mom & Dad,"

through letters painstakingly labeled "Sis." And then, the sight that raised my small neck hairs: the writing was the same boxy, thick-lined pencil I'd seen on Max's camper application; the envelope was grungy with graphite. *Bryce Dawson, 119 Avenue A, New York NY 10009.*

I slit the envelope.

Yo Bryce!

Something happened. Badness. What you told me used to happen with you and your dad? Except other stuff, too. I fucked up, as usual. I guess even in the forests of VT you can't escape! Lions and tigers and bears ha ha ha. I thought I knew what I wanted, but I should have stuck with you. One dude's pretty nipple, though. Jeremy. I think he gets it.

Hey, you seen my mom? Haven't heard from her. I've got a gut that she's back in St. Vincent's. Damn.

Well, steal some Yoo-Hoo from the Koreans in my honor. Play safe. I'll write more if it gets worse here. Which direction should I run?

Later,
Max

The letter was a calligraphic minefield, each word explosive with innuendo. Even now, after all these months and mishaps, there are meanings I'm unable to parse.

Nipple? A compliment, surely. He cared enough to mention me. My neck flushed.

Other lines were more troubling. The one that stabbed most was "I fucked up." Max shouldn't feel at fault. It was Charlie! I resolved then to use Max's letter as evidence, to nail Charlie to the wall.

But when I examined the page again—through Max's cryptic slang—I realized he hadn't *named* Charlie. Without a name, the letter lost its power.

Max had said I "got it," but what did I really get? I didn't get this letter's best-friend lingo, as Bryce would. I didn't get what Charlie got—what he'd *taken*.

In the choke of jealousy I crushed the page and tossed it in the fire. Just as quickly, I pulled the letter out. Only its outer edge was singed. I smoothed it as best I could, then folded it and the envelope in my pocket. Then I noticed a close, carbony stench. Had the letter turned toxic when burned?

When I saw the dark creep of smoke leading to the kitchen, I remembered and ran for the stove. My tea water had boiled down to nothing. The steel pot was black and brittle, wrecked.

THIRTEEN

I did something I'd never done before: I slept through breakfast. I had counted on my body's circadian obedience to shove me off the plank to wakefulness. But my subconscious refused the plunge. I missed the half-hour bell, the ten-minute warning, even the clanging come-and-get-it.

What roused me at last was the ear-splitting cheer, a wave that slammed the ridge and surged back. Charlie sometimes gathered the campers on the lawn after breakfast and led them in shouts. Yell, he incited them, louder, give me more! until their voice boxes burned. Then he calmed them to a rumble, then to silence. The kids felt they'd gotten away with something.

As the boys segued into morning sing-along, I overcame inertia and got up. Fatigue dogged me, stomping at my heels. I crested the hill to the strains of "Here Comes the Sun" and saw above, indeed, a brilliant morning. A sky the color of first-place ribbons was broken by a single heart-shaped cloud. But the clarity only heightened my confusion. I was mired in last night's memory and indecision, now metastasized into system-wide dread.

Dread edged to dismay when I rounded the Lodge and saw Charlie dressed as the devil. Razor horns, red suit, a goatee. With fire-and-brimstone fury he ranted and declaimed—something about the coming end of days. For emphasis, he brandished a pitchfork. Then his voice rose and he declared with an emcee's enunciation: "Today's all-camp game is . . . Armageddon!"

Wild whoops from the campers, and a slap to sense for me. The reason for his costume clarified.

Whenever Charlie thought Ironwood's mood was sagging, he cancelled plans and called an all-camp game. Given our outsize population, sports like soccer and football weren't practical. Instead we cooked up wacky games, introduced by slapstick skits to mask the fact that nine out of ten were capture the flag, barely veiled. All we did was substitute another object for the flag, then develop a lunatic backstory. For example, when the "flags" were cans of Penzoil, we played "Gulf War Showdown"—the Bush Leaguers against the Saddamites.

"Armageddon" was our latest invention: Lucifer's minions against St. Peter's angelic host. We'd concocted the game and its silly skit at the last staff meeting. By oversleeping, I'd just missed my role. I skulked into place between Charlie and Doug Rose.

"What happened?" Doug hissed. "You were supposed to be St. Peter!"

"Sorry. I had to . . ." I struggled for an excuse, then answered truthfully, "I overslept."

"Thanks a lot. Too late now. Look at me."

He had curtain rods shoved into his jeans, the curtains billowing as wings. Above his blond brush cut, a tinfoiled coat hanger made a preposterous halo.

"You look . . . heavenly," I said.

He rolled his eyes and mouthed, "You owe me one."

"Okay," Charlie was saying, "above the road is Heaven; below is Hell. The road is Purgatory—no-man's-land."

At stake, he explained, were campers' "souls," represented by orange life preservers. If the angels captured Satan's preserver, Goodness would prevail; if the demons were first, Evil ruled the day. In addition, there were two groups of rovers—the Apostles and the Apocalyptic Horsemen—who would convert boys to their respective teams.

Like startled birds, hands flocked into the air. The game's rules were perforated with ambiguity. And the strained, bewildered faces of these answer-begging boys sent me back to my own anxiety. How could we play games with the trouble in our midst?

I found Max by his jaded baseball cap—in the crowd, body-guarded by cabinmates. Behind them sat Simon, plucking tufts of clover, as much a boy as a counselor himself. (Should I tell him? Could he handle knowing?)

I wanted to give Max a wink, a private nod, but he never looked anywhere above the ground. I was heartened, though, by the way he and Eli lolled together like puppies from the same runty litter. He appeared safe for now, stabilized. His broken wrist rested easily on his chest.

Charlie pulled a cheat sheet from the pocket of his costume. "It's pretty simple," he said. "Say the Horsemen want to get an angel to their side. First they catch him, then they say the follow-ing: 'In the name of Satan's blasphemy and deviant catastrophe, we steal your soul into our depthless hole.'" He beamed. "Nice ring to it, don't you think?"

No, I didn't. It sounded too much like the formula for Amish excommunication. When a member is expelled, the bishop in-tones, *"dem Teufel und allen seinen Engeln übergeben"*—the guilty is committed "to the devil and all his angels." Beulah Glick had told me this was what had frightened her the most, hearing herself marked with this ancient curse. She felt a weight, she said, a hopeless crushing weight, as if yoked to all the evil in the world.

Charlie flipped his paper to the other side. "The Apostles' in-cantation goes like this: 'In the name of Holy Trinity and Iron-wood Divinity, we bring your soul back to your Father, whole!'"

Groans of perplexity. Blank stares.

"There's obviously some confusion," he said. "Let's do a dem-onstration. I'll be an Apostle, but I need a couple of assistants."

Once again, hands lifted to the sky.

"All right, Duncan, you can come on up. And . . . Jared."

The anointed boys made their way to the front, high-fiving mutual congratulations.

"And for the sinner?" Charlie said. "Let's see. Max? Okay, sure, come on down."

Max hadn't even raised his hand. He cocked his head for an instant, the way a magician's helper, summoned to be "sawed in half," might briefly pause. But he didn't seem to be bothered by impressment. He ambled to the front, ushered by chants of "Max! Max! Max!" His eyes were trained downward as he stood in the camp's spotlight. His slump was that of someone hypnotized.

"You've got to hold him," Charlie said, his face flushed nearly to his costume's fiendish hue. "One on the left arm, one on the right, and then the head."

Jared claimed Max's left wrist with executioner's force, while Duncan, on Max's injured side, gripped the elbow.

"Keep in mind," Charlie said, "that he's going to be struggling. You've got to say the words fast as you can."

Max, though, was anything but resistant. His arms were all calm accommodation; his All Stars flatfooted the grass.

A tickle at my elbow made me jump. It was Doug, batting his wings for my attention. "Told you Max was wicked," he said, but kiddingly—Max's winsomeness had tempered his dislike. "Just hope the parents don't get wind of all this sacrilege."

Was this, too, meant in jest? Or did Doug sense the underlying villainy?

Charlie faced me with his pitchfork. "Mind holding this?"

I had no choice. I took the tool.

"Right," he said. "So we've nabbed the little devil, and we're going to hold him while we say the formula. You got him?"

Solemn nods from his deputies.

"Good, I'll hold him, too. On his head, see, like this?"

Charlie laid his hands on Max's temples. The gesture was clinical, with a surgeon's cold precision, but also with the implicit hint of violence.

"On three. One, two, three: 'In the name of Holy Trinity—'"

But the rest was inaudible for my shout. I dropped the pitchfork and dashed to Max's aid.

"No," I said, ripping Charlie's hands off of him. Duncan and Jared backed away.

"What are you doing?" said Charlie.

"Stop! That's enough!"

My voice froze the crowd to a still life. In the quiet we could hear my words echoing off the ridge, as the campers' shouting contest had before.

"It's not safe," I sputtered. I appealed to Doug: "Someone's bound to be hurt."

"I guess," he said. "But if the kids are careful?"

Charlie placed a hard hand on my shoulder. "It's a good point, Jer. Totally valid concern. But our usual safety rule should be enough: Never put someone else in jeopardy."

He smiled at me, then at the boys, with sovereign condescension, seeming not to guess my reason for alarm. In our scuffle, his paste-on goatee had been ripped. It hung like a bloody afterthought from his chin.

Beside him, although now perfectly free to move, Max stood as if waiting for someone's orders.

Charlie split the camp into its teams. He announced that he was walking down now to the camp bell; when he rang it, the game would begin. He reclaimed his pitchfork from me and waved it. "Take your marks. The end is near!"

As Charlie and the other boys trundled down the hill, Max retreated to the lawn's bramble edge. He signaled that I, too, should stick around.

I knew what I had to do. Legally, I had twelve hours left. But foremost in my mind wasn't the law, it was safety: his, mine, all the other campers'. I would call Child Protective Services.

"Hey," he said in a minuscule voice.

My whisper back to him felt furtive, criminal. "You okay? They didn't hurt you?"

"The wrist? Nope. Hardly even feel it."

"Great. That's great. That's progress."

In the silence that ensued, I whiffed his body odor (a smell that now, when I pass certain boys in Harvard Square, floods my sinuses with reminiscence). There was the dirty-sock stench of unwashed adolescence, commingled with a sharp, grown-up sweat. Max's face, normally plaster-pale, was blotchy with distress. His cheeks looked as though they'd been sandpapered.

I was wondering how to break the news. CPS would keep things confidential, I could say. His safety would be guaranteed.

Before I could speak, he said, "About last night?"

"Yeah," I said. "I think we have to talk."

He cleared his throat and made to spit, then swallowed the phlegm instead. "What I said? Last night? Just forget it."

"Forget it? Max, what do you mean?"

"It was just a . . . I mean, it's really nothing."

"It's not nothing. You were right to tell me." I offered him the buttress of my hand on his shoulder, but he shrugged away and out from under it.

"Maybe it didn't even happen," he said.

From downhill, the steely certainty of the camp bell resounded. Yelps of gleeful gaming filled the air.

Max looked at me: Was there apology in his wilted blue eyes? That, and a bloodshot trace of fear.

"The game's starting," he said. "I gotta go." He loped off, not quite running, down the path.

FOURTEEN

I didn't call CPS. I didn't tell anyone.

What would I have said? That the moment I was moved to molest a teenager in my care, he accused my boss (who happened also to be my oldest friend) of beating me to the kill—but that the next day, the kid had recanted? It wasn't exactly "Book 'em, Dano" material.

Was Charlie threatening Max? Possibly. Or maybe Max was terrified by the prospect of intervention. When his mother went to rehab, he'd likely been a ward of the state. Had the welfare folks in New York mistreated him?

On the other hand, maybe Max's retraction was honest. Maybe he'd really made the story up. The wishful thought struck me that he'd invented the abuse as a desperate plea for contact: not to dissuade my touching him, but to inspire.

Time slunk by, dragging its feet. A day, three, five. I lost track.

Rain again, a stalled front that punished us with damp; ceaseless static like a shipwreck's radio. Wet, windless mornings turned to wet, windless noons as the sun grudged its rut behind the clouds.

We had planned this week to build the long-postponed log shelter. We'd cleared the spot and poured foundations before camp, and now were set to start with sills and joists. But outdoor work was indefinitely rain-delayed.

We sought sanctuary in the Lodge. All hundred of us, all at once. At first we tried to maintain a semblance of routine. Doug

Rose brought out *The Ashley Book of Knots* and distributed lengths of thong to the kids; they fashioned sheet bends, Dutch cringles, monkey's fists. Bill McIndoe coerced some boys into varnishing canoe paddles. Teddy Trimble taught how to fletch arrows.

But after a simmering day of claustrophobia, forestalling lunacy became our only goal. From dusty bins we retrieved boards for backgammon, Chinese checkers. Ken Krueger warmed a bottomless vat of cocoa. I played every harmonica tune I knew.

The Lodge assumed the pall of a refugee camp. Mud smeared the floor, then the benches, then our clothes. Ponchos dripped on every nail and peg. The air was dense with wet-wool musk and smoke.

Max's closeness worsened everything. There he was in all his inscrutable beauty—near enough to count the freckles on his nose—but speaking with him privately was hopeless. I can't say he specifically shunned me (although the one time he was partnerless for cribbage and I approached, he decided he was suddenly sick of playing). But in the barracks climate, we kept communication to the functional: Are you warm? Do you have dry clothes to wear? My deeper questions—Which story was the lie? Whom do you want?—snagged within me thick and choking as the smoke.

Charlie, too, was cooped in our refuge. He spent his time flitting among the boys, telling jokes, attempting to bolster spirits. At intervals, we consulted on logistics. Could the Seward's truck make it up the slick drive with our milk? Had the radio predicted any break of sunshine? Nothing was said of our confrontation. Our nimble choreography of avoidance brought to mind log-rolling stunt lumberjacks: never sure which direction meant sinking, which being sunk; hotfooting at top speed to stay put.

On the second night of captivity, Cornelio set up a slide projector. Max's counselor was shaky in his command of English, but photography is a universal tongue. Boys shouted as he clicked from slide to slide: a cabin cookout, Caroline's apple toss. As I might have searched the police photographs of a crime scene, I scrutinized these images for Max. Perhaps from this angle, or from that, I'd glean a clue.

Night shots, hard to fathom, black on black. Then eruptions of color: July Fourth. In person, the shells had soared perfect, overwhelming, but in stasis they glared garish and unreal. Magic was unmasked as trickery.

On my day off, I was more than ready to escape. A project I had in mind required the hour's drive to Dartmouth, where I could put my research skills to use. I worried about leaving Max unsupervised at camp. But he'd have ducked my supervision anyway.

As I came upon Dartmouth's campus—precisely ivied bricks, lockjawed charm—I tried to imagine Ruff here in college. How had a quirky farm boy like him ever fit in? (He'd once told me that his boyhood hobbies ran more to bird watching than baseball.) But somehow he had managed to adjust. Witness his devotion to the Dartmouth Outing Club, his choice of "Dartmouth green" for Ironwood. If once he'd been a misfit, Ruff had clearly been retooled: first Dartmouth, then the army, then camp—all-male enclaves where conformity ruled. It was as though he were a square peg who'd sought out round holes, hoping they would shave him down to size. Was there something in his natural shape he feared?

The college library was a churchlike building with a weathervaned bell tower. Its waxed chessboard floor foiled my plans for a subtle entrance. Sneakers squeaking, I walked a gauntlet of purse-lipped librarians, as though I'd been audibly flatulent. But I marshaled my own Ivy League arrogance and strode on as though I'd meant to make the noise. Unlike Widener, where guards sternly demand Harvard ID, in this library all you needed was attitude.

I battled a moment's homesickness for my monkish book-filled carrel, my unencumbered academic life—to be disentangled from the mess of boys. Lee Miller had done it, or something similar. He'd left behind the painful complications of his Amish past and was now answerable only to his books. But was that honestly the kind of life I wanted? Lee's library existence was enviously serene, but serenity and deprivation are kissing cousins.

I settled myself at a gray-faced computer terminal and out of habit, before today's project, searched all databases for keyword "Amish." During my brief absence another two monographs had appeared: something about tractor use in the Elkhart, Indiana, settlement, and a job survey of Amish-raised women who decline baptism. That last was a bit too close for comfort. Scholars were finally realizing interest in the ex-Amish, nipping at my intellectual heels. Every day increased the risk of my dissertation's being (if brought to term) stillborn by obsolescence.

There were also a slew of citations from daily newspapers, a breaking story in late June that I had missed. Lexis-Nexis brought up a *Philadelphia Inquirer* article:

Plain but Not So Simple: Amish Men Accused in Cocaine Ring

Prosecutors in Lancaster County yesterday accused two Amish men of distributing cocaine to other members of their strict religious sect at Sunday night parties known as "hoedowns." Noah Stoltzfus, 23, and Christian Zook, 22, have been released on their own recognizance, awaiting arraignment.

The Amish refer to their Sunday party groups as "gangs," but until now this seemed a quaint misnomer, as the gatherings have been characterized by softball games and occasional beer drinking, not the criminal activity associated with inner-city youth. Recently, however, say local officials, the Amish rite of passage known as "rumschpringa," or sowing of wild oats, has gotten out of hand.

Between the years of school and their baptism into the church, Amish men take a break from the rules of their tight-knit subculture, which requires them to be "separate from the world." Some get driver's licenses, attend movies, or wear flashy clothes.

And now, apparently, some indulge in the worldliest of drugs.

I was saddened—what a terrible disruption of Plain life. I also knew it was great material. If the men were banned, I would need to speak with them.

The article discussed the steady encroachment of temptation that made it difficult for the Amish to stay untouched; many were leaving, it said, starting settlements elsewhere. And then, at the story's end, after court dates were noted, I read a final devastating sentence: "According to prosecutors, a juvenile identified only as JY also participated in the conspiracy, but it is unclear whether he will be indicted."

Jakie? It couldn't be. No way.

The J could be Jonas or Jonathan or Joe. The Y could be Yutzy or Yost. I'd heard of Amish folks with all those names. Besides, the inbred Amish are famously same-named; there must be a dozen Jacob Yoders in the county.

The Jakie I'd witnessed tipsily kissing some girl was a far cry from a dealer of cocaine. But a far cry from the previous Jakie, too. What if he'd strayed even more? That's why the Amish draw their line so bold: One step across puts you on a slope so slippery that you can't help but plummet fast and long.

From this distance, what could I do to help? Probably nothing.

The boy I might possibly help was Max.

From my pocket I removed his letter. By now it was limp like an old dollar bill and smelled, too, of money's flimsy hopefulness. Bryce's address was smeared but readable.

I'd already tried Information, to no avail. The day after Max told me to "forget about" his accusations, I'd snuck into the Dump during lunch. I called Manhattan and spelled Bryce's name. There was a B. Dawson on East 83rd Street and another on West 110th, but nothing on Avenue A. Just in case, I dialed both numbers, then promptly hung up on a Barbara and a Bernice.

I was not without detective experience. Amish folks, after they're shunned, sometimes change their surnames, but almost always tell a neighbor where they've moved. I had learned to track a person not by name, but by address, using a reverse phone directory. Not only did Dartmouth possess such a listing, they had it conveniently online.

I keyed in the Zip Code, followed by the street address. With a blink of the computer's omniscient gray gaze, I hit informational pay dirt.

The reference librarian directed me downstairs to a phone. The booth was a relic: three metal walls and a glass-paneled door. It reminded me of a quiz-show "isolation booth." Inside, I felt the heady mix of doubt and self-assurance I imagine contestants must endure.

On the ninth ring someone finally answered. I was greeted by some words, against frenetic background noise, like a drunk slurring "Yes, sir" to a policeman.

"Excuse me," I said. "What did you say?"

"Odessa," the man spat. "What you want?"

"Odessa? What's Odessa?"

"Odessa Restaurant. You call, so what you want?"

Now the background noises clarified: the cold clank of dishes, a griddle's greasy hiss. A waitress called, "Two cabbage, one kasha."

"I think I have the wrong number. Is this"—I glanced at Max's runic writing—"119 Avenue A?"

"Yes. Already I tell you: Odessa."

"Does someone—is there someone there named Bryce?"

"No. Nobody." He hung up.

Back at camp, a letter from Beulah Glick, forwarded from my Cambridge address. I recognized her looping, guileless script. She must have written, I surmised, about the cocaine controversy. Jakie was her nephew, after all.

"Dear friend Jeremy," she began—still conforming to quintessential Amish style. "How are you? I sure hope you're doing well. It's been a long while since I put pen in hand for friendship's sake."

What followed was a two-paragraph weather report, about

"suitable sun for haying" and "creeks so low the watercress just wants to wilt." After that, more chitchatty catch-up. Benny, she wrote, was almost ready for first grade; his hair had lost its baby blond. Lancaster County was busier than ever. Had I heard they might turn the Petersheim farm into a retirement village?

Then, tacked to the back end of what I thought was just another filler sentence, came a stunner: "The quarter moon just hardly seemed to shine on June the 12th, the night Jonas was riding in Steve Hutchinson's convertible and they hit a deer, which sent him up and over the hood. We held the funeral the next day. None of his family came."

In meek but measured prose, she tried to make sense of Jonas's death. "Maem always said, 'Never put a question mark where God has put a period,' so I'm trying not to ask why this happened. But my own life—well, that's a sentence I've got to keep on writing." She could confess and return to the Amish church, she wrote. The door was always open to those who repented. Benny was young enough to switch back with no problem, and Beulah herself wouldn't much miss living "fast." Freed from Jonas, maybe she'd find a new husband.

Once a shunned person has confessed and been restored to the church, her transgression is never mentioned again; the silence signals absolute forgiveness. But what if the sinner herself *needs* to talk? Even if an Amish man would accept her, Beulah wondered, how could she ever accept herself? She would always know exactly what she'd done.

I must have met a few people in her situation, she mused. All my traveling, talking to folks, my research. What would I, with my book learning, think was best?

I took this, finally, after all these one-way years, as an invitation to write Beulah back. For the life of me, I didn't know what to say.

FIFTEEN

—◄○►—

My first dream of Max. (If only it were the last.) We're in Peach
Bottom, riding in the back of a pickup truck on a fog-hushed,
tepid, moony night. Ruff is driving. A swerve, a screech, the burn
of brakes. With one hand I reach for the solid spare tire, with the
other grab urgently for Max. Before I can, he is launched skyward, gone.

"Beautiful," Ruff is saying as he slinks from the cab. "Did
you see? A little fawn. So beautiful."

Then, in the way of dreams, Ruff transforms into Charlie.
And then Ruff/Charlie disappears.

I find Max flopped on the yellow median as though hung on
the post of a crucifix. In the moonlight his blue eyes are milky,
mirrorlike—the only part of him that seems alive.

"I have to tell you something," he says.

"Okay. You can tell me anything."

"He touched me."

"Who touched you?"

"He did."

I know and I don't know who "he" is. I ask Max to show me
where exactly he was touched, but his paralyzed arms don't respond. Dark blood seeps behind his skull.

"Was it here?" I ask. My hands meet his face, his chilling
cheeks.

"No," he says.

Next, his gulping throat.

"No. Not there, either. Lower."

Scalloped ribs, open kiss of belly button.

"Here?"

"No."

"Here?"

"Unh-unh."

Then the one place in him that still beats with warmth. Its pulse, like mine, is quickening.

"Here?" I ask.

"Yes."

"Like this?"

"Yes . . . yes." But then: "*Duh net! Shick dich!* Behave!"

His voice fades, the light fades, blood rushes from his flesh.

"So beautiful," I hear—or do I say it?

And I'm crying, huge tears that swirl with his fleeing life. It all mixes: yes and no, blood and tears.

I awoke hard and touched myself as I'd touched Max in the dream, felt the same fluid pulse beneath my skin. I beat myself. My fist came away wet.

The rain, finally, had stopped, giving way to a muffled, moody haze. I spent a day sulking through routine: paperwork, a guarding stint at the waterfront (the lake was urine-warm, unrefreshing). The names Bryce and Odessa clattered around my mind, loose bearings that stalled its normal spin. Did the riddle have an answer I was blind to? More confounded than ever, I huffed my way to dinner.

Caroline stood at the Lodge door with spread-eagled arms, blocking a thick camper mob. On her head, in place of the usual Red Sox cap, bobbed a ten-gallon Stetson; a toy gun belt slipped down her hips. "In this town," she drawled, "I'm the law and the only law. And the law says: Y'all got to be clean to eat."

Hoots and hollers: "We're starving!" "Let us in!"

"Heck no," she said. Her cowpoke accent sounded like a Dolly Parton ballad played too slow. "Too many a y'all's slackin' off, not warshin' up. Well, I'm tuckered out from cleaning up your puke. Vomit, upchuck—I'm up to my ears in sick."

As always, her lunatic style enthralled the boys. But I detected, behind her smile, the weariness.

"Seriously," she added, back in her normal voice. "There's fifteen kids and counting with this flu. So when I say 'No washy,' what do you say?"

"No eaty," came a sputtering call.

"No washy?!" she said louder.

"No eaty!"

"Not bad. But to help the lesson sink in, I want y'all to go back to the warshroom and scrub up. Get along dogies, hya!"

A few kids grumbled, but astonishingly, the horde backed away. As they single-filed for the washroom, I approached. Even in this moment of distress, Caroline retained a reassuring solidity. It was a physical sensation, a coherence, as though she magnetized the scatter of our world.

"Hanging in there?" I asked. (It was the question I wished someone would ask me.)

"Depends. Are you Jeremy the assistant director and my sort-of boss? Or Jeremy my pal?"

"Either. Both. Up to you."

"Well, this sucks. Why'd they all get sick at once?"

"Anything I can do?"

"Sure, make the Sox win the pennant. Or maybe just invent a wonder drug."

What would Sadie do—brew a vervain tea?

"The worst thing?" said Caroline. "Charlie's totally on my ass. 'This whole camp better not be sick when the parents come. The infirmary's not our best selling point.'"

"God. Visiting day. I'd blocked it out."

"Join the club. But it's only"—she counted on her fingers—"four days. When the Volvos come, I swear I'm going AWOL."

"Speaking of . . . where's Charlie now?"

Caroline rolled her eyes. "The camp's falling apart, but one of his favorites is in the dumps, so they were going off for some one-on-one time."

My gut clutched: Max. What should I do?

A steady flow of campers, hands pink from scouring, began

streaming back to the door. "Nice work, pardner," said Caroline, inspecting each.

As more and more passed through, the Lodge's noise swelled to bedlam. Something banged. There was the gasp of shattered glass.

"Aren't there any counselors in there?" I asked.

"Apparently not." She admitted two more kids.

"Jesus. If you want something done around here. . . ." I plugged my ears to enter the fray.

"Whoa! Not so fast!" Caroline snagged my belt loops, stalling me midstride. "How 'bout those paws?" she said.

"Ha ha. Lucky for me, I'm friends with the inspector."

She held me fast. "I'm serious. You can get sick just as easy. Go back and wash."

"Come on. They're perfectly clean—look!"

Bottlenecked, the campers voiced impatience. "What's the holdup?" "Out of the friggin' way." Then the nearest boys tuned in to our standoff. (Adult arguments emit a special frequency that kid antennas pick up instantly; if grown-ups disagree, they must be fallible.)

Dylan Shallot, with smug pleasure twisting his face, said, "He didn't wash! Jeremy didn't wash!"

The phrase zoomed bee-like through the crowd, spreading a pollen of righteous accusation.

"Caroline," I whispered. "This is ludicrous. Let me in."

But Dylan installed himself between us; he could hear every heated syllable. A knot of boys leaned behind him combatively, ready to balk at any sign of special treatment.

"Can't do it," said Caroline. "Rules are rules."

"Send him back," Dylan cried, and the crowd picked up his chant.

"Send him back! Send him back!"

I retreated through the campers, and they gave me a wide berth, as if my condition might be catching.

That night's staff-meeting agenda revealed standard Week Three issues: day-off swap requests, understaffed swims. In the wake of the long deluge, Jim Talbot would assess trail-repair needs. Under "Health," Caroline's topic was: "What happened?"

Charlie guided the meeting in his kingly, commanding style. If his conscience suffered about Max, it didn't show.

When the time came for discipline concerns, Simon asked the group for help. His Mansfield boys were usually sweet-tempered, he said, but their squalls of insubordination wrecked him. "Like the other day, at rest hour, I asked Toby to stop humming, so then Dylan started up, then everyone. Pretty soon they were shouting, jumping on their bunks."

Simon hadn't mentioned Max as especially bothersome. How often was Max the problem? The solution?

"Any advice for Simon?" Charlie asked.

"At rest hour?" said Jim Talbot, smiling saucily. "Try ear plugs. I sleep like a baby."

"Easy enough for the maintenance man," said Charlie. "Any cabin counselors want to give it a go?"

Doug Rose raised his arm. He'd been Simon's counselor five years ago, when he was nineteen and Simon fourteen. "In an avalanche, Si, the only safe thing is to jump out of the way. So prevention's the most important thing."

"I try," Simon said. "I think I'm really strict."

"Maybe *too* strict is the problem. You know how ski patrollers set off mini-avalanches on purpose? Or out west: those burns to prevent forest fires? Maybe you need to loosen up sometimes."

I'd often given the same advice. It was gratifying to watch the handing down of wisdom from someone besides Charlie or me. I fancied us sometimes as those cloud-seeding scientists who bring rain to drought-ridden lands: We raised boys into competent, compassionate young men, then released them to spur thunder-bursts of the same.

But tonight, despite Doug Rose's nurturing shower, the world seemed a lifeless badlands. Detachment was increasingly the air I breathed.

I doodled in the margins of my notebook, mindlessly scribbling camper names. Petey, Toby, Abe. Then Abe became Abner, and I listed Amish names. Jakie Yoder. Emma Riehl. Christian Zook. I wrote *Beulah* and toyed anagrammatically.

Be.

Blah.

Blue.

A shoulder tap. I turned to find Cornelio, who informed me it was my turn to patrol. I nodded and forfeited my seat.

Bill McIndoe was my patrol partner tonight. Since his grandmother's death he'd been skittish and broody. In a better time, I'd have taken the chance to console him, but just now his mournfulness matched my mood. We spoke only long enough to divvy up the cabin area, then walked separately into the murk.

As Bill's footfalls dwindled, the night enveloped me with an unaccustomed tightness, like a favorite shirt shrunk in the wash. There was a stingy moon, cataracted by clouds. I relied instead on my headlamp, seeing only within its slim wedge of light.

I stalked through the cabin area, step by nervous step, as though the ground might be laced with mines. But from the bunks I heard only narcotic murmuring, the anodyne rustle of sleeping bags. I poked my head into Shrewsbury, then Saltash, then Pico, and all eyes were peacefully shut.

Mansfield, by the lake with its coy kissing sounds, was my last stop; I switched the headlamp off. Would they be Jekylls or Hydes on this dark night? I tiptoed inside. There were the mouth-breathers' mantralike emissions, the occasional whisper of a snore—barely enough noise to wake a baby.

Then a new noise, an animal sniveling. But a human animal, I was sure. I shielded the headlamp and turned it back on, aimed its dim beam around the room.

There again—a wheeze, a tiny moan. It led me outside and down below the cabin, where the scree dove steeply to the lake. Hugging the cabin's foundations for support, I hunched underneath the deck. I slipped and slid into something, hard.

"Unh," I heard, and knew I'd kicked Max, but he didn't acknowledge my "sorry."

He sat where I'd found his Hershey's bar. Despite the head-lamp's glare his pupils were huge: puncture wounds from which some lifeblood leaked. The skin of his eyes and cheeks was redly puffed.

"Max?" I said. "What is it? Talk to me."

He didn't. He shook. He sank away.

His sneakers, at the end of his mantislike legs, had nudged into the gurgling lake.

"Your shoes," I said.

He didn't move. Water wicked slyly up the toe.

"They're getting wet," I said. "Come on."

When he still didn't answer, I pulled them out myself. His pliant heft reminded me of a thing recently dead. It reminded me of the paralyzed dream-Max.

"He did it again," finally came the waifish voice.

"Again?" I said. "I thought it never happened."

"I was lying."

"And you're not lying now?"

I was angry at Max, but mostly at myself. In my wavering, I'd placed him back at risk.

"I need you," he said, "to believe me."

He sobbed once, then silenced himself with the thumb of his bad hand. He didn't suck the thumb so much as gnaw it. I glimpsed torn skin, a dark bead of blood.

My headlamp was still squarely in his eyes, so I trained it down. But I kept it on; I needed to see some of him.

"Can you tell me? What happened this time?"

"Like before," he said. His words emerged laggard and mushy, as though his tongue were swollen, unfamiliar.

"He touched you," I said.

Max nodded.

I wanted to ask where—how—but the discomfort of last night's dream prevented me. Instead, thinking of Ruff—of what I'd wanted at Max's age—I asked, "And did you touch him, too?"

"He just wanted to, you know, do me."

"Did he threaten you?"

"He said . . . he said that if I . . ." But that was all he could manage. With his thumb, he traced a pattern on his jeans.

I placed a taming hand on Max's cast. "I'm going to have to tell people now."

Max flinched, but at the same time he nodded. On the denim, his thumb had left a bloody circle.

"The social service folks," I clarified, trying to make them sound friendly, different from the ones Max might have met in New York. "They're going to have to check this out. But I think your family should know, too. We tried to get hold of your mother. Have you heard from her?"

"Unh-unh." Max worried his jeans again, drawing an X through the previous shape. "She's sick. In the hospital, I think."

"Sick how?"

"You know, *sick* sick. AIDS."

"Oh. Oh god, I'm sorry."

Max snorted. "Yeah, well so is she."

I hadn't spoken with my own mother lately. Superstition lit a sudden burn to call.

"How about your grandparents?" I asked.

"They're not her parents. They don't care."

"But you can . . . I mean, if something happens?"

"I don't think they like me," he said.

"Of course they do. Didn't they send you here? And what about, um"—feigning a lapse of memory, nonchalance—"that friend of yours?"

"Bryce?"

"Bryce. Is he someone you can count on?"

Even now, having just learned about Max's mother and realizing how truly adrift he was, I was focused on damping my confusion.

"I thought I could count on him," Max said.

"But?"

"But I sent a letter. He never even wrote back."

"Give it time," I said, "maybe he'll come around."

The lie made my mouth taste like soap. A breeze swirled between us like a ghost.

"I'm scared," said Max. "I can't sleep."

"I know. But you're going to have to. They're expecting me soon at the staff meeting."

"What if Charlie comes back?"

"In the middle of the night? With the other campers around?"

"But what if he does?"

Max listed sideways, onto me. The way a kitten will stretch to stay in a patch of sun, his body followed when I inched away.

"Can I sleep with you?" he asked. "In your tent?"

His cast weighed thrillingly on my thigh.

"Can I, Jeremy? Just tonight?"

Now his hand found its way into my lap.

"No," I said, with a vehemence to match my body's instinctive *yes*. "But we'll find somewhere. Stand up. Can you walk?"

There was a room at the Lodge, adjacent to the kitchen, where Ken Krueger sometimes napped between meals. But with the staff meeting, I was nervous we'd be seen. The infirmary would normally have been the easy choice, but it was filled with diarrheic campers; every bed, Caroline had said, was spoken for.

"Not every bed," said Max. "There's still one."

"You sure? Caroline told me she was booked."

"Not the meds room. There's a cot in there. I've seen it."

"The meds room's locked."

"Don't you know where the key is?"

I had to admit that I did.

At the road, we met Bill McIndoe. He'd been hunting for me; it was time to switch patrols. I told him Max's stomach was terrible with cramps and that I was looking after him. I'd rejoin the meeting as soon as I could. Bill said fine and walked on, self-absorbed.

We padded into the infirmary, feeling our way by the glow of night-lights. The place was chalky with the smell of pills and sickness. From the bunk room, patients' ill-breathing chafed the air.

I retrieved the key from its cache—a Red Zinger box in the cupboard—and freed the meds-room door of its padlock.

"You can't tell anyone, all right?"

Max zipped a finger across his lips.

"I'm serious. In the morning, I want you to head back to your cabin. Early, before Caroline comes in. Tell Simon you were showering, or something."

Max already had his shoes off and had settled on the cot. A blanket covered everything but his head.

"Are you going to be all right?"

Max said he would.

"Okay. We'll talk more in the morning." And then I bent and kissed Max, dryly, on the spot between his brows. "Dream rainbows," I said. "Dream pots of gold."

SIXTEEN

The day before induction, Amish baptismal candidates are given a last chance to "turn back." Amish life is difficult, a minister reminds them; it is not the right path for everyone. Once baptized, they'll be enjoined to stay separate from the world, to keep the *Ordnung,* to live "without spot or blemish." If they doubt their will or their ability to conform, then it's better to wait and reconsider; better never to make the vow than make and break it.

What I lacked, it occurs to me now, was such a guide: someone to help me recognize the point of no return and decide whether to pass or stop short. Ruff Peterson should have been that person.

First thing in the morning, I checked the meds room. The door was locked. Just to be sure, I got the key and took a peek. Max was gone. The cot was made. It looked pristine.

While Ironwood busied itself with breakfast, I called Child Protective Services. The officer who responded was Don Fisher. (Fisher: the third most common Amish name in Lancaster; should I ask where his people came from?) He sounded easygoing but methodical, with a bricklayer's step-by-step persistence. He asked when the child had first alleged abuse, and I lied; I said just last night. He kept calling Max "the child." I wanted to convey to him how unchildlike Max could be, how he often seemed more knowing than most adults.

"Anyone else been informed?" Fisher asked.

Not Bryce. Not Caroline. I told him no.

"Okay," he said, and promised to send some officers the next day. In the meantime he would reach Max's family. Could I supply contact information?

I battled misgivings. But CPS, I reminded myself, was on Max's side; they and I were perhaps the only ones. I gave Fisher Max's home number, cautioning that it didn't seem to work. I mentioned the dead father, the distant grandparents.

"We'll see if we have better luck," Fisher said. "But even if not, we'll move ahead. Now, tell me, can you keep the child under watch?"

"Under watch? How do you mean?"

"He should never be out of sight of an adult. And no contact with the alleged perp."

The phrase was like a razor at my eye. I tried to picture Charlie on a "Ten Most Wanted" poster, but saw a different, less conclusive image: Charlie, at eleven, collecting candy.

"Mr. Fisher," I said, "this is summer camp."

Silence strangled the line. I wondered what Don Fisher looked like. He sounded older, but not too old, maybe forty. There was a pinkish tone to his voice that made me think him overweight. What kind of man spent his life protecting kids?

"Is there maybe something like kitchen duty?" he said. "Some place where the kid would be supervised?"

"The infirmary," I said. "The nurse is there. Or, if not her, lots of kids. We've got a flu."

"Fine. Tell him to play sick. Give him ginger ale. Just make sure he keeps mum about the reason."

We agreed to talk again that afternoon.

I hit the road as the boys loafed to first activity, a heel-nipping, puppyish herd. Summoning indifference, I beelined for the infirmary. I would find Caroline, explain to her our ruse.

Past the shade maple, around the dogleg curve, and there she was. But she wasn't alone. Next to her stood Charlie.

Right away I could tell something was wrong. Normally, like

a polished lens, Caroline focused the world; she was a clarifier, a bringer-down-to-size. Now she emanated a scattershot distress.

Charlie, too, appeared disarranged. His copper hair had been messed—by wind or nervous pulling?—to resemble a match tip, just igniting.

"We've got a problem," said Caroline. "Max."

The name was a cuss word, an indictment.

"Max? What about him? What did he say?"

"Nothing yet," Charlie said. "We haven't confronted him."

"We've had a break-in," said Caroline. "The meds room."

Shit. Had I forgotten to relock the door?

"Are you sure? Maybe the door just got left open by mistake." If only I could explain everything to Caroline. If only she hadn't told Charlie first.

She glared. Her jaw muscles swelled in small bullets. "I don't 'just leave the door open.' Ever. But it's not that the door was open. It wasn't. A bunch of Percocet is missing."

"Jesus, really?"

"Almost half a bottle. Gone."

"But what makes you think it was Max? Just because it was prescribed for his wrist?"

Charlie stepped forward, too close. His breath was morning-stale in my face. "We think it's Max because he stole some before. July Fourth, when we were all at the apple orchard. We just warned him then, gave him a second chance."

"July Fourth? Why didn't I hear about this?"

That was all the protest I could manage. I would like to have argued that it couldn't be so, that Max wouldn't do a thing like that, but the truth was disappointingly blatant. Max's spaciness, his weird dilated pupils. The mood swings, the disassociation. He'd been that way last night, and the Fourth of July, too—both times when he laid the blame on Charlie. In Rutland, after the doctor refused a new prescription, that's when Max had tossed his temper tantrum.

"We didn't mention anything," Charlie said, "because a) we

didn't have physical evidence, and b) we know his home situation. We thought if we kept it quiet, asked him to shape up . . ."

"But he blew it," said Caroline. "No one fucks with my meds. No one."

"What do we do now?" I asked—thinking of Don Fisher and his CPS procedures, of my own late-night promises to Max. Every nugget of certainty dissolved to sludge.

Charlie pressed his temples, as if to keep his skull from fissuring. How had I been so ready to condemn him?

"My instinct is to kick him out," he said. "The kid's too big a risk—to us and to himself."

In all the summers I'd worked at Ironwood, only two campers had been expelled: one who attacked his counselor with a Swiss Army knife, and one who stole a van and drove to town.

"Shouldn't we at least talk to him?" I protested. "Give him the chance to explain?"

"We gave him the chance already," said Caroline.

"But you said there wasn't actual evidence."

"His weasel face was evidence enough."

"Whoa," said Charlie, patting her on the back. "He's still a kid, not some evil force. Jer's right, we should make our case tighter. Make sure we do this properly. For starters, we can search his bunk."

Camp rules precluded searches without the camper present. "But he's gone to first activity," I said.

"He's pushed too far," Charlie said. "He's lost his rights."

Charlie stripped the bed, shook out Max's sleeping bag, jimmied his trunk and combed through its mess. When he started palpating Max's mesh laundry bag, my mind was a deadweight of apprehension. What if he unearthed *my* underwear? Would he note the size difference? Would he know? But all Charlie found were some raveled tube socks, two T-shirts skunky with boy-sweat.

Caroline upended the cabin's trash can, poking through

crumpled Kleenex. She, too, came up empty-handed. "Probably got scared," she said. "Dumped it."

"He could still be carrying it," Charlie said.

"Maybe we should just keep him under watch," I suggested. "See if he gives himself away."

Charlie stuffed Max's laundry back into the bag; frustration was stitched into his brow. "All right, let's give it a couple days. I don't want him to move an inch without us knowing."

It was precisely what Don Fisher had advised.

Charlie excused himself—a meeting with Cornelio—and I followed Caroline to the infirmary. As we neared the building I broke into a sweat: on my neck, behind my ears, in my fists. I was queasy. Had I caught the stomach bug?

Caroline must have sensed my neediness. "You got something to say, you'll have to do it while I clean. I've lost a ton of time, thanks to your pet camper."

"Actually, it's about him," I said.

"Then grab these and come outside." She handed me a stack of kidney-shaped trays, colored a regrettable porcine shade. "Jeremy, meet the puke pots; puke pots, Jeremy."

"Yuck!" I held the trays from my face.

Caroline filled a bucket with steaming hot water and splashed in a toxic dose of Clorox. "Be a big boy," she said. "You can handle this."

She led me out back and handed me a hose. I began rinsing the vomit-spackled pans. As I did so, I told her the story. I recounted what Max had said on the Fourth of July, then his backtracking, then last night's reversion.

Caroline's expression gelled along unpleasant contours: disgust layered over anger and disbelief.

"I was the one who let him into the meds room," I admitted. "He convinced me it was the safest place to sleep."

She snorted as if hearing a stooge routine.

"And this morning, before I found you, I called CPS. I reported suspected sexual abuse."

Caroline plunged a tray into the bucket of Clorox. "That shithead. That wily little weasel."

I didn't know whether to protest or agree; was she referring to Charlie or to Max?

"Does he honestly think we're going to fall for that?" she said. "If he cries 'abuse,' he'll get away with everything?"

"But what if it's true? What if it happened?"

"He's just trying to save his skinny ass."

"You're not sounding like you. What happened to 'kids come first'?"

"*Is* he a kid?" she said. "His break-and-enter skills seem pretty grown-up."

We lapsed into a hard, concussive silence. I'd worried she would chastise me for not calling CPS sooner. Now I wondered if I had acted too soon.

I aimed the hose at a recalcitrant bit of puke, cold water numbing my good fingers like the fifth. The comatose feel of Max, the pendulous not-thereness as he leaned onto me, now returned.

"How did I screw up so bad?" I said.

Caroline wiped her brow with the blue bone of her wrist, her bleachy fingers held away. "No, I'm sorry," she said. "I'm way at the end of my rope." She dunked the last puke pot in her rinse. "Reporting was right. Of course it was. Even if Charlie's innocent, it's best."

"Should I call again? Tell about the missing drugs?"

"Yeah, guess you better," she said.

"But listen. We can't say anything to Charlie."

"What do we do when he wants to send Max home?"

"I don't know. But he can't find out that CPS is snooping. That puts Max in too much danger."

Caroline dumped her bucket over a patch of brown grass.

"All right?" I asked.

"Okay," she said. "All right."

For the time being, we stuck with Fisher's plan: Max would

fake illness in the infirmary. He wouldn't leave, and he wouldn't be alone.

I took Caroline's bucket and hosed a final rinse. The hush-up smell of bleach hung in the air.

On the chance I might find Max, I hiked back to Mansfield. I met only a brazen chipmunk gnawing something cottony, illicit. It scudded to the deck and leapt away.

I followed the chipmunk and sat on the deck, kicking my legs at empty air. I was staring through the cracks of the weathered one-by planking when what I should have guessed all along finally struck me. I retraced last night's hazardous route outside the cabin, down the loose scree and underneath. There, in a shallow hole next to the deck piling, I found the bottle. Three pills remained.

In my palm it felt like nothing—a bauble, a piece of trash— hardly enough to condemn a boy. But it was. In the wrong hands, it could be.

The bottle was not much thicker than the thumb I'd watched Max sucking. We all have private ways of killing pain. I reared back and chucked it in the lake.

SEVENTEEN

—◄○►—

I found Max, finally, at the waterfront, immersed in a game of Drown the Clown. (When I was a kid we called it Smear the Queer, but political correctness now prevailed.) On doctor's strict orders to keep his cast dry, Max couldn't fully join the sport—which involved piling onto whoever grabbed the ball until it was gaspingly surrendered. But still he'd made himself the action's center. He'd waded as far as he could from the shore and stood up to his nipples in the water, his cast hoisted Liberty-torchlike.

Teddy Trimble and Rick, a crafts-barn assistant, purported to guard the group of Mansfield boys, but seemed more mindful of their own tan lines than safety. Were parents crazy? Entrusting their sons to teenagers—to me?

It would have behooved Eli, Toby, and the others to swim out where escape would be easier. But they orbited near Max in the shallows; he was a sun from which they feared losing warmth. Max called "Here!" and his playmates tossed the ball. He batted it and sent them wildly diving. "Every man for himself" became "Every man for Max."

It galled me to see him this giddy and carefree when I'd been so distraught on his behalf. But this didn't curb my compulsion to be near him. In a way, the anger only intensified my yearning, the way a noxious smell can draw you close to sniff.

Max's braces, when he cheered, caught the sun and briefly flashed, a semaphore of carnal rowdiness. When he leapt to swat

165

the ball, water sheeted off his chest—he looked as if he'd been enamel-glazed.

"Max," I called, but he was deaf by splashing, tuned only to the back-and-forth mayhem. I called out a second time, louder.

As he turned to look, the ball squirted free. It shot past him and landed in front of Eli, who scooped it and hugged it to his chest. At once the kids all yelled, "Drown the clown!"

The pile-on was instantaneous. Boys pawed and thrashed in mirthful viciousness, limbs churning a smother of foam. And swirled through the foam like a trail of spilled blood was the red of Eli's bathing suit.

Teddy and Rick gaily egged the boys on. For a second, I thought they might join.

Since the scare with Simon, all those many years ago, I brooked no more gambles in the water. "Stop!" I said. "Enough. Let him go."

It worked. My voice still commanded deference.

Eli emerged from the lake rubbing his skull, as if buffing loot to judge its worth. His face wore a stunned kind of smile.

"You okay?" I asked.

"Yeah. Fine."

"Just go easy," I said. "Please watch yourselves. And Rick. Teddy. Let's get on the ball."

Then I summoned Max. My tone was blistering.

"What?" he said. "The cast's dry. I'm being careful."

"Get out of the water!" I said again.

Max scuffed over and stood shivering in his cutoffs, despite the morning's stultifying warmth. In the scoop of his chest, goose-flesh looked painful.

"I was having fun," he said.

I told him to get dressed.

He pulled on a black Zoo York T-shirt, its right sleeve stretching over the cast. He stomped into his All Stars without bothering to untie them. The cutoffs darkly dripped. He looked marooned.

When I told him we were going for a walk, he asked why. I couldn't tell if he knew how much I knew.

I led him through the cabin area to the old logging road. I had to check on the shelter project anyway; this would kill two birds with one stone. The humidity hovered in the nineties. As we clomped up the rutted incline, breathing was like sucking through a straw. Max's sneakers squished a soggy beat. The only other sound was a white-throated sparrow's doleful, unrelenting innuendo.

A caul of doubt trapped me, delaying confrontation—doubt not of Max, but of myself. The role of inquisitor sickened me.

Mose Ebersol, the bishop of Beulah's church district, had spoken to me about the onus of enforcement. Amish clergy do not aspire to lives of ministry, nor are they specially trained; they are farmers and blacksmiths, leather harness-makers, picked from the brotherhood by lot. Mose himself was a humble dairyman. We met in his milk house, where antiseptic didn't quite mask manure. Mose was hunchbacked, but the deformity seemed a mark of fortitude, his shoulders canted as if from long ardent leaning into life. His thick gray beard divided in two tufts.

I asked Mose how he found the confidence to be bishop. How did he threaten his own neighbors with the ban? Beulah, for instance, had been his wife's hired girl. She'd served Mose's supper, washed his clothes.

Mose tugged on the left side of his beard. He tapped a thumb on the stainless steel milk tank. "It's a blister growing on my heart," he said. "I've never done it without tears in my eyes. Beulah, I cried a lot over her."

"But don't you ever doubt yourself? Forcing her to leave the church like that?"

"No one forced her," he said sharply. "I pointed out where the fence is. She chose to jump."

Mose dipped his boot in a puddle of muddy milk. As the ripples pulsed away he seemed to soften. What made his role tolerable, he said, even heartening, was knowing it was vital for the church. "See, it's not so much to punish the offender. It's to give *us* a chance for forgiveness. We need people to kneel down before us sometimes so we know what it's like to lift them up."

"And you're sure what you did to Beulah's worth it? To help the church but maybe wreck her life?"

"The door's still always open for her. We only ban someone in the hope of *Busz* and *Besserung*."

Busz and *Besserung*: repentance and reformation.

But aren't there some sins beyond repentance, I wondered—transgressions of thought, of the heart?

What I didn't ask Mose then, but now wished I could, as I climbed the old logging road with Max, was: What if the minister himself needs reformation?

The shelter was weeks behind: just foundations. In the past, campers clamored to take part in building projects, but this year their enthusiasm hadn't sparked—the rain, partly, but also my own failings. I should have spun the activity in all its Daniel Boone mystique, but Max and his troubles stole my focus. Without hype, the task looked thankless: lugging logs.

To make things worse, the rain had destabilized the foundations. Hence this unhappy check for damage.

Max and I still hadn't spoken. Maybe he sensed his game was up. Or maybe, I thought bitterly, he was high on Percocet, far away in chemical seclusion.

I surveyed the site. Even this long after the deluge—a week? two? I'd lost count—the soil was grabby with moisture. Mosquitoes inflicted themselves. Just eyeballing, I could tell the foundations were off, but I couldn't tell exactly how bad. The hill's slope played tricks with perspective.

I was readying to take measurements when Max spoke.

"Thanks for last night. I was freaked."

I nodded noncommittally.

"So did you talk to whoever about Charlie?"

His voice was fluid, but with a scum of overconfidence. Did he think the coast would clear so easily?

"Yes," I said. "I talked to them."

"Cool. Are they going to arrest him now?"

"It's not quite so cut-and-dried, Max. They've got to hear

everybody's side, try to figure out what really happened. When people lie, things get complicated."

Max gripped the frayed bottom edge of his shorts and wrung a splash of water from the fabric. "I'm sorry," he said. "I'm really sorry."

His cheeks flushed the sunset pink of regret. It was almost enough to be convincing.

"I won't bullshit anymore," he said. "I promise."

He didn't specify what he meant. The Percocet? The sexual abuse? Bryce?

"It's out of my hands now," I told him. "So you don't have to bother with promises."

"But friends keep their promises," he said. He sidled closer, stepped joshingly on my toe. "We're friends, right? Buster buddies? Special?"

I pulled my foot away. "You've put me in a tough spot."

"I know. I shouldn't even have told you. It's between me and Charlie, not you."

"That's not what I'm talking about, Max."

He did something pouty with his lips. "Then what?"

I stared into the rapturous blue of his eyes, wishing that it hadn't come to this. "Caroline's missing some drugs," I said.

I expected a protest, some stuttering excuse, but his mouth remained cowardly slack. Was there guilt in the bob of his Adam's apple?

A mosquito gorged on my forearm's blue vein; I clenched my fist and the pest detonated.

"They say it's you," I said. "Apparently they'd accused you before? So Caroline thinks you made up the story about Charlie. To frame him, get yourself off the hook."

Max shifted. His sneakers belched a desolate, mucking sound. "What do *you* think, Jeremy?"

I could have told him I'd found the evidence. I could have told him I'd tossed it away. But I wanted to know if he'd confess uncoerced; I wanted his choice to be clean.

"It's not about what I think," I said. I left him standing in the snare of his footprints.

At the northeast foundation sat an old spackle bucket, now filled with brackish rainwater. With that and with the coil of plastic tubing beside it, I could craft a workable water level. I sank one end of the tube into the bucket, then sucked on the other to start a vacuum. I mistimed, and a jet of water sprayed into my mouth—sweet but stale.

Much as I would have liked to do this all myself, I needed help. I handed Max the tube.

"Hold your end at the northeast foundation," I instructed. "Do you think you know how to hold it right?"

A shrug.

"First, find the meniscus."

Now his shrug was verbalized: "The huh?"

"The meniscus, where the curve of water flattens."

(Would this term enter Max's private lexicon, another word to endearingly misuse? *"Dude! You're the apocryphal meniscus!"*)

"Okay," he said. "Check. Think I got it."

"Now hold that spot at the lip of the concrete."

The water at my end of the tube was way off—three inches below the southwest foundation.

"Sure that's in place up there?" I called.

"Yeah, right at the . . . whatchamacallit."

"Wow. This is a pretty major mess."

I was pondering our options when Max stood. In a small voice, he said, "I took the pills."

I forgot the tube long enough to lose a spurt of water. "Oh," I tried to say, but nothing came.

Would he also now admit that the second part was true, that he'd fabricated Charlie's abuse? He said nothing. He stepped to the next foundation.

I took another measurement: worse.

"Do you realize how serious this is?"

Yes, he said. He did. Of course he did.

"You'll have to tell it all to the investigator. And apologizing to Caroline wouldn't hurt."

Max was crouched by the far foundation; from my angle he appeared as though kneeling. I imagined him an Amishman in Mose Ebersol's district, someone shunned but now asking to return. "This kneeling is not before me," Mose would say, "but before the all-highest God and his church. Do you believe that henceforth you will be able to guard yourself better against unrighteousness?" If the member pledged yes, Mose would lift him from his knees and grant the forgiving kiss of peace.

But restoring Max wasn't in my power anymore. A kiss from me would bring nobody peace.

I explained Fisher's plan: the infirmary as a hideout. "For now," I said, "if anyone asks, you're sick."

EIGHTEEN

◄○►

The infirmary's A.M. smell: whiff of vomit in every inhalation, the curdled stink of normalcy reversed. The place looked ailing, too: clunky light through muslin drapes. If Max were persuasively innocent, I'd have felt bad for cooping him here. But it was Caroline who earned my sympathy; she'd weathered the night on a swaybacked canvas cot to ensure that Max stayed safely put.

I arrived to unburden her at eleven. The night duty had cricked her neck and her temper. "At last, the cavalry," she said. "Excuse me if I don't jump for joy." Her eyes were beleaguered by hangover bags. On her shirtfront, a forlorn stain of something.

"Any problems?" I asked.

"Six upchuckings count?"

I cringed. "But no escapees, no visitors?"

"Nah, nobody but us chickens. If you're taking suggestions, though, I think the meal service could be improved. That kid who brought my breakfast? He'd give a slug a run for his money. The pancakes were practically compost."

"Sorry. That's Eli. He tries. I could bring you back a deep-fried treat. Clam basket? Scallop roll?"

She flashed her tongue. "The smell alone would kill me."

I was taking Max to the Sea Haven Snack Bar in West Woodstock. The place was Don Fisher's suggestion. ("It'll loosen the kid up—comfort food.") When I'd told Fisher of the new developments—Max's drug theft, his admitted deception—I expected him to call the case off. But his officers, he said, were trained in sifting truth from lies; they should meet Max in person to gauge the mix.

He asked if the "perp" suspected anything. All clear so far, I told him. Charlie and I had spent the previous evening together, co-leading a support group for new staff. (Bill McIndoe attended, and Simon and Cornelio, Teddy Trimble, Rick, a few more.) We tag-teamed the meeting with almost marital synchrony, adroitly blending humor and advice. With work at hand—work we loved—scruple slipped away, leaving just our old-line partnership. We had years of practice skating the thin ice of denial.

"Fine," said Fisher. "Then the only other thing's the guardians. Mom's hospitalized, too sick to factor in. But Moss might call Grandma if he plans to kick Max out. I'll have her record a new message, saying she's out of town for a while. Then she screens. If it's Charlie, she doesn't answer."

"Wow! This is so *Starsky & Hutch.*"

"It's for the child's protection. It's not a game."

Shame shrank me to a useless mote.

Caroline mounted her swively drafting chair and began sorting noontime meds. On her desk sat a 1986 photo of Bill Buckner, who'd lost that year's World Series for the Red Sox, bungling the would-be last out. The photo was a kind of memento mori for Caroline, a totem of her Soxaholic creeds: that loyalty is more important than (and probably precludes) winning; that every silver lining has a cloud. I was starting to understand the team's appeal.

"Sure I can't tempt you with some onion rings?" I asked.

She pantomimed gagging on puke.

"Is the—what do I call him, prisoner?—all set?"

"He's just getting dressed," said Caroline.

"Did you guys have a little pillow talk?"

"Yeah. He apologized. And apologized and apologized. Even said he would have returned the bottle, but he'd finished all the pills, so he just chucked it."

Another lie. Needless. Was he compulsive?

Caroline hugged herself as if chilled. "I feel so rotten for accusing him of lying. I guess the drugs thing made me go a bit ballistic."

"So now you believe him about Charlie?"

"I kind of think we have to. Don't you?"

I couldn't tell her I knew more of Max's fabrications.

"Just seems like you changed your mind fast," I said. "I mean, you really think Charlie's the kind of guy who would do that? And if you think so, why have you been working for him all this time?"

She opened a chubby bulk bottle of Ritalin and parceled pills into Ziploc bags. "You know as well as I do, Jeremy. *Everyone* is a potential abuser."

"So it's guilty until proven innocent?"

"Not guilty," she said, "but possible." She torqued the cap back on her container. "And there *is* something creepy about Charlie when it comes to sex. Like accusing me of sleeping with Bill."

"Come on, Care. Just because you and Charlie haven't always been best friends doesn't mean he molested Max."

"Just because you *are* friends doesn't mean he didn't."

"Who's friends?" came Max's scratchy voice. "You mean Jeremy and me? Yeah, we're pals."

I turned to see him slouched against the sick room's doorjamb, face pale as though he'd swum in too-cold water. His BLAH BLAH BLAH cap was insolently atwist.

"How's the patient's stomach?" I asked.

"Okay," he said, not rising to the joke.

"Then maybe *you'll* split my onion rings?"

Shrug.

"Well, we better get going. We'll be late." At the door I whispered a PS to Caroline: "The alibi is a checkup in Rutland. To see if his cast's ready to come off."

"Gotcha," she responded. "Ten-four." Then to Max: "Bye,

pumpkin," and a quick buss on the cheek. "You'll be fine. Just be honest, like last night."

I guess I wasn't the only one he'd seduced.

In the van, we settled into a gray neutrality, neither chummy nor particularly tense. Max buckled up, but given the wreck of our summer, this puny precaution seemed beside the point. The shaded camp road gave way to fry-pan highway. Clouds flabbed in the bland, uncertain sky.

Max set in on his air-drumming routine, index fingers rotely slicing space. Hard to tell, but I thought the beat was softened, contained, more subtle than his usual punkish seethe. Then again, how could I know? With Max, everything was finger-to-the-wind conjecture, hurricane as likely as calm.

He didn't ask for the radio; I didn't offer.

At the one-pump gas station where the road hit Route 4, Jim Talbot stood filling the camp truck. He waved. I answered with the horn.

Then, turning right, as Jim dwindled in the rearview, I realized we were traveling the wrong way. Not for our destination, but for our alibi. If Jim learned we were supposed to have been Rutland-bound, he'd remember we turned east, not west. And why wouldn't he infer the worst? After all, he had seen us in this same van weeks ago. My hand on Max's neck, my almost-hug.

Who else had spied us in suspicious circumstances? Bill McIndoe, during patrol? July Fourth? How easily I could be framed, if Max accused. I wondered what he would snitch to the cops. That I'd delayed in reporting? That I loved him?

He drowsed in the passenger seat. On his face flickered shadows, alternating with bright sun—erasure and then sudden clarity.

The Sea Haven was a fish out of water; the nearest seashore was two-plus hours' drive. But alongside maple-syrup stands and other landlocked New Englandry, here stood this greaseball clam shack. It was tucked between Route 4 and the Ottaquechee River, whose trickle mocked its oceanic airs.

Cars from New York and Connecticut crammed the lot. A Winnebago hulked dunce-like in the corner. I swung the van into a space between two boxy, official-looking vehicles. The door of one boasted the State of Vermont seal; a police bubble rested on the other's dash.

Among the madras-clad tourist families, the men were as easy to spot as their rides. They sat at the rivermost picnic table, two middle-agers in wrinkle-free solids. The detective, to my surprise, was uniformed, which perhaps explained the vacant nearby tables; who wants to eat lunch beside the law?

The man in civvies—lean-meat face, leftover Beatles hair—raised his cup of Coke in welcome. "Started without you, I'm afraid." Fry crumbs marred his otherwise clean plate. He wiped his bony fingers with a Wet Nap. "I'm Peter Morgan, Social Rehabilitation Services. Call me Peter. You must be Max"—he waited a beat for Max's hand to come forward—"and Jeremy. Glad to meet you. This is Bureau of Criminal Investigations Detective Mullen."

In front of the walrussy, mustached detective sat his own picked-over plate, plus a half-gone basket of oysters. As if destroying evidence, he popped one in his mouth. "Pleasure," he said, showing oily palms to excuse the skipped handshakes.

"Got a nephew named Max," Peter said. "Cute as hell. Motormouth. Not like some *silent* Maxes."

Wink wink, nudge nudge. No response. Max faded half a step behind me.

"What—the cap says 'Blah Blah Blah' but he won't say a word?"

Max remained stubbornly silent.

"You know," Peter kept trying, "Max is the only guy's name ends in x?"

"Not true," barked Mullen, voice of the law.

"'Course it is. Tell me another."

"Tex." Mullen fed his smile an oyster. "Ajax."

Peter snorted. "Ajax?! That's a household cleanser. And Tex, that's just a nickname."

Mullen licked his pinkie. "Rex," he said.

"Well, like I said, it's *one of* the only names."

From Max came a mouse-squeak of giggle; for an instant, the sun found his braces.

I liked these guys, too—their odd-couple ease. They must have worked in tandem frequently. (Catch-22: the more abuse, the more time they had together.)

"Camp chow must get awful old," Peter said. "Order all you want. Our treat."

Max's eyes glistened with jackpot gleam. He ordered the seafood sampler: clam bellies, oysters, calamari. Side of fries. Jumbo Coke, extra ice. For me, just the basic fish and chips.

Detective Mullen paged through a greasy *New York Times* that he'd swiped from a tourist's trash. "Paper stinks," he said. "Look at this sports section. Practically nada."

He knew exactly what he was doing.

Hoisting himself from his usual slouch, Max sat tall with hometown pride. "Best paper in the world. All the news that's fit to print."

"Sure, if you like reading through a magnifying glass." Mullen granny-squinted, pressed newsprint to his nose. "Me, I'll take the *Boston Globe,* thank you."

"No one's forcing you. Let me see."

"Good riddance to bad rubbish," Mullen said. He pushed the newspaper across the table, and Max accepted it with proprietary fingers.

While Max filled himself on news and fried food, the men resumed their lazy banter. Mullen had the bloaty look of suddenly gained weight; his belt's abandoned crimps confirmed my guess. Then I noticed the burnt stains on his fingernails, the way his hands searched constantly for fidget fodder: a saltshaker, a confetti-in-waiting napkin. How recently, I wondered, had he quit smoking? And wondered, too, if a man in this fretful, withdrawing state was the best choice to investigate abuse. But then, he understood control and its lack.

Peter, too, sent mixed signals of persistence and surrender.

With his razor-burned cheeks he looked just-woken, alert; in his eyes sparked a cobalt optimism. But his haircut suggested a man past caring.

Such were the inherent paradoxes, I imagined, in the lives of abuse investigators—or perhaps their profession's consequence. Every day you'd face the worst of human wickedness, knowing it could never be defeated. And yet, each new case—each moon-faced, hurting child—would renew your faith in redemption. Or why go on?

Max and Mullen split a last basket of fries, Max's cheeks like a bird stuffed for roasting.

Peter shook his head. "The kid's starving! You guys running a summer camp, or a concentration camp?"

The joke skirted the edge of tastelessness. The mood darkened. Time for grim business.

"Listen," he said, blue eyes fixed on Max. "You know we've got to ask some tough questions?"

Max trained his own blues down, seeming to focus on his frayed cast. Mud nearly obscured all its doodled get-well-soons, my own naïve, "We'll share everything."

"You've done the hard part," said Mullen, "coming forward. Now we just need some details. We'd like to tape it, BCI procedure. For your sake, so you only have to do this once."

Max braved a look as to a battlefield surgeon: Go ahead, Doc, amputate.

Mullen removed a Dictaphone from his pocket, set it tactfully by the empty boat of fries. "I'll just grab my notepad from the car," he said. "Jeremy, why don't you come with? Fill out an incident report form while we're talking."

"Shouldn't I stay here with Max? Maybe he'd feel more comfortable."

"Or maybe just the opposite," Peter said. "Nothing about you, personally. We find it best interviewing subjects on their own."

Why was I always kept away from the action? But Peter's jaw was square, uncompromising. I followed Mullen to his Crown Vic, unmarked but unmistakable for a police vehicle, carnivorous-looking, malevolent with antennas. He reached across the driver's side to let me in.

"You can listen," he said. "Just didn't want the kid to know."

I didn't understand; from this distance, how could I possibly hear?

"We videotape, too. I'm wearing a wireless." Mullen pointed to a black box clipped to his belt—what I'd assumed was an emergency pager—then to a camcorder mounted on the dash. On a miniature LCD screen, a scene lit to view: Max and Peter, sitting at the table. "Not trying to hide anything. But video's scary. A kid might freeze up."

I saw how he had parked the Crown Vic strategically, how deliberate was the choice of picnic table.

Mullen's voice came at me doubly, from his mouth and the machine: "Don't worry, the kid'll be fine." Then he scooched across the vinyl and was gone.

This wasn't a bona fide squad car; there was no cage separating front from back. Still, I felt the boxed-in loneliness of the suspect: handcuffed, on his way to jail. In the tiny gray world of the camcorder's LCD, I watched Mullen settle next to Max.

"Let me ask first," he said, "who all knows so far?"

"Well, there's Jeremy," Max said.

In the audio my name rang flimsy, ridiculous.

Mullen jotted a note. "Jeremy. Who else?"

"Caroline," Max said. "The camp nurse." He brought a thumb to his mouth and bit the nail. "And one other person. I sent a letter."

I was flooded with the sensation of the library phone booth: duped, dumb, confused.

"Can you tell us who you sent it to?" asked Peter.

"Bryce. He's like my best friend. Back home."

"And so you wrote him."

"But he never wrote back."

Mullen shifted, scratched his potbelly. The hidden microphone burst with static. "Is that unusual for Bryce?" he asked.

Max doffed his baseball cap, shook out his dirty hair, and slowly replaced the hat, now backward. On the screen, his lunar forehead shone.

"I don't know. I never wrote him before. I mean, this is my first time away."

"I see," Peter said. His voice was as tight and scraped-clean as his face, devoid of either skepticism or belief. "Could you give us his full name and address?"

"That's the thing," said Max. "Bryce is homeless. Not a bum, he just doesn't have a place. So he usually crashes in Tompkins Square Park, or sometimes this abandoned building next to mine. That's how we met. I let him come in one day to use our shower. Anyway, we planned a system. I was supposed to send him letters to Odessa, this restaurant across the street from the park."

Odessa: I *had* found the right number.

"The waitress said she'd make sure to hold a letter for him. But I don't know, maybe it got lost."

The truth was so ruthlessly dull. And instead of relief—to know that Bryce was no threat—what I felt was a dazy sense of loss. Was Max's mystery what I relished most of all?

He waded into his story—his broken wrist, the stubborn doctor—and soon was knee-deep in narrative.

". . . I ask that mastoid if he's ever broken anything, and he says no, nothing, including his oath not to harm a patient, so don't worry, Motrin'll be just fine. Screw that! I knew where they hid the meds-room key. So on Caroline's day off, I snuck to the infirmary. Get the key. Let myself in. Bam! Find the Percocet and—wait. You promise I won't get arrested?"

Detective Mullen X'd his chest. "Hope to die."

"Okay. So I take the pills, and I've just downed a couple when I hear the door. Shit. Try to hide, but I'm such a doofus, I kick a box of, I don't know, something that rattles, splints? Then Charlie's voice: 'Max? I know you're in there.'"

Could Peter and Mullen be buying this? It struck me as a kid's narcissistic fantasy, a plot cribbed from *NYPD Blue*. The telling was coming too easily for Max; he sounded more thrilled than traumatized.

He pried the lid from his drained jumbo Coke, shook a shard of ice into his mouth.

"I keep still, but no way, he's got me cornered. The pills're in my pocket. I'm doomed. Sure enough, Charlie busts in. 'This is way off limits, Max. You know the rules.' What can I say? I mumble some dumb shit. 'You take anything?' 'No, I was just looking—' But he grabs. Quick. Frisks my pockets. He goes, 'Looking? Looks to me like you're *taking*.'

"And for a long time we're just standing there. I'm thinking about when Bryce and I swiped some Yoo-Hoos from the Korean deli on Second and A. The owner started yelling, 'Thief! No take! No take!' So we chucked the bottles, *pop,* and busted ass. But what could I do here? Woods for a million miles.

"So I'm waiting for the shit to hit. But it's weird. Instead of yelling, Charlie gets all goopy-eyed. He closes the meds-room door, bolts it. Steps up to me, puts his thumb on my chin. He says, 'These pills make you feel real good?' He shakes 'em, this creepy sound. *Tsk tsk tsk.*

"I didn't say anything. I kept telling myself: Play it cool, no big deal. 'Cause the thing is, Charlie was cool before. Gave me an extra chocolate bar one time. But next thing his hand's on my neck. He's like, '*I* could make you feel real good, too.' It's dark with the door shut, I can't really see his face. 'I could,' he says. 'I promise. Real good.'

"I knew what he meant, then. I knew it. But I couldn't quite believe it. I just stood there."

I couldn't quite believe this story, either. Was Charlie really that hard up—and that incautious? Or was I just too jealous to believe?

"Charlie goes, 'Come on, Max. I'll let you keep the pills.' My wrist was killing me. But I told him I was fine. 'Then why'd you come here?' he said. I said it was a mistake. He's like, 'I don't think so. I think you knew just what you wanted. And you know it now, too. Don't be afraid.'

"I went for the door but he blocked it: 'Think about it. Don't make this so hard.' I said, 'Come on. Let me go. Please? You can punish me. Just please let me go.'

"But he says he wants to help, not punish me. He knows about my dad and everything. A boy needs men in his life, he says, to teach him things, like it's good to admit how much you hurt."

I shuddered; I'd almost used this same speech. But Charlie twisted it. He twisted everything.

"I said *no.*" Max threw the word like a punch. "So Charlie said how my grandma would be awfully disappointed. How there wasn't any refund on tuition. He put his hand on my hip. I twisted to shake him off. But he moved it to the middle, then down. I said 'I don't want to,' but he grabbed and he was like, 'Oh really? Feels to me like you do.' And it's true. I couldn't help it. I couldn't."

I was torn between the actual Max, fifteen yards away, and the tiny flickering image of him onscreen. Video Max, reciting all the graphic details, was a talk-show confessor, overacting. But when I looked with my own eyes at this boy, hunched over, trying to disappear behind his hands, I thought I saw the shimmer of honesty.

"Afterwards, I wanted to get the fuck out of there. I start to zip up, but Charlie says, 'Wait.' He looks around. He takes the bottle, empties the Percocet, puts all the pills in my pocket. 'This'll just have to do,' he says. Then he lifts my shirt and scrapes it on my stomach—where it was all, you know, still sort of sticky. I was way too freaked to even move. He goes, 'I've got you now, forever,' still scraping, collecting it. 'It's beautiful. You're so beautiful.'"

I shrank into a distant place deep inside myself, the boy I had been at fourteen. Cold and wet. Star-crossed. Alone.

There was a whimper, which at first I thought might have been my own, but I realized it came from the video. I saw Peter touch Max, heard him say, "Hang in there, kid." Detective Mullen patted Max's hand.

I wanted to rush forth and comfort Max myself, but I was blocked off, behind glass.

NINETEEN

<del>◄O►</del>

We drove home from the snack bar in silence. I felt reamed. I should never have doubted Max.

As we curved into Bridgewater, he groaned and doubled over. Immediately I pulled to a stop. He opened the van door and managed to aim the vomit; stream after brown stream coughed forth. It seemed he might turn inside out. Another heave in Bridgewater Corners—and again, just in time, I pulled over. A mile later, he barely got the window down.

On top of everything, now he really was sick.

Back at camp, I saw that puke covered the van's IRON-WOOD logo. I half-carried Max up the infirmary ramp. I longed to let him know that I had heard and knew the truth. But that would require telling my own truth. I couldn't, not yet, not out loud.

The infirmary smelled even worse than before. Caroline was pouring cups of Coke syrup. "Warm Coke!" came her best ball-park voice. "Flat soda here! Lukewarm Coke!" Then the sight of us sank in. Her smile dulled. "Ouch," she said. "Double ouch. That bad?"

"You don't know," I started, but my voice snagged in my throat. "You don't even know the half of it."

The bed where Max had faked was still vacant. We tucked him beneath a wool blanket's shroud. "Try to rest, pumpkin," said Caroline. "Don't fight it." She placed a puke pot by his head.

I saw the first staff casualty: Simon. He lay on a bunk, knotted in discomfort. His face was the color of oatmeal.

184

I whispered his name.

"Nnnhh," was his response, a mournful, buried-alive sound.

"When did it hit you, this morning?"

"Nnnhh."

I had a vision of the ten-year-old Simon: that squirmy minnow, gasping, terrified. He lived today because of what I'd done. I'd found him, placed my mouth on his, I'd breathed. But Charlie was a counselor back then, too. What if he'd messed with Simon? What if Ruff had? I'd saved Simon, but perhaps not kept him safe.

I asked if there was anything I could do for him now. He was too miserable to reply.

In the exam room, I asked Caroline, "Don't you worry about the germs?"

"What do you think I've crusaded about all summer?"

"I mean *you*. Aren't you scared of getting sick?"

She ran the faucet and wrung her hands in soap. "You get immune, I guess. And the Lady Macbeth washing routine doesn't hurt."

I soaped my own fingers, rinsed, then repeated.

Caroline hopped onto the exam table. "So, what happened? Max tell them the truth?"

"I don't know," I lied.

"What do you mean you don't know?"

"He told his version, same as before. The officers didn't say if they believed him."

And what if they *didn't* believe him? Would I tell my own story as crude corroboration? Expose Ruff to bring Charlie down?

I could barely look at Caroline. With no conclusive evidence, she still supported Max; I, despite my certainty, was fudging.

Max still fudged, too—on my behalf. When he told the investigators about Charlie's second assault, Mullen asked why he'd waited to seek help. "Why didn't you report the first incident right away? Why didn't you tell Jeremy, for example?" And Max, without blinking, had dissembled; he said he was scared to be expelled. Would he have covered for me if he knew my true desires?

Caroline joggled a jar of tongue depressors, then plucked one out and tapped it on her chin. "If CPS needs more evidence," she said, "they should just come down and watch Charlie. He's obsessed with cleaning up before visiting day. Talk about displaced anxiety."

Another Lady Macbeth—an entire staff of us.

"He didn't come to check on Max?" I asked.

"Nah. I've been here the whole time."

"Good. We should still keep them apart."

She bent the tongue depressor till it snapped. "How much longer can we, though, Jer? And what about all the other kids? While we're looking out for Max, Charlie could be with some other boy."

"He's not a monster," I said reflexively. "He's Charlie."

"He's a monster if he did those things to Max."

The coldcock of a headache hit my eyes. Until now it had felt like any charge against Charlie was just as much a charge against me—weren't our differences merely circumstantial? Now I saw more fundamental distinctions. I couldn't explain the coexistence of Charlie's impulses: healing and harming in one man.

Caroline slumped like an enervated patient, her face an ideogram of fatigue. "I'm just scared, Jeremy. I'm really scared."

"Why? Charlie wouldn't do anything to you."

"Not that. *Me.* What I'm turning into. When Max accused Charlie, I called him a liar."

"He'd lied before. Of course you were skeptical."

"But good nurses always side with hurting kids."

"You're a great nurse. The best. It's who you are."

(When I was passed over for director and nearly quit, Ruff had pep-talked me likewise. "You're a counselor, Jeremy, *inherently.*")

"If I'm so great," Caroline said, "why's the whole camp sick?"

"We'd be ten times worse if you hadn't been here."

But the strain of overprotest caved my voice. I'd been asking similar questions of myself.

"Jer," she said, "I really need a hug."

I don't think she noticed my moment's hesitation, the skin-flint leadenness in my arms. I reached for her and held her flagging form. "You're doing fine," I said. I pulled away.

Rest hour hadn't quite yet ended, but I heard commotion somewhere down the road, the boyish sound of things about to break. I walked toward it, blinking against a sense that camp had changed. It seemed as though the world's tint control had been disturbed, adulterating all the normal colors: the greens way too blue, the yellows bloodied.

At the camp bell, I saw the racket's source: Charlie, amid a swarm of boys. Each boy's right arm was adorned with a red bandanna; each clutched a shiny clipboard.

"What are you?" Charlie goaded them.

In unison, they cried, "Inspectors!"

"And what are you gonna do today?"

"Inspect!"

Charlie pumped his fist. "That's the spirit!" He looked disturbingly Hitlerish. "Normally, of course, people's cabin space is private, but today, you're authorized to look around. Anything that doesn't belong—what a parent shouldn't see—jot it down: dirty laundry, graffiti."

A boy raised his twiggy, quaking hand. He was Petey Wooster, Jay Wooster's kid. "What if they don't want to let us inside their cabin? Like, someone a lot bigger than us?"

"Tell 'em you've been deputized by me," Charlie said. "That red bandanna is your badge." Like Ruff, he could heighten the lowest stakes.

Petey nodded, mouthing "deputized" like a password.

"All right, now go to work. Get the mess!"

Charlie thrust his fist again, and off the campers trooped, the shields of their clipboards held aloft. He turned to ring the end-of-rest-hour bell. He saw me, though, and came to me instead. "Hey, Jer. You see my hound dogs, sniffing?" He tried to chum a hand onto my shoulder.

I shrugged away to scratch a phony itch. This was Charlie, same as always, my old partner. But *not* the same. Everything had changed. I was scared of him, and piteous, and jammed with envy.

"What's up with this inspection stuff?" I asked.

"Just want us looking good. Those snooty parents . . ."

"It's a camp. They don't expect hospital corners."

"But they need to think they get their money's worth."

Including sexual initiation for their boys? A claustrophobic pounding closed my throat.

Maybe Charlie sensed my unease. "With all those campers sick, we need *something* to be in order. Speaking of which, nothing new on Max?"

"No," I lied. "Still laid up in bed."

"Well, I've been thinking. It's time to send him home. Still haven't reached the family yet, though. Mother's in the hospital, grandparents on vacation."

"Then maybe we should sit tight," I said. I tried to sound neutral, uninvested.

"No. He's a bad seed. I spoke to Ruff."

"Ruff?"

"Yeah. You know his new program? Bringing juvenile offenders up to his farm? Since he'll be here for visiting day, I figured he could take Max back with him. Toss him in with the city kids till we can deal."

Charlie's plan made only a vague impression as I pictured Ruff's annual appearance: greeting parents who still considered Ironwood to be his, letting newer ones catch a guest-star glimpse. Would I have the guts to say anything when I saw him?

"We can tell Max first thing that morning," Charlie said. "Minimize the chance for disruption."

Objecting or stalling more would only rouse suspicion. In an iffy voice I said I'd go along.

"Shit," Charlie said, checking his watch. "This has been more like rest *two* hours."

Before I could plug my ears he whipped the camp bell. The sound drove its barbs into my skull.

At five o'clock, I telephoned Don Fisher. He'd watched the tape of Max. He was convinced.

"Does that mean you'll take him away?" I asked.

"We might. But if you can keep him there, safe, we could use that. Use him to catch the perp off-guard."

The hardened pitch of Fisher's voice scared me. I kept wanting to check behind my back. (It might not have been a bad idea. I was in the Dump, fooled into a sense of hiddenness, but Charlie could enter any second.)

"We wire Max," Fisher explained. "Set him up to talk with Moss, prep him with what to say: 'I've been thinking about what you did, and I'm worried,' or 'The things you did to me made me angry'—lines to prompt Moss to incriminate himself."

"Face-to-face?" I said. "That seems dangerous."

A ghostly creak came through the phone: Fisher tipping back in his desk chair? I pictured brogans landing on a blotter.

"We'd have officers, listening in, ready to jump."

"That's legal? Taping someone without their knowledge?"

"In Vermont, you only need one-party notification."

From outside, a clamor: "Me!" "Over here!" The kids were playing Frisbee down the hill. Their guileless fervor sang up through the woods.

"Don't worry," said Fisher. "We've done this. It's not that risky."

"Hit me," yelled a kid, "I'm in the zone."

"What about Max?" I said. "Seems like a lot to ask."

"We only do it if he's comfortable, of course. But when he sees how big his role could be, I bet he'll want to. If he can get Moss to say the magic words: bingo! We can arrest him. And then follow up with a search warrant. Look for photos of kids, et cetera. With preferential molesters we almost always find something."

Right here! Right here is where they'd search. They would snoop through all our files, our history.

There were dozens of picture albums, compiled in summers past: boys in Speedos, boys shirtless in the sun. My own Cambridge apartment harbored similar "evidence": my friends, my family, my life. Was there anything questionable in my tent? No, just my gear, my sleeping bag.

If I felt this anxious, how must Max feel?

"Okay," I said. "If he says yes, let's do it."

"Good," said Fisher. "Sooner the better. Tomorrow?"

"No. Max'll still be too sick. But before Saturday. That's when Charlie's kicking him out."

I told Fisher of Charlie's callous scheme.

"Perfect," he said. "We'll do it Saturday. Visiting day's great cover—all those extra folks in camp. And if Moss is already planning to talk with the kid that morning . . ."

"Okay," I said slackly. I couldn't correlate our Charlie with Fisher's "Moss," couldn't fathom these cop machinations as real.

"Let me work out some details on this end," Fisher said, "and tomorrow I'll chat with Max."

"Okay," I said again. "Okay."

"You all right?"

"Yeah, I'm just—it's hard to think."

"It's tough, I know. This kind of thing gets ugly. But it's just the way things have to be sometimes."

We said good-bye. I hung up. I was numb.

The stark lonely silence of the Dump's dinginess was broken by a burst of downhill voices: "Come on. I'm open. Come on, hit me!" Somewhere, beyond my view, a Frisbee ripped through space; half the kids cheered, half groaned. A boy had made the catch, or fumbled, I couldn't tell.

TWENTY

—◄o►—

After breakfast, Charlie sprung a surprise. The schedule—swim instruction and a hike to Lookout Rocks—was preempted for a special event: the Pre-Parent Prophylactic Prettification Protocol. I could see him trying to conjure up his old magic, transforming the chore into a game. He plied flourishes of gesture and voice. But his hands twitched, and the bombast jammed up in his throat, and the boys merely groused and rolled their eyes. They recognized exploitation when they heard it.

We drudged through our assignments, checking items off an endless-seeming list: scythe the puckerbrush, creosote the fishing dock. In each cabin were bunks to repair, laundry to be bagged. Every path was desperate for sawdust.

The sun fussed its heat through the day: now moderate, now fleeting, now caustic. Victims of warm-bloodedness, we donned and doffed shirts. The air was ridiculous with bugs.

The inspector Nazis had included on their list of eyesores the foundations of the would-be log shelter. The foundations were admittedly useless, but the thought of destroying them drained me. Maybe I still blamed myself for the shelter's sorry state, as for so many other recent blunders. Or maybe it was the futility of superficial cleansing: Wouldn't it show our deeper failings all the more?

The erasure only took a few minutes. I did it with a sledgehammer, alone. The concrete exploded in deprecating clouds, as if sorry for its worthlessness.

—◄o►—

That night I visited Max to review the next day's plan. I don't recall much of what was said. Can I not bear to remember my willingness to use him, or how eager *he* was to be used? (Earlier, speaking to Fisher on the phone, Max had appeared almost excited; dare and revenge glinted in his eyes. He was getting better, had kept down saltines and chicken broth. His fever had eased by two degrees.)

Next, I remember sitting in my tent. Camp was suffused with that tight, casket silence that is soothing or spooky, depending. Everyone slept. Even the bugs.

The parents who'd arrived in prep for tomorrow were cloistered in Route 4 motels, watching cable, making country-weekend love; ice machines and Magic Fingers hummed. But here in the woods all was savage. In the corner of the tent, an unaccountable scampering. Then a rustle, a whoosh—I flashed my light. Nothing but dull nothingness. This silence, I decided, was spooky.

My finger, tonight, throbbed with hankering pain. That's why I couldn't sleep. Partly.

I'd been picturing Charlie, duped to self-incrimination, then . . . what? led away in handcuffs? I wouldn't know if I should cheer or cry. I assured myself that whatever was truly meant to happen, would. The outcome wasn't up to me.

But no. There was choice. Always choice.

Peach Bottom: my first day with the Yoders. The smell of old barn hay—sleepy, moldering—mixed with the tang of new-mown. The patient knock of horses in their stalls, the cries of calves; the beat of life itself like one large heart. Into this equilibrium I stepped. Jakie handed me a currycomb. I can do this, I thought. I can *be* this. Fear itself was something to hold onto—solid, unlike my normal life. I leaned into its rough and heaving flank.

I'd told Max that my downfall had been an ill-timed sneeze; that's how I'd always told the story. But far more dangerous and damning than the sneeze was my posing as someone I was not.

When I dropped the comb, I should have asked for help. Instead, I attempted to act nonchalantly Amish, and the horse, sensing fraudulence, stomped.

I'd told Max, too, of Sadie's turpentine. It killed the pain perfectly, I bragged; my choice—my new self—was vindicated. But in the long run, how was I to know? Perhaps if I'd refused Sadie's stopgap remedy and held out for proper doctoring, I'd have been spared this years-later throb. Maybe the cure did more harm than good. Maybe, in fact, I'd chosen wrong.

I sat there, flipping a mental coin of loyalty—the same coin that Beulah had been tossing. I retrieved her recent letter from a bag within my trunk, where I'd stashed it in case of further floods.

Dear friend Jeremy . . .

The situation, at first glance, was clear. With Jonas dead, why should Beulah not rejoin the church? Leaving hadn't ever been her wish. But the very fact of Beulah's indecision posed a problem, indicating how far she had slipped. An Amishwoman doesn't question. She just *is*.

Her closing humbled me with its appeal:

It wonders me, Jeremy, what you would say to do— you with all your fancy college learning. You're used to making hard decisions, ain't? Me, I'm used to having them made for me.

Benny's crying now, and if I don't quit this soon, I will be too. With all good blessings to you.

Your friend,
Beulah

Without any inkling of what wisdom I could offer, I found a pen and pad of dampish paper. The paper barely took my ballpoint marks. "Dear Beulah," I began. "My friend, how are you?"

It feels strange writing you after so many years. I cherished your letters, and always wished I could respond. Now I can—an occasion for happiness!—although the reason is your own recent sorrow. My condolences for the death of your Jonas.

I considered wishing Beulah patience and grace, the traditional Amish consolation, but those were the words her sister Ruth had slung. I longed, too, to tell her of the sister that I knew, to pass on loving sentiments from Sadie. But I wasn't sure if Sadie felt that way.

Your letter made me think of when we met at the Plain & Fancy—could it really be three years ago? You seemed trapped then as I imagine you're trapped now. You looked like you were on a roller coaster. It's been a roller coaster here, too, at the summer camp where I work. Too much to explain in this letter. Suffice to say I'm tired, and confused, and getting queasy. I might not be such a good decision-maker.

How strange it must strike you, this notion of summer camp—people paying to be separated from their families, when all *you* want is to be reunited. How much money would you pay for that?

And I know, too, that you're wondering if you'd even belong at "home." All your life you believe that you're one kind of person, then you leave and see you're maybe someone else. Everything you knew about yourself might have been wrong.

I met a man one day in Chestnut Level. He'd grown up Amish, with two brothers who were dwarves. He wanted to help his brothers, and also the Amish who were anemic, or who had six toes. He wanted to understand why. When he asked his parents and his bishop, nobody had convincing answers. So he hitched rides into Lancaster, to the public library, and found books on human genetics.

He ended up going away to high school—which of course meant he couldn't join the church—then to college and medical school, too. He became a doctor at Johns Hopkins University. The research he did on genetic diseases led to better treatment for Amish everywhere—his own family and thousands of others. But as proud as he was, he wondered why he'd been forced to choose. He'd saved lives—but what about his own?

Maybe your choice is simpler, Beulah. The church would have you back, if you confessed. But you have to ask, how wrong was what you did? Did you choose yourself over what seemed right, or did you choose what seemed right over yourself?

I wish there could be some middle ground. I know that sometimes when an Amishman is under *Meidung,* his family cuts corners in the rules. He can't eat supper at their table, so his wife pushes another next to it. She drapes a single tablecloth over both. Technically, they've kept the ban; they've shunned him. All the same, they're still a family.

Can you be loyal to your old self but also to the new? To outside laws and also inner ones?

Which is where I quit and crumpled the page. I'd written the letter less to her than to myself.

Leaving the tent was a semiconscious compulsion. Like a homing signal, my finger's ache steered me.

Charlie still had a light on, the Dump's windows ablaze, two startled eyes. I listened for his typing—some nights he worked late on the laptop—but the gnash of wind in trees was all I heard. A smell of coming thunder edged the air.

"Come right in," he said, before I'd knocked on the screen door.

He wouldn't be so calm, I thought, if he knew.

"Oh, Jeremy. I figured it would be another puker. You haven't come down with this bug, have you?"

"No, not me. Stomach of steel." (In truth, my stomach felt composed of worms.)

Charlie leaned back in the desk chair. "What're you doing up this late?"

"Guess I could ask the same of you."

"You're the one out prowling."

He was right, I needed an excuse. "Couldn't sleep. Worrying about tomorrow."

"Me, too," he said. "I keep feeling like I'm forgetting something."

I noticed the rumple of Charlie's sleepless bed, two mugs stained with coffee residue. At the desk, his PowerBook was indeed turned on, but must have lain untouched for some time; a screen saver dominated the display. *Green camper dodges cold capture the flag* chugged across like digital ticker tape. It was one of those randomizing programs: You type in a list of words and proper names, and it spews them back as gnomic poetry.

Edible Ruff Peterson roasts buggy Ironwood.
Smiling misery whip counsels mountainous Charlie Moss.

I imagined Don Fisher impounding the computer. Exhibit A: the alleged perp's screen saver. Was there evidence encoded in these nonsense epigrams? Everything now meant more than it seemed.

Charlie must have noticed my staring. "Kidding myself? I'm not doing any more work tonight." He spun the mouse ball and shut down the machine. The absence of its hum was somehow morbid.

Then he lit a Coleman lantern, hung it from a rafter hook, and switched off the electric gooseneck lamp. The night's surrounding darkness choked closer. Charlie retreated to the clutter of his bed, above which hung his Lifesaver ax.

"Just make space," he said, patting the mattress. "Throw stuff on the floor if you have to."

I didn't. There was plenty of room.

We settled on either end, feet almost abutting, as if poised for a tug-of-war. Through its charred glass, the lantern cast a shifty votive flicker, as fickle and as hope-filled as friendship.

"Quiet," he said. It could have been an observation or a command—just as he and I, sitting here, could be pals or adversaries or something else again, I wasn't sure.

I kept wanting to see his hands. I wanted there to be a sign, something like my own scarred stump, but from the outside he was only ordinary: fingers, veins, lifeline.

The lantern flared, then dimmed, then brightly danced again. The Dump's walls were leaky with knotholes.

"Time to patch this shack up pretty soon," he said. He corked his thumb into an inch-wide gap. "Patch it up, or . . ."

What: Tear it down? Build another? Forty years ago this had been just a common scrub of woods; Ruff had cleared it, framed the cabin, pitched a roof. Just as quickly as this haven had been summoned into being, the whole thing could surely slip away.

I said, "Maybe some cedar shingles. Would that hold her?"

"For a while, maybe. Couple of years."

But there might not be that much time anyway. Because of Charlie. Because of what he'd done.

"Or maybe we should go ahead and wreck it," I said. "Like the shelter. Right now. How about it?" I could taste the bitterness in my voice.

"The shelter's not wrecked," Charlie said. "We'll pour new foundations. Deeper this time. Same site."

"Trash something just to do it all again?"

"Ruff always said, 'It's the process, not the product.'"

I grimaced. "Ruff said a lot of things."

But no matter how acidly I challenged his responses, Charlie wouldn't budge from his calm. The screen saver was right: mountainous Charlie Moss. He shrugged with geologic stoicism.

As kids, I'd sometimes thought we could read each other's minds: that we *were* the same mind, in different flesh. And if I could no longer read Charlie as I used to, perhaps it was because we'd grown too close; you can't focus on an object at your nose.

We sat in the sag of his bunk. He rolled his hips to the right, which sent my own to the left. Our legs knocked for an instant. We pulled away.

"About tomorrow," he started. "I guess the plan"—but the lantern flame guttered and was gone. "Shit," he said. "Damn it. That wick."

"You sure it's not just out of fuel?"

"No, the wick. I've been meaning to replace it."

He didn't move, didn't reach to turn on the gooseneck lamp, as though the darkness had trapped him in its pitch. To me, too, the night seemed suddenly crystallized, ambering us in memory.

"Remember the time—"

"Of course I do. The ax."

Ruff had owned his five-pound Australian ax since his stint on the Woodsmen's Team at Dartmouth, where he won felling champ three years running. On its fourth handle, but with a tempered head still sacramentally sharp, it remained his totemic obsession. The ax hung in his truck where some lesser men keep rifles. He'd christened her with his mother's name: Molly.

We knew not to touch her. It was privilege enough just to watch Ruff chopping, wielding his muscular love. He would feist his way through a stand of ash or oak as though punishing each tree for its own good. So perfectly was Molly's wide cutting blade whetted that each of her blows was like a gift. "Your tools are an extension of your soul," Ruff often said. "Do unto them as you would have done unto you."

Was it Charlie's idea or my own? Perhaps the whimsy struck us both at once. It was the same year we vied to be Lifesavers. A muggy midnight in July.

Charlie and I lay head-to-head in our bunks, insomniac with prankster energy. One counselor was on his day off, the other snoring. Show me the boy who could stay put.

We fled randomly into the cabin area. Mischief was our only destination. We stopped by the waterfront and stole a skinny dip, which did nothing to relieve our vagrant itch. "Raid the fridge?"

Charlie proposed, but we had the key already—there's never any jazz in what's allowed.

It was Ruff's truck that finally inspired us: his old Ford, parked by the Lodge. We clambered in, Charlie calling dibs on the driver's seat, and pretended to dodge phantom traffic. Then Charlie popped the clutch and we really were moving. Three slowpoke feet had never been so thrilling.

He caught us again with the emergency brake but it couldn't halt our roguish momentum. We ransacked the glove box, discovered Ruff's pipe, and got high on cherry tobacco fumes. Then Molly smiled—how else can I describe it? Before fear or conscience or good sense could stop us, she was down from the rack and in our hands. No bickering, no fuss for custody. We regarded her with common reverence.

Just one chop each, we agreed. Maybe two. Up the ridge so we wouldn't be heard.

We would need light, so we rummaged in the Lodge and found a Coleman. I pocketed some Ohio Blue Tip matches. Charlie lit the lantern and led us out back, past the trash shed, up into the woods. My fingers like a lover's on Molly's satin throat, I felt the smooth of Ruff's longtime caress. She weighed only a pound and a half more than the axes I was used to, but that was all the difference in the world: who we were versus who we might soon be.

We came to a cluster of white pines. They were giants, three feet across; we picked the biggest. Because I'd had the honor of carrying Molly, it was only fair for Charlie to chop first. I held the lantern as he dug his heels and swung. There's no word for the sound he made. It came less from his lungs than from every inch of skin, like the all-body astonished breath of sex.

"God," he said. "Oh, God." He swung again.

I felt the shudder deep within my bowels.

Charlie chopped a third time, a fourth. Bark split, unmasking a grin of virgin wood. He sent Molly's blade again to kiss it.

My turn. We traded ax and lantern. I'd say I swung Molly, but truly she swung me. The steel seemed to know just where to go. Pine fibers snapped along with something inside me. Everything was opening.

I reared back for another swing, but: blackout. The lantern was dead. Stone dark.

Charlie struck a match but the flame wouldn't take; the wick was less than a stub. "Damn," he said. "Should have checked it at the Lodge."

"Try again. There's got to be some left."

"Nope," he said, wasting another match. "Oh well, it was fun while it lasted."

I wasn't done. I'd had a taste and wanted more. "Look out," I said. "I'm taking another chop."

"You shouldn't."

No. Of course not. But again, I say: Show me the boy who wouldn't.

It ended predictably. The blow glanced off the trunk, and Molly jumped from my grasp. When she landed, a spark cracked the darkness. Why couldn't it have been my leg? At least then Molly would be intact. But as we saw soon enough in the Lodge's sober light, the rock she'd hit had been unmerciful.

"I'm fucked," I said. "I'm fucked. I'm fucked." I might have turned the ax blade on myself.

Charlie was the one who kept his head. "It's just a ding. Totally fixable."

"It's not. Look. The whole tip's smashed."

"Nothing a whetstone can't repair. Don't worry, we've got all night."

We: sweet generosity.

"No," I said. "You were smart. You said stop. Get back to bed. I'll say I was alone."

But he took Molly and marched to the toolroom.

We holed up in that dank chamber for hours. We started with the coarse gray side of the stone, then switched to the finer, smoother blue. We took turns—oiling, honing, wiping—but the damage appeared implacable, as though Molly wanted us to get caught.

I said, "Get out of here. I'll keep my mouth shut." But Charlie insisted on remaining.

Reluctantly, the ax began to yield. The bent steel sludged away, the edge regained its sheen, and by dawn it could shave our knuckle hairs.

Ruff never knew, or never said.

Charlie finally turned on the lamp. His Lifesaver ax, on its mount above the bed, caught the beam with a monitory glare. I twisted the lamp's neck to a shallower angle, absolving him with a soft, backlit aura.

"Charlie," I said. "I know everything."

He scratched an ear, knuckled his nose, uncomprehending.

"Everything," I repeated. "The whole deal."

Now fear skittered across his eyes. "I don't know what you're talking about," he said.

"Max."

I watched the name work its way beneath his skin, a sharp nib to pierce denial's hide.

"Max what?"

"Charlie, it doesn't matter if you lie to me or not. Truth is, it doesn't matter what I think. The state's involved. They're going to hit you hard."

He winced at this new information. He waved his hand as if swatting smoke from his eyes.

"Max told me a while ago," I went on. "Didn't want to believe him. Figured chances were pretty good he'd made it up. I mean, the drugs, and . . . you know how he can be kind of . . ." I stopped short of saying seductive, even though that's how it still felt. All summer, Max had been leading us to a cliff, daring me: Who would jump first? Charlie had stood on the same edge with Max. But that was different. Charlie had shoved.

"Charlie," I said, "you're my oldest friend. But I had to. I called CPS. I'm sorry."

Why did I still feel the need to apologize? Why wasn't *Charlie* apologizing?

"Is it just his word? Or do they claim to have evidence?"

"It doesn't matter. What matters is that it's true."

Charlie's eyes were distant with shock or calculation. He might yet attempt to resist.

"Listen, Charlie. When Max told them, it was very detailed. He said things. Things that only—"

How could I say it? Charlie sat inches away from me on the bed, but he seemed as beyond reach as the past.

I said, "You think I don't know about you and Ruff? I do. I was there. I heard it all."

A long breath left Charlie's lungs. He shifted on the bunk with arthritic brittleness, as though my words had suddenly aged him.

"I tried to forget," I said. "For years, I mostly did."

I'll give him credit for not prolonging the bluff. Accused by someone else, I think he might have. But not me. Not after everything. Surrender edged its way into his brow, two thin lines like an equals sign: You solved me.

What he said, in a knotty voice, was, "I'm sorry."

Sorry for what? For whom?

There were so many questions I longed to ask. What had it felt like being held in Ruff's grip? Did his calluses tickle or hurt? And how, in Charlie's own grip, had Max's flesh felt? Was his skin *there* as pale as the rest?

"That night," Charlie said, "at the Point? I wanted to give you my place in the shelter. But if I had—don't you see? I couldn't."

For a long time, nothing more was said. This was enough. For now, it would have to be.

Accustomed to the lamplight, we could look without squinting. Charlie's gaze was watery and benign. I noticed the hatch marks on either side of his mouth, remnants of long-ago smiles.

The air was sedative with silent remorse and with something else, too, maybe love. I wanted to fall asleep, head in his lap, let the bad leach out into the sea of dreams.

But I had to warn him.

At first he wouldn't believe me when I told him of the sting:

Hidden microphones? Undercover cops? But I unlaid the plan in all its hard-nosed detail, and gradually he recognized the truth. He wanted to know what time the cops would be arriving. And who else knew about it? Did Ruff? He might have been a reporter gathering a story's routine facts.

"I really didn't want to put you through this," I said. "Or Max. It'll be terrible for him."

Charlie nodded.

"And the parents," I said. "What are they going to think?"

A thud against the screen door sent us jumping. Who could be knocking at this hour? But a moth, not a person, had hit the screen—a sphinx moth with scalloped brownish forewings, the left of which was crumpled, fluttering.

For a moment we watched it wheel on the ground. Then Charlie made his way to the door. He stooped and cupped his hands for the moth to crawl inside. When it did, he clapped once. The flutter stopped.

TWENTY-ONE

—◄○►—

Beulah and Sadie both told me of their last time together, the day before Beulah was banned. It was March, an icy Saturday; the world was dazzling and dangerous. The sisters had been working on a Sunshine & Shadow quilt featuring oxblood red, electric blue. Their grandmother Zook had pieced the top years ago but had died before she could stitch the quilting. Beulah took a taxi to Peach Bottom.

Abner and the boys were sequestered in the barn, diligently stripping tobacco. In the house, Anne baked "friendship bread" from a schoolmate's sourdough starter, and Lydia needlepointed a wall hanging. ("JOY," it read in cheerful yarn letters. "*Jesus is first, You are last, Others are in between.*") Sadie and Beulah sat in the modest living room, on opposite sides of the quilting frame. My memory provides the scene's details: the bird's-eye-maple hutch and the books on its top shelf (a stout German Bible, *Martyrs Mirror*); Hoober Feed and Musserman's Dry Goods calendars on the wall; the overdry, propane-smelling air.

The sisters had quilted together since they were girls—a thousand and some hours, Sadie guessed. Effortlessly, they slipped into the rhythm. The only words spoken were those crucial to the task: "Roll the frame?" "More batting?" "Another spool." It was unconscious artistry, like breathing.

When their eyes were overstrained and their index fingers ached, Sadie served popcorn and tea. Beulah had been qualmish with morning sickness lately and she asked if Sadie knew a remedy. "Blue cohosh," she said. "Or raspberry leaves. Either'll suit just fine." But she didn't brew a batch, or say she would.

They returned to their boldly colored patchwork. In each ox-blood square they stitched a trim rosette, using thimbles to push four stitches at a time. Their sewing was identical—tight, unwavering; no one could have told their work apart. Gradually, they rolled the fabric in and shrunk the frame so they could reach the middle without stretching. Now their knees knocked. Their heads sometimes bumped.

In Beulah's version of the story, the name Jonas was never mentioned; there was no talk of banning or changed hearts. Sadie remembered differently. She tried to persuade her sister one last time, she said. "Don't turn away. It's a death certificate on your soul!"

But after that, silence. Stitching.

Each woman told me that she glanced at the other, studying the face that matched her own. Sadie memorized her younger sister's lineless forehead, the brow she'd kissed when baby Beulah stumbled. Beulah said she noticed Sadie's left ear hung too low. What else had she missed before? What would she now?

They'd still be allowed to visit if they wanted; *Meidung* doesn't call for total separation. But once Beulah was banned, Sadie wouldn't confide in her; they would never talk *intimately* again. And if no longer sisters as they'd known all of their lives, they wouldn't be real sisters anymore.

As evening hemmed in, they stitched the last rosettes, their knees touching beneath the finished quilt. Their fingers were green from the metal of their thimbles. Any moment, Beulah's taxi would arrive to retrieve her and bring her back home to Quarryville. Then supper, a steaming bath, and sleep. By noon-time tomorrow she'd be banned.

Originally, they'd spoken about sharing the quilt, trading it every few years. Now that was out of the question. Sadie told me that if Beulah had only asked to have the quilt, she would have gladly handed it over. Beulah told me she was waiting for the offer.

They sat there at the frame, saying nothing. The sleety winter light was ebbing fast. A minute later they heard the taxi's honk.

Beulah gathered up her sewing things. She appraised the two thimbles resting on the quilt frame's edge, and took the one that seemed to her familiar. Just as fast, she doubted her decision.

"Yours or mine?" she asked, holding it out.

Sadie took the thimble back. "Mine."

It was the last word that ever passed between them.

I don't have a sister or a brother. The nearest I ever came was Charlie Moss. When Sadie and Beulah each told me their story, I made a solemn promise to myself: If a rift ever arose between me and my best friend, I'd make sure not to squander our last chance. I would tell him what he meant to me, everything, good and bad. I'd find words to echo through the silence.

But life is hardfisted, full of tricks. When the moment came, I didn't even know.

Rain again. A wrathful soundtrack for my nightmares. I was up at five, five-thirty, again (or still) at six, but dawn never clearly bared itself.

A chill wind bullied its way into the tent and baited me into getting dressed. My shirt and socks were tissuey with damp.

On my way to the Dump, I worried about the weather, one more crimp in a convoluted day. The parents, accustomed to their climate-controlled lives, would panic: ruined picnics, penny loafers! I couldn't think of the last rained-out visiting day. Surely, though, we'd faced inclemency. Ruff must have finessed it with some whipped-up solution, that famous impromptu wizardry.

The Dump was dark. Had the power gone out? My knock brought no response, so I let myself in. I flipped the switch and there was sudden light.

I knew right away that he was gone. Moments later, I would register his missing clothes and shoes, the PowerBook absent from the desk. But what I noticed first—all I needed to—was the blank space where Charlie's ax had hung.

Caroline sopped in for our daily meeting. "How bad does this suck?" she said. "Where's Charlie?"

A squidging noise: my feet, tapping a puddle. The roof was dripping. Everything leaked.

I pointed to the computerless desk. "Gone."

"What do you mean 'gone'?"

"Out of here. Split."

"You sure?"

"I'm not sure of anything."

But our quick further inspection confirmed it. He'd left his master keys on the hook beside the door, a "to do" list taped to the gooseneck lamp ("Call ACA about fire safety standards"; "Van 3 needs transmission fluid"). Outside, in his parking space, only the dash prints of tires, punctuation for an interrupted thought.

"How did—?" Caroline started, then caught herself. Who else could have tipped him off but me? "Oh, Jesus Christ, Jeremy. How *could* you?"

We stood in the void of Charlie's car. Caroline stared at me—or, rather, at not-me. It was a look I'd once seen aimed at Beulah. Three Amishwomen strolled past us as we left the Plain & Fancy. I watched them notice, then unnotice, Beulah. They didn't turn away, didn't make a show of shunning. They didn't need to: for them, she wasn't there.

Detective Mullen wasn't so reticent when he learned Charlie had fled. "He what? Who the fuck spilled the beans?"

Who the fuck, it went unsaid, was my new name.

I'd met him and Peter where the camp road hit the highway, and climbed into their idling Crown Vic. My skin was water-logged, shrunken-feeling.

"That's just great," Mullen said. He pulled a pack of Camels from the glove box.

"I thought you quit," I said.

"And I thought you were going to help us catch him. Instead you aid and abet. Are you psycho?" He lit a cigarette and sucked urgently, as though removing venom from a wound.

"Help us now," Peter said, "and we'll try to forget this." His cheeks were even redder than I'd remembered, like those of a man recently slapped to sense. "Give us a description— physical stats, vehicle. How far could he get with troopers on the lookout?"

But if anyone could disappear, it was Charlie. Ruff had taught him—had taught us both—the skills. *Save yourself to save the rest.* By now he could have ditched his car and holed up in the woods; he could hunker down for days, weeks, a month.

That's not what I told the detectives. I told them: red hair, five-feet-five, orange Saab. Mullen CB'ed it to the dispatcher. It was done.

He was now on his third cigarette, the car's air choky and tight. A set of parents turned past us into the camp entrance, then another, then a steady stream. I explained that I had to get back.

"We'll come with," Peter said. "Check up on Max."

There was no need, with Charlie gone, to sneak. The Crown Vic bombed up the sloppy road. Mullen parked behind an over-waxed Range Rover, and we emerged into a flood of families. Like a crook dodging courthouse cameras, my instinct was to duck and hide my face.

"What's going on?" said one mother with taut, patrician cheeks; her slacks were creased in all the right spots. "We've been waiting here, but no one's come to greet us."

"My son isn't with his cabin, is he sick?" asked a man whose hair was grizzled and see-through.

Then Jay Wooster stepped forward, a woman and a young girl at his side. "Jeremy, great to see you again. This is Julie, my wife. My daughter, Carrie."

The girl had Jay's immeasurable blue eyes. She gazed at him with undiluted adoration.

"Hey, how's the foot?" Jay said. "No more wild ax chops, I hope?"

"No, no. Everything's—" I looked to Mullen and Peter, who stood waiting, as grim as undertakers. *No matter what happens, act like it's supposed to.* "Why doesn't everyone head up to the Lodge?" I said.

The upper-crust mother began to protest, but I promised I'd be there in a minute. The men and I headed for the infirmary.

Max cinched Mullen in a hug so fast and tight that he had no real choice but to hug back. Peter received a similar greeting. And for me? A weak smile, a fleeting glance. When the seduction was full-on, Max was profligate with affection, but later, once he'd hooked you, miserly.

"Hey, how's your belly?" asked Peter. He patted Max's concave gut. "I heard you got sick on all those clams."

"I ate French toast this morning," Max boasted. "With syrup. And a bowl of oatmeal. And a banana."

Caroline, who'd been tending to campers in the sick bay, walked shrugging into the room. "I told him to take it easy. He won't listen."

"I'm starving," Max said. "I could eat an elephant."

"Too gamey," said Mullen. "Stick to oatmeal. Or I've got some chocolate Pop Tarts in the car."

There was a humming, happy-ending levity in the room; I thought, for a moment, that we'd be fine. Then Peter cleared his throat.

"Well," he said. "So"—two verbal pricks to deflate the swell of cheer. "I guess we all know the sting is off."

"I still don't get it," Max said. "How'd Charlie find out?"

So he didn't blame me—at least, not yet. I wanted to explain, to speak of boggling loyalties. But I didn't fully understand myself.

"It creeps me out," Max said. "Him taking off in the middle of the night."

I couldn't gauge his attitude. Relief, clearly, and a sense of victory, but also a rising bitterness. He'd been cheated of his chance to get back.

"We'll do everything we can to track him down," said Peter. "It'll help if we keep things on the q.t. for a while. Don't tell the other kids, or the parents."

"Not anybody?" asked Max.

"Not for now."

Max seemed torn again between letdown and relief. It struck me that this incident, for all its harmfulness, had placed him where he thrived: on center stage. The flu had pared his face to its callow, bony essence. But when all was stripped, who really was this boy? Freed from all our projections, was he anyone?

He trod joshingly on Mullen's toe. (He had done the same to me, once, hadn't he?) "Can I at least get out of here?" he begged. "I'm so totally over being sick."

"Fine by me," said the detective. "Then again, I'm not the medic."

With moony eyes, Max appealed to Caroline.

"Just go slow," she said. "Rest. Wash your hands."

"Hot diggedy," he said. "Free at last."

"Careful," said Mullen. "It's raining cats and dogs."

"Siamese and dachshunds," added Peter.

Caroline dressed Max in a large Hefty bag to wear until he got to his cabin. He stepped out, then paused in pelting rain.

"Thanks for coming," he said. "I'd given up on visiting day applying to me."

With Max gone, the mood ossified. The men grilled Caroline about camper-behavior patterns, indicators of widespread abuse. Was there anything suspicious she had noticed?

No, she said, nothing she could think of.

What had I noticed? Only Max. Only myself. I should have been looking out for more boys.

Had other kids presented with bruises or cuts, they asked. Any other broken bones, like Max's?

I explained that Max's injury had nothing to do with Charlie.

It was the truth, but still my voice wavered. Detective Mullen scribbled in his notebook. Did he figure me an accomplice? Wasn't I?

They demanded to search the Dump. I didn't want to watch them. I couldn't. Excusing myself to attend to antsy parents, I brought them to the door and took my leave.

(The next morning, though, in the desolate aftermath, I would return and study the files. To an outsider, all might have looked in order. The men hadn't found a thing. But if, as I did, you knew the past years' rosters, you'd have noticed conspicuous gaps. Scotty Allen, Matt Sheehan, Chris O'Rourke . . . half a dozen dockets had been purged. Guilt and anger twisted in my ribs.)

The Lodge, when I arrived, was explosive. At the door I smelled a pungent volatility, as though restlessness were a leaking fume. Hats, wool jackets, and ponchos all dripped; a humidity of unrule steamed the room.

Boys and parents feasted on cornucopic spreads. Soda cans and wrappers trashed the floor. Around every table gathered visitorless campers who pressed in pleadingly for scraps.

I saw counselors monkeying in the crowd: Simon, Bill McIndoe, Rick. They were difficult to distinguish from the boys. At the staff table, Jim Talbot plugged his ears.

Tripping over heaps of abandoned rain slickers, I budged my way up to the stage. No one else would calm this place down. I stood, right arm lifted in silent urgency like a child begging permission for the toilet.

I pumped my arm higher. No one noticed.

From the back of the room rang a gunshot. People shouted, people ducked, all heads turned. But it was just a jumbo bag of Fritos popped open. Abe Rottnek held up the evidence.

For the millionth time I told myself: If I were director, I'd eliminate junk food entirely. Even on visiting day. But Charlie—

Then it hit me. He was gone.

I caught the eye of Petey Wooster, sitting in the front row, by his dad. I grinned, and he grinned in return. He likes me, I thought. Most of them do.

"Excuse me," I called to the mob—a pebble into their smooth inattention. Again, a little louder, "Excuse me!" I waited five seconds, raised my voice a third time. Now a true quieting rippled.

"If we could just settle down. Thank you. Thanks. I know you're all soaking wet. But the important thing is, everybody made it!"

Even the visiting younger siblings now turned. They all faced me. Everybody looked.

At this point, Charlie normally voiced another version of Ruff's old ironwood speech: strength through bending, each tree part of the forest. Silently, I'd revise it in my head. What about focusing on ironwood's diverse uses—bats and handles, play and work, a balance. Handles might inspire a longer riff: how an ax handle is used in the felling of a tree, which in turn can be lathed into handles. A perfect cycle, just like Ironwood. Here, men taught boys how to grow up into men who would teach boys, and on forevermore.

"It's so great to see you all," I started. "Now, you may have noticed I'm not Charlie Moss."

One mother laughed. "We thought you'd grown six inches."

"And dyed your hair, too!" called someone else.

"Nope," I said. "Just me, all natural. I'm the assistant director, Jeremy Stull."

The first mother asked, "Where *is* Charlie?"

"I was just about to get to that. Charlie left unexpectedly this morning."

Could I blame them for their quick disgruntled huffs? They'd come here expecting to see the eminent headliner, and here I was, the flustered understudy.

"He sends his best to everyone. But a . . . personal emergency came up." My voice was all chickenshit quaver.

"What kind of emergency? Is he all right?"

"Charlie's fine, there's no need to worry. But I really can't say anything more."

Their whispers sounded like a pit of snakes. To forestall further distraction, I began. "I'd like to talk for a moment about who we are at camp, the sort of people we strive to become. It's built into our name: Ironwood."

When I paused for effect, a backbench camper shouted, "Wait. You forgot about the song."

I smiled the tight smile of an interrupted speaker. "The camp song? We can sing it when I'm done."

"No!" the boy hollered. "The other song."

"I'm afraid I don't know which song you mean."

"'Here Comes the Sun.' Charlie said that if it rained on visiting day, we should sing it, and the sky would clear up."

"Yeah," came two more voices. "He said so."

I dimly recalled Charlie rehearsing the tune, but not that he had deemed it magical.

Petey Wooster stood to his full four-feet-nine. "It's tradition. Charlie said we *always* do it."

What does an eleven-year-old know about tradition? I'd been at Ironwood more than half my life.

"I'm not sure I even know the words," I said.

The boos were instantaneous. Raspberries, catcalls. They might as well have hurled rotten fruit.

"Okay," I said. "Okay. I'm game to try. One of you want to join me here and lead?"

But my backpedaling was too little, too late. A camper in the rear—my guess was Dylan Shallot—raised his fist and chanted, "We want Charlie!" He repeated the cheer, and more boys caught the cadence. By the third time, mob rhythm ruled the room.

"We want Char-lie!"

"We want Char-lie!"

I jigged a self-deprecating dance to the chant, trying to brush it off; no one laughed. My face felt brittle and rickety with faults, my fake smile a wedge that might crack it.

"We want Char-lie!" they persisted.

I looked around for backup—Jim Talbot? Doug Rose?—anyone who might be on my side. I had one foot lowered from the stage in retreat when all of a sudden the chant stopped. There was no "shhhh" or angry shout for order; everyone, as if dumbstruck, simply quit.

Then I heard the unmistakable oaky voice. "I agree, it would be great to have Charlie. He's wonderful, isn't he? What a guy!"

I turned and saw Ruff standing behind me on the stage, where, seconds earlier, I had stood. He must have entered the back door while I was clowning.

"Yes sir, it would be nice to have Charlie. And if only he were here, and if only we had some ham, then we could have a ham-and-egg feast together . . . assuming, that is, we got our hands on some eggs!" Ruff held up his own hands—those roughened ax blades—and turned them over, miming emptiness. "But we don't have any of those things, do we? So we'll have to make do with what we've got. And that's us. And this glorious rainy day."

He brushed a hand through the wet, silver broom of his crew cut. Mist sprayed me. I banished myself to the side.

"Since I don't know each and every one of you," Ruff said, "allow me to introduce myself. I'm Ruff Peterson. I started this place."

His words were comically redundant, as he stood below the portrait of himself. It was like Abraham Lincoln tossing you a penny and saying, "Name's Abe. You might've seen me around." But Ruff was even loftier in person than in his likeness. His sharp jaw appeared quintessentially Scandinavian, as though honed by northern wind and snow. Nearly seventy, he still stood monument-straight. An amphetamined alertness lit his eyes.

"Now, this seems like a pretty big storm," he said.

He tossed me his checkered hunstman's jacket, which looked big enough to make a tablecloth. It was the same jacket, I was certain, he'd worn ten years ago, musked with wood smoke and history.

"And it *is* a big storm," he continued, "if you've never seen Mother Nature *really* angry."

He plucked something from his shirt pocket and poked it in his mouth. Everyone strained to catch a glimpse. When his hand moved, we saw a wooden toothpick. The man even cleaned his teeth with charisma.

"But I'd like to tell you now about a true storm," Ruff said. "The Great Hurricane of '38."

Dramatically, he sucked on his two-inch-long splinter, then pointed to a reedy boy in front. "Son, how old are you? Ten? Well, picture me at your age, actually a little younger. But it feels just like yesterday . . ."

And off he was on a classic yarn.

He knew nothing of our current imbroglio. He didn't know why Charlie was AWOL. All he knew was a roomful of malcontented folks who needed a leader, so he led. It was a beautiful, frightening thing to watch. Ruff could have asked them all to drink cups of poison, and probably, eagerly, they would. But he also could have told them to be kind and love each other, and they'd be just as faithful to his will.

Ruff winked at Jay Wooster, his long-ago favorite, now a husband, a father times two. How different Jay's path was from mine. He gazed at Ruff the way his daughter Carrie gazed at him, with absolute, uncomplicated affection. And I knew that Ruff had never done him harm.

". . . at the tippy-top of the ridge," Ruff said, "way way up, at the spot where the sun sets in summer, stood a monster white pine, a real giant. It was one of the King's pines, marked by British surveyors, the mast for a royal battleship. But they'd missed it. It had never been chopped. Seven men could join arms around its trunk.

"Well, that tree had been fighting off the howler all day, feinting like a heavyweight champ. But at two o'clock in the morning, the hurricane at its peak, a wicked wind swept up the ridge. The tree snapped. Just like that. Like a twig."

Ruff paused to let the crowd tingle in its hush. Even the rain lulled in deference. With the toothpick, he fiddled at his upper incisors, then downed a deep breath and resumed.

"The tree crashed—they could hear the echo all the way to Rutland—and she started sliding down the ridge. Now, most of the other trees had long since been felled, so the hillside was pretty much clear. That old pine kept sliding, faster and faster. It gained so much momentum that when it hit bottom it kept going up the far side!"

"No way," called a boy. "That couldn't happen."

"Yes sir, I kid you not," said Ruff. "Up that tree went until it almost kissed the top, and then it started slipping back again. Back through all the other trees, the boulders—everything—past the bottom and up the other side.

"And then? It slid right down again.

"Back it went, then up. Then back and up again. From one side of this valley to the other. Each time it landed just an inch shy of the last, and each time it got whittled by the rocks.

"It kept going like that through the night and into morning. By the afternoon, she'd barely slowed a bit. But she'd been shaved to a telephone pole.

"The storm pounded through a second full night. In the morning a pipe-sized piece of pine was still shuttling, too fast for anyone to grab hold.

"Two days later, when the hurricane finally quit for good, and the dawn came up quiet and calm, we went out to survey all the damage. There, smack dab in the middle of the debris, was what was left of that monster King's pine." Ruff smiled a huge hambone grin. "You guessed it: this little toothpick."

He held it high for everyone to see.

Exasperated heckles and generous groans were followed by a wallop of applause. Fathers elbowed gullible sons.

Then I saw Max on the far side of the room. I wondered how long he had been there. His mouth was agape, his eyes trained to center stage. He stared at Ruff with the fixity of an addict.

TWENTY-TWO

—◄○►—

For once, I did right; I kept the kid away. Sent him griping down the hill on an errand. Ruff never laid eyes on him, or hands.

But Ruff and me—that couldn't be avoided.

We sat face-to-face in the tight kitchen pantry, on five-gallon tubs of peanut butter. Fusty with cornmeal and other raw smells, the air suggested future gluttony. A lightbulb dangled on its long hangman's cord, casting faint pendulous shadows.

Through the thin walls to the mess hall leaked the noise of merriment: Cornelio was reprising his slide show. The audience's delight came through as muffled mirth, like the dub of a dub of canned laughter.

But in the pantry, just our deadlock breath. Ruff stroked his chin as though testing a blade's sharpness. I chewed a stub of cuticle.

". . . some explanation," he mumbled through half-clenched teeth (the toothpick still stuck between his molars). A minute later: "If Charlie told his side . . ."

Then more silence, the ache and scrape of it.

Was Ruff's distress that of a disappointed mentor? Or did he worry that he, too, might be fingered?

"This business about stolen drugs," he said. "Charlie was just discrediting the boy?"

"No, it's true. Max did it. He confessed."

"But CPS believes him anyway?"

"Charlie wouldn't have skipped town if he was innocent."

"No," said Ruff. "No, I guess he wouldn't." He tongued the

217

toothpick around his mouth. "Does the press know? This'll kill us if it gets out."

Now he was the threatened businessman. How quickly he abandoned Charlie's cause.

"Not yet," I said. "But the *fact* of it isn't necessarily so harmful. It's how we respond. It's up to us."

Ruff went on worrying the toothpick. I could tell he was searching for just the right spin if the *Rutland Herald* asked for a quote: unhesitating, compassionate but firm. From outside, a drumming like the march of an enemy; a martial clap of metal against itself. It took a moment to peg it as only the garbage shed, buffeted by rain and wind.

"Maybe if we find him before they do," Ruff said. "Convince him to turn himself in? Or we issue a statement. 'This will not be tolerated.'"

Onstage, Ruff had flashed with invincible sheen; this close, I could see timeworn flaws. His face appeared chafed by a lifetime of shaving, close to its bedrock of bone. His eyes were a cornered animal's.

The thought came to me: Ruff would die. It might take a year, half a dozen, a decade. But he was an old man. He would die.

Death brought me, as usual, to my father—my father who had never grown feeble or flawed, stuck a scant year older than I was now. It hurt my head to think that I would pass him. My father had talked of change and changelessness, the afternoon he took me underground. He steered us to an offshoot of the main subway tunnel, found the breaker and switched off the lights. Then he killed even his hard hat's pale bulb. In that vast black murk, borders blurred. There was no front or back, only dark.

"Do you like it down here?" my father asked.

I was scared to tell the truth: I wanted out.

"Me, too," he said. "Up top, seasons change, people die; down here you can count on things forever."

"Then why don't people live down here?" I asked.

"We'd ruin it. We're human. We screw up. Much better to leave it be, don't you think?"

"Yes," I said, gladdened by the thought of permanence. I relaxed into the infinite dark's embrace.

But Dad himself had ruined it so soon! He had buckled the very ground beneath my feet.

Which is how things remained until I came to Ironwood, and met Ruff, and found a place to stand again. Like trees, Ruff said, we could grow with roots so deep that our limbs could endure the cruelest gale. Then he, too, uprooted everything. I hated him.

I had never before let myself admit it. But as much as there was love, there was hate. The two feelings wrenched so hard in opposite directions that they met at the back and were one.

Ruff tapped a rhythm on his peanut butter tub, telegraphing unaccustomed panic. From his chin hung a liverish wattle of skin that shook with his slight unsteadiness.

He said, "There's still the boy. What's the plan?"

I pictured Max, across the stage, transfixed by Ruff's performance; I saw the troubled hunger in his eyes.

"Maybe I should still take him back with me," Ruff said. "Bring him to the farm, get him away."

"No," I said. "He'll be just fine here."

"But don't you think—"

"No! Max stays."

I had never challenged Ruff so forcefully. Like a new flavor, the words stunned my tongue. He eyed me with the intimation of resistance in his gaze, and I leaned back to dodge his outrage. But the blow, when it came, wasn't aimed at me.

"Damn that Charlie. I can't believe he'd do this."

It wasn't clear what Ruff meant by "this." Hurting Max? Getting caught? Running away? I wanted to say: Of course he would; you taught him. *Predator*, I thought. *Asshole. Thief.*

But Ruff was the one who spoke first. "I'm sorry. I made a mistake." He lowered his head; the toothpick fell. "You're a good kid. I should have picked you."

A flurry of confusion gusted in me. How dare he suggest that the sin of his misdeed existed in the *whom*, not the *what*. Then again, perhaps it really did, for I'd wanted it—wanted him—so much. Was it possible that Ruff's touch, if only he'd chosen me, could have mended (or prevented) all our wounds? If so—if a man and boy, together, could find healing—then I could still hope for me and Max. I could still, despite everything, hope.

"So," I asked, "why? Why not me?"

"I'm not really sure I can explain. It was tough. I thought so much of both of you."

"But you must have had a reason," I insisted.

A mild, recuperative light blurred his eyes, and I saw in them the Ruff from before: the man who had held me as I shivered hypothermic, who fixed my busted boots, dried my tears.

"I guess when it came right down to it," he said, "I thought Charlie'd be better with the parents. And he was. He was an awfully good director."

Did he think that's what we were talking about? "Not that," I said. "That wasn't the mistake."

"It was. It was definitely a mistake."

"No. Before. When Charlie and I were kids."

The cords in Ruff's neck pulled tight. "You were *my* kids," he said. "I loved you both."

"I know. And we both loved you, too. But that's different from"—what? Physical desire? With Max and me, it was all the same.

"I told you I made a mistake." Ruff's tone was glazed, amnesiac. "But now I can do something about it. Better late than never, don't you think?"

"Now? What could you possibly do now?"

Tear time apart and restitch it with new seams.

Give me back my childhood.

Choose me.

Ruff placed a heavy hand on my thigh. "I'm counting on you, Jer. Don't say you won't. I'm asking you to be the new director."

As if he'd overheard my silent plea.

"We'd say 'acting director' for the rest of this season, announce it as official in the fall."

I wasn't certain how I should respond. Amish farmers like

Mose Ebersol, "struck" by lot as ministers, often weep or get sick with the news. The call is more a burden than a boon.

"I don't know," I said. "We've got no idea what'll happen with Charlie. The state might decide to shut us down."

Ruff tightened his grip on my thigh. "If anyone can lead us through, it's you."

A gasp—a collective intake of astonishment—was audible through the pantry's walls. Cornelio must be flourishing the slide show's climax: the Fourth of July fireworks.

"I'm too old to direct again myself," Ruff said. "You can do it. You're young, you've got the smarts. The camp would be yours. Really yours."

Now a sudden swell of applause—the slide show had reached its final frame. Glowing on the screen would be a last chromatic burst, a brilliant tableau of Independence. I remembered sprightly mortars, the canoe's beguiling sway. Then my hand on Max's thigh—closer, closer—just before he mentioned Charlie's name.

TWENTY-THREE

◄○►

After that, things ran smoothly, more or less. Like the weather, camp alters but always persists; it jet-streams resiliently on.

I was "acting director," and felt just so. I could do the stentorian basso profundo, the "Stop that *right this instant!*" scowl. But acts that before had been natural, instinctive, now felt dictated by script. *Director sees boy crying in corner of Lodge, crosses to him, kneels, consoles.*

Thankfully, no one else appeared to notice, and the "We want Charlie" sentiment soon waned. Boys have such brief attention spans. In absentia, how could Charlie maintain the campers' interest through the onslaught of in-their-face action? Vans teetered down the road, ferrying kids to Lake Umbagog and the Presidential Range. In the crafts barn, the hot trend was handcut jigsaw puzzles. A Grand Circuit swim was organized. The freight train of fun could not be stopped.

Events conspired to buttress my leadership. The stomach bug, like a cat bored with tormenting a mouse, hurried off in search of fresh prey. Even the weather cooperated. After parents' day, the sky atoned with blue. Mornings, before breakfast, I looked up for clouds, trying to suss out a coming front. But the fluky windfall calm held for weeks.

With Charlie deposed, counselors spoke critically of his reign. According to Doug Rose, Charlie sometimes stole candy from care packages. Bill McIndoe told of how Charlie would come to his cabin and badmouth him in front of the boys: "He undermined my authority just to give his own a boost." These anecdotes were inevitably contrasted with affirmations of my own benevolent leadership. I was praised for staying flexible within my firm command, for knowing what to say, and when to stay mum.

I kept expecting contact from Charlie: a postcard, a midnight phone call. Don Fisher hinted that somebody somewhere had seen something. But every trail ran lukewarm, then cold.

Rumors connected Max to the mystery. Had he leaked red herrings? Who knows how these things start? One story had him poisoning Charlie's oatmeal, and Charlie now comatose in Rutland. In another, Charlie had lost an exorbitant bet with Max and was hiding from knee-break debt collectors. Spooked by the notion of Max as black magician—a boy who could make a man vanish—the other campers shied away from him. While he waded in the lake, keeping his cast high and dry, they swam to the farthest-flung rafts. When he asked if he could join their rambunctious Frisbee games, they shouted, "Next goal wins!" and wrapped things up.

Max couldn't tell the real story; he'd promised Peter and Mullen that he wouldn't. The truth might not have helped him anyway. Boys shun nobody more quickly than a victim. Peer-rejected, he latched back on to me. Where once he'd been guarded, only hinty with affection, now he blurted testaments of fondness. His eyes glowed with drug-free devotion.

His transformation had begun back on visiting day—only hours after Charlie had absconded. Once the parents left, we segued into cabin cookouts to stave off postpartum homesickness: intimacy as preventive medicine. With no cabin, I was liberated for the night. I decided to indulge myself with a shower.

I carried my toiletries and towel to the washroom, along with a heap of clean clothes, and left them on the bench outside the stalls. Adjusting the spray to a purgative sting, I stood stuporous, a junkie for the heat. I was off-duty, untouchable, alone. Charlie washed away, as did Ruff and his request. Don Fisher, high-strung parents: down the drain.

I stepped, steaming, out of the stall. Half-blind from billowing mist and dripping hair, I groped for the towel on the bench. Instead I felt the shock of human flesh.

"Jesus," I said. "Max, you scared me shitless." I found the towel, tied it to my hips. "Why aren't you with your cabin? What are you doing?"

But I could see his actions plain enough. His T-shirt was pulled halfway up to his armpits, exposing his taut abdomen. With my razor he shaved at the thin fuse of hair that trailed teasingly from his navel.

"What is this all about?" I said.

"Don't know, just feel like it," he answered. He took another swipe at his skin. He worked carelessly, as if unafraid to cut himself, or maybe more than that—maybe hoping.

"Quit it, Max. You're worrying me."

Another strip of hair was erased.

"And hey, who said you could use my razor?"

That finally made him stop.

"Sorry. It was just sitting here, in your bag."

He set down the razor on the bench. It was matted with hair, the blade ruined. I saw now that he'd also shaved his arm, the healthy one. It looked as though he *had* cut himself.

"Max. Show me your arm. Right now."

There were two sets of parallel scratch marks near his wrist from drawing the Sensor blade sideways.

"Talk to me," I said. "What's going on?"

"I miss you. You've been acting weird and whatnot."

"We've all been. We've had to. You know why."

"But it's different. We don't hang anymore. I'm lonely."

I faced him sternly. "That's no reason to hurt yourself."

"Don't freak. I'm not, like, suicidal. I just wanted to see how it would feel." Max tapped the sections of his xylophonic stomach, as if malleting a melody. "Lean and mean," he said. "Feel how smooth."

I declined. I turned my gaze away.

I couldn't gauge how seriously to take this. Max sounded edgy, erratic, forlorn, but not at all deranged or self-destructive.

Maybe he really was just curious. He'd probably never shaved before. (This was the very washroom where Ruff had taught me.)

"Do Simon and Cornelio know you're here?"

"It's cool," he said—a standard Max nonanswer. "The kids were being dicks to me, so I left. I'm sick of them. I'd rather be with you."

He tugged puppyishly on my towel, which I realized was still all that I was wearing. The thought came: If I wanted, I could have him.

I pulled on a T-shirt, then underwear and shorts, undoing the towel only when I was dressed.

"Max, do you promise you're not going to hurt yourself?"

He shrugged. "Never say never."

"I'm serious. Do I have to tell Caroline?"

"Jesus, can't I just be in a bad mood sometimes? What do you want? Should I sign something in blood?"

"Not in blood, that's the point. Pencil's fine."

A smile unlocked his lips with a quick mercury flash: his orthodontic mood barometer. My gut told me he was out of danger.

I asked if he'd had any dinner, and he said no. "Me neither. Let's go raid the fridge."

As we munched leftover meat loaf I could see Max settling, returning to the shape of himself. And yet an off-kilterness remained. More than once he took a bite and then forgot to chew, as if even this task were flummoxing.

"Listen," I said, "this stuff with Charlie." We were now onto Seward's maple ice cream: huge, convalescent, bribing scoops. "It's okay to be *not* okay about it. It's okay to need to talk. You know that, right?"

Max cringed at the nip of a big mouthful.

"Still worried about Charlie?" I asked.

"Nope," he said. "I think he's gone for good."

"Me, too. He wouldn't take the risk."

Max licked his spoon thoughtfully. "By the way, I wanted to thank you. For whatever you did to make him leave."

"Oh. Well. You don't have to thank me."

"No, I do. You've been totally cool to me. It means a lot. There's nobody else."

The clipped but articulate sorrow of his words made me realize the progress he'd made—the sign language of shrug and slouch and feint now translated to actual speech.

"Have you been thinking about your mom today?" I asked. "Must be tough, all the other parents here."

"Whatever," he said. "No big deal."

But I saw the tightening at the corners of his jaw, two corks of muscle keeping in the pain.

"When I was a kid, I hated it. Everyone's dads, patting their backs. My mom never visited, either. 'Too far.'" I served Max the last of the ice cream. "How'd you like to call your mom?" I asked.

"I thought campers weren't allowed phone calls."

I ruffled the mop of his yarny, nightshade hair—the first touch I'd permitted myself all evening. "I believe we can make an exception for you, Max. You're nothing if not exceptional."

I led him through the door into the Dump—another violation of camp rules. (As director, the rules were mine to break.)

"This is where Charlie lived?" he said. "This is the big secret HQ?" He kicked a ball of socks on the floor.

"No big secret. There just needs to be a place in camp that's for adults and only for adults."

His smirk was tight. "Except for right now?"

The room remained a mess from the CPS inspection. Files and notebooks spilled across the desk. First-aid manuals had toppled from their shelves.

Max took a seat at Charlie's desk. I spied him perusing an ink-jetted letter resting in the printer's output tray.

I said, "I'm trusting you. Keep your eyes to yourself."

"Okay," he said, as he stole another glance.

The answering machine blinked evidence of half a dozen messages. From the *Rutland Herald*? Don Fisher? Worried parents? I'd play them when Max wasn't around.

I dialed the hospital and asked for the extension. When it rang, I handed Max the receiver. I sat on what had been Charlie's cot.

Max, for a second, looked lost again, drugged, a dozy trepidation in his eyes. Then he came to life with fawnish energy. "Mom? Hey! Surprise surprise!" In a useless, fledgling wave, he raised his hand.

"No," he said. "It's me. Come on, it's Max." His hand dropped to the desk and gripped its edge. "Me, Nicky. Nicholas. I'm at camp. It's awesome up here. There's this guy named Jeremy"—he ravished me with a wink—"and they've got a bombing oldies station. 'Duke Duke Duke, Duke of Earl . . .'"

He tried to smile, but his thin lips crumpled.

There was a long pause during which Max scratched futilely at his cast, unable to quell an itch within. He twisted the phone cord around and around his wrist in a tourniquet of nervous disappointment. Finally, faintly, I could hear his mother's voice, a girlish unbridled monologue.

Max tucked a leg beneath his butt. His forehead was crimped with concentration.

"Yesterday?" he said. "An audition? 'Cause I thought . . . haven't you been in the hospital?"

He persuaded a pencil into the cast to tame his itch.

"Wow. *One Life to Live?* Maybe when you get better, they'll offer another part. I mean, if they saw how good you are."

He listened again, all loyalty and suspension of disbelief, his eyes alight with filial optimism. On his wrist the tourniquet wrung tighter.

In time, the other end fell quiet. I couldn't discern if his mother had quit talking or perhaps had simply lowered her voice. Pensively, Max stroked the shaved patch on his arm, fingering the double incisions. The cuts might have been a geometry illustration: parallels, the failure to intersect.

When more than a minute had passed silently, Max said,

"Mom? You okay? What're you thinking?" The coo of his voice was parental. But when, hearing no response, he called for her again, he reverted to the child he truly was. "Ma?!" It was the pleading of a lamb. "Oh. Okay, thanks." He hung up.

For a while he faced the wall, rigid, motionless. I couldn't even tell if he breathed.

"Max?" I said. Then again, softer, "Max?"

"She fell asleep," he said, still turned away.

"She must be wiped out. That's natural."

"The nurse said to try another day."

"Sure," I said. "Whenever you want, just ask."

Something between a laugh and a sob left his throat. "What's the use? Another day'll be the same."

"Come on. You just caught her at a bad time."

In his eyes, when at last he looked up and turned around, was a pointed, tunneling misery. "She didn't even know who I was."

"Don't be crazy," I said. "You're her son!"

"No, she didn't. Not at first. Maybe never."

"Your mom is sick, Max, she's—"

"She's not sick, she's *dying*."

Those eyes. I was hollowed by his gaze.

The room was tricky with baleful half-shadows. Max trembled. His face looked erased.

"They all die," he said. "Everyone. They disappear."

"That's not true."

"Yes it is. It fucking sucks."

"*I'm* here," I said. "Always. You know I am."

In seconds he was nestled against me on the bunk, shuddering, enfolded in my arms. There was a gasp, a ragged release of breath and spit—his fluids on my skin, emollient.

"You're okay," I said. "You're all right. You're with me."

We were touching all over: his back against my chest, my chin kissing the top of his skull. I held him like gravity, like an axiom of nature; my hand on his heart was absolute.

"You're okay," I said again. "You're with me."

What would someone barging in have seen? A man and boy coupled in comfort or in pain? The tangle of passion or control?

I wanted to be inside Max but also be his armor, at the same time to penetrate and protect. I wanted things to be what they were, and something else. I wanted to destroy dividing lines.

Max snuggled closer, conforming to my shape. His lips brushed the pulse point on my wrist.

"I love you," he said rawly. "More than anyone. I do."

"I love you, too," I said. "I love you, too."

TWENTY-FOUR

◄○►

And so, from the worst, I'd gotten the best. I now had everything. Almost.

Max was my sidekick, my tagalong mascot, heeling me everywhere. ("My hero," he would croon, as in the old vaudeville routine, but with candor beneath the foolery.) He sported my Jockeys and made sure I noticed, the waistband tugged high above his jeans. He made gifts: gimp wristbands, a granite paperweight, a valentine's wholehearted curve. Some toughened husk of him had been peeled, exposing the sweet, essential seed. He kept his oddball genius and saucy, quick-draw wit, but was newly unlocked, accessible.

Ruff returned, ostensibly as a judge for Talent Night, but in truth, I knew, to check on me. As much as he watched the exhibitionists onstage, he watched me watching over them. After the jew's-harped "Star-Spangled Banner" and the mimed episode of *South Park*—while campers toasted one another with bug juice—Ruff mingled with his former acolytes. A full third of the staff had been campers under Ruff; he was still godfatherly to all. Bill McIndoe challenged him to a bout of arm wrestling: "Come on, I'm finally big enough to win." But he wasn't. Ruff pinned him in four seconds. Doug Rose showed a snapshot of his pearl-eyed fiancée, asking for Ruff's blessing on the union.

Simon, in turn, had his audience. I overheard him telling Ruff of his freshman year at Williams, of how he'd joined their fledgling Woodsmen's Team. "At the meet, Dartmouth whipped us, but I got third in single bucksaw. Next year I'm going to train for the ax throw." "Attaboy," said Ruff, and tousled Simon's hair. "Come to the farm, check out my M-tooth saw." Eagerly, Simon promised that he would.

Later, while Ruff was reminiscing with Jim Talbot, Simon and I chatted at the back.

"It's so great to see Ruff," he said. "Isn't it?"

"Yeah, you can tell he misses this. But can I ask? Did Ruff? Back when you were a camper?" I couldn't even formulate the question.

I studied Simon's face for some memory's overclouding—or the opposite, a reflex of forgetting. He stayed sunnily oblivious.

"Back when I was a camper, what?" he said.

"Nothing. I was thinking out loud."

At evening's end, I walked Ruff to his truck. It was the first moment we'd had to ourselves. Even in the dark, I could see his dewy eyes. He clapped my back and let his hand remain. "Jeremy, I never meant . . ." he started.

His fingers on my back slowly tensed and then released—the touch that might have changed everything, once. If it had, though, might I now be in Charlie's predicament? Which butterflies trigger which hurricanes?

Ruff's voice came out husky with emotion. "I only meant to help you—all the boys. It'd kill me if I did the opposite."

"I know," I said. "I know. I understand."

Perhaps Charlie had been to Ruff what Max was to me: his one and only, his snapping point. Perhaps Ruff had never snapped since. Or perhaps that's what I had to believe.

A swirl of air caught us in its updraft. Laughter tinkled from a distant cabin.

Ruff moved his hand to my neck. "This helps a lot. Seeing you, tonight. The boys love you. The staff. Everyone. You make me pretty sure I did okay."

Before I could react, he bent and kissed my scalp. He climbed into his truck and drove away.

At midnight, sleepless in the swelter of my tent, I thought: *Dream rainbows. Dream pots of gold.* I began to have faith that we might all make it through this, perhaps even stronger than before. Fantasizing no specific person's body or encounter, but eased into an overall calm, I stroked myself until I found release. The ghost of Ruff's kiss lingered on my head.

Into August, camp burned with terminal intensity. The last fortnight found everything heightened. Blue cloudless skies, we all agreed, were heaven-sent. We became metaphysicians of summer.

And why not? The transformations were undeniably charismatic. Boys who'd never climbed more than Upper West Side walk-ups now summitted Camel's Hump and Mansfield; they returned with calves and confidence bulging. Food brats who in June had fought for heaping plates now waited and philanthropically shared.

Even the most hopeless cases flourished. At summer's start, Abe Rottnek, ashamed to be albino, had swum in shirts and clamdigger shorts. Now, at every chance, he streaked the waterfront, as if his birthday suit were the smartest of tuxedos. Eli, definitionally a loser when he arrived, had parlayed his geekiness into shtick. Each night he took the stage to deliver knock-knock jokes with irresistible, aw-shucks aplomb.

As the banquet neared, we urged kids to varnish crafts projects and to clinch Red Cross swimming ranks. But we tried not to pressure, only nudge—for equally as crucial as these tangible achievements were the personal bonds campers forged. If boys spent their last days cementing friendships instead of supergluing model boats, so much the better for their growth. You could be a man and still be *human,* was our gospel.

I conducted the closing movement of our summer symphony, driving toward its final, fraught chord. For that harmony, I needed Caroline. But she had been keeping her distance. When we met with Ken Krueger to plan the banquet menu, her voice was stiff and businessy. One night she dyed her hair without asking my opinion. She took her morning mugs of tea alone.

I couldn't fault her; I had let Charlie walk. But now, with him gone, my loyalties were clearer, and I wanted the chance to make amends. I had a vision of the future, starring her.

What finally got us talking was a game. On the next-to-last Saturday of the season, as the lunch plates were being collected, Simon announced a hiking afternoon. From the mess hall came an upchuck of groans. The kids were jonesing for an all-camp game.

We hadn't indulged in more than two weeks. Charlie's mind housed the only playbooks.

"We can't," Simon said with circular insistence. "This afternoon we're going on hikes."

But the campers were rallying for revolt. One kid hollered, "Ar-ma-ged-don!" and soon the Lodge resounded with a chant. Boys clanged cutlery in time with their demand.

"Hey," I said, mounting the stage to rescue Simon. "We can't play Armageddon twice."

"What about a different game?" asked Toby.

"Sure," I said. "We'll play a different game."

Before I'd closed my mouth, he challenged, "When?"

A hundred gazes turned toward me like searchlights. I didn't have an inch of breathing room.

"Now," I said. "Today. This afternoon. Head on down to rest hour, and when you hear the bell, meet right back here for the skit."

You'd have thought I said they won the lottery. They stampeded, hip-hooraying, to their cabins.

Caroline was obviously annoyed. She'd been planning to take off the rest of the day to listen to a Red Sox doubleheader. Plus, all-camp games almost guaranteed sprained ankles, or worse—another broken bone? But it was too late to turn back. She joined me and Doug Rose for a powwow.

We racked our brains trying to devise a clever theme—something current, something punny, double-edged. Names of ridiculous celebrities were bandied: the Osmonds, Celine Dion. "Kenneth Starr Wars" was my best idea, President Loose

Slytalker battling the Independent Counsel. But Caroline vetoed the plan; even kids, she said, were bored with that old story.

Doug finally pulled from his memory's bottom drawer the plot of a game from years ago. Ironically, it was I who had invented "Avoidance," but I had long since forgotten it. On either end of the camp road were two Amish "church districts"; in between was the tainting English world. All the boys except one began the game as Amish, half in each settlement. Their goal was to move back and forth between districts without getting caught by the apostate. They were caught by having bandannas—representing obedience—yanked from their back pants pockets.

The odds appeared wildly unfair: ninety-nine boys against one! The handicap was that the Amish must travel by "horse"—one camper piggyback on another. This slowed them just enough for the sole English boy eventually to execute a nab. The caught boy was excommunicated and joined the English side. (His "horse" returned safely to base.)

Inexorably the numbers would reverse. Two boys were "in the ban," then three, soon ten, and accordingly the Amish ranks diminished. The boys pirouetted and leapt to save their faith in a madcap ballet of evasion.

Dylan volunteered to start as shunned. "Horses and buggies? You're living in the past!" He commanded the center of the dusty camp road in the pose of a matador awaiting bulls.

Doug Rose was posted at one finish line, Caroline and I fifty yards down at the other. Together we counted out "one-two-three-go!" Not a single Amish horse or rider moved.

"What's the matter?" goaded Dylan. "Are you scared you'll be corrupted? Don't you think you can handle the temptation?"

The pre-game skit had been an Amish church service. I'd sermonized on their core points of faith: unspottedness, not being yoked with sinners. I'd brandished every theological blade.

"Hey, come on with darkness," Dylan said, meaning "commune." He shimmied a lurid dance of enticement.

At this, brave Toby took the dare. He hoisted a ten-year-old camper on his back and galloped down the center of the road. Barreling full-speed, directly at Dylan, he aimed for a head-on collision. But a yard shy of crash, with fullback expertise, he spun and darted just out of reach. He and his rider crossed the line to safety.

"Do not love the things of the world," he shouted, fist pumping fiercely in the air.

"Don't eat yolks with sinners!" his teammate added.

I wondered what the Yoders would make of this irreverence. Or Beulah. Or Mose Ebersol. I'd cooked up the game in a spirit of respect, but now it seemed rude and trivial. The kids didn't understand how real people's lives rose and fell on these heartfelt beliefs. They'd never seen the vanishing points of Beulah's eyes.

With a war cry, another charge began. Again the horse and rider eluded Dylan by a hair. But denial only made him hungrier. When a third pass was made he nearly tackled his opponents and stole the rider's polka-dot bandanna. At last, he was no longer alone.

With two boys in the middle, the action picked up pace; the game began its automatic shift.

"Looks like we fooled 'em again," I said to Caroline. "Don't they realize it's just glorified tag?"

"They like to think they're part of something more important."

"You mean we're not fooling them, they fool themselves?"

"We *all* fool ourselves that way," she said.

"Wow, you're a nurse *and* a shrink?"

Normally, Caroline would have laughed at such a dig or sniped another right back at me; but our friendship, in the strain of these last stressful weeks, was like elastic pulled past the point of give. She stepped a long, hard step away.

"No, you're right," I said, attempting to mollify her. "It's why religions—and summer camps—stay in business."

She didn't acknowledge my acknowledgment. She glared, unyielding, at her feet.

There was a blur of moving bodies, a slide, a burst of dust. Immediately, contentious voices rose.

"I made it! Tell Toby I made it," said Owen, a sorrel-haired twelve-year-old.

Toby, in the brief time we'd ignored the game's flow, had apparently been caught and shunned. He was now one of the predators in the middle.

"No way," he said. "That's total bull, I caught him." A checkered handkerchief proved his point.

"But I'd already crossed the line," Owen said.

"The horse had, not you," countered Toby. He pointed to a panting, older boy.

"Is it true?" I asked the winded horse.

He nodded. "I was definitely across. But Owen? To be honest, I don't think so."

If a sinner dies midway through his last holy confession, does he get sent to heaven or to hell? Is it possible to be *partly* saved?

"Let's give the benefit of the doubt," I decided. "If the horse made it, so did Owen. You're still safe."

The kids were slapping an exuberant high five when Caroline called, "Whoa, now, hold on. I thought Amishness was about boundaries."

"It is," I said. "Like the line this horse just crossed."

She folded her long, bossy arms. "Say an Amish guy got caught, I don't know, going to college. But he rode to his classes on a horse. He'd still be excommunicated, right?"

I said he would.

"Right. You're in, or you're out, no halfway. Owen, face the music: you were caught."

The boy stomped in protest, but Caroline wouldn't budge, so he pocketed his handkerchief and left.

"Wow," I said to Caroline, "you sure know how to call 'em. Maybe next summer we should make you head ump."

She ran a hand through her newly auburn hair.

"Actually, you know, I'm serious. Someone's got to take Charlie's place. You want to be in charge of games next year?"

"I'm not sure there's going to be a next year."

"Care, what are you talking about?"

The ruffian chatter of boys bubbled around us, the hoopla of triumph and near-miss.

"This hasn't been the best summer," she said.

"These last two weeks have been good, haven't they?"

"Define 'good.' Charlie's god-knows-where, and we cruise along like everything's just fine."

"We've talked about this. It's triage. When the season's done, we'll deal with everything."

She looked at me then with sore eyes. "Thing is, Jer, we *haven't* talked about it. Maybe Ruff and you came up with some grand strategy, or you and the CPS guys. I've been cut out of the loop."

"You know I totally count on your opinion."

"Did you ask for my opinion before you spilled the beans to Charlie? How can I work for someone . . . you still haven't told me why."

Abe Rottnek dashed past on the back of a boy, arms skyward in the symbol for goal. But when he patted his pocket with champion pride, he discovered only emptiness. He'd been nabbed along the way and didn't know.

"I'm sorry," I said, as Abe trudged to his new team. "I made some mistakes. We all did." I wanted desperately to stay part of a *we*.

"Maybe I was crazy," Caroline said. "To think I could fit in at a boys' camp."

"Now you're just being silly. You're as much a part of camp as anyone. Not just a part of it—you *make* it. I want you to be assistant director."

I hadn't intended to blurt my plan like that, but her threatening to leave had cornered me.

"Assistant director? Give me a huge break."

"Maybe it is. For both of us. A clean start."

"Wake up, Jer. What would the parents think? A woman?"

"That's *their* problem. There's a waiting list for enrollment."

Caroline turned her face away. She might have been reacting to an off-color joke or to a rumor she wasn't sure was true. But I saw the unveiling of possibility in her eyes, a glint of daughterly aspiration.

"And Ruff?" she said. "The good ole Dartmouth boy?"

I grabbed her by the shoulders and held her at arm's length, making her look at me. "Ruff needs me," I said. "And I need you. He'll have to go along. End of story."

"I don't know," Caroline said. "I don't know."

But she let my hands stay firmly on her shoulders.

By this point, more than half of the boys patrolled the middle. The survivors had trekked back and forth so many times that their feet barely left the ground. (I thought of Brown and Betty, Abner's sturdy Belgian geldings, at the end of a long plowing bout, their hooves belled with burdensome earth.) With most of the younger campers already caught, older boys were forced to ride each other. They were heavy. They stumbled. They fell.

Not Max. His twiggish figure made a manageable load, even for the haggard, slow-foot boys. He always ran the gauntlet unscathed.

"I have no spots," he bragged after another winning pass. "I am pure. I do not commune with darkness."

His streak was uncanny, almost supernatural. Or duplicitous — that's what Dylan charged.

"He's cheating! His bandanna's tied to his belt loop."

"Frig off," said Max. "Sore loser. You *wish* you were fast enough to catch me." He planted his hands on his hips in defiance — or was he fiddling with the handkerchief?

"See? See there?!" Dylan's voice was thin with anger. "He was fixing it! I swear I got him, but it was tied."

"Guess you didn't pull hard enough," Max said.

"Oh yeah? Would *this* be hard enough?"

Dylan lunged, but Caroline caught him. "Watch it, or you'll both be sitting out!"

"But it sucks. He screws up *everything*."

Caroline briefly caught my eye. Dylan didn't know how right he was.

"If you're so sure," said Max, "then go ahead and check me." Twerpishly, he hula-hooped his hips.

"Well, now you untied it," Dylan said.

"Then you don't have any evidence, do you?"

The scot-free vainglory of Max's tone was ugly; for an instant, I imagined disliking him.

"Did you tie it?" I asked.

He said no.

"Show us," I demanded, and he did.

Caroline stayed quietly neutral; she knew this was between Max and me.

The delay-of-game was making other campers antsy; their impatience crept toward us like a fog. "Come on, let's finish," called one loudmouth boy. Another said, "So the kid cheats. Big deal."

I couldn't help but agree. Life had consistently sucker-punched Max; if he swung back, occasionally, a bit below the belt, wasn't that just evening the odds?

"Sorry, Dylan," I said. "It's his word against yours."

"Well, we know whose word you care about more. Why'd I bother? You'd do anything for him."

It was true. I would do anything for Max. I didn't see yet how that could be other than good.

"Where is he going to go?" asked Caroline, as the game returned to full tilt.

I'd told her about Max's phone call to his mother—that there might be no "home" to send him to.

"His grandparents', I guess. They don't really want him. They feel like they've done their part already."

With her shoe, Caroline traced a large circle in the dirt, then another, smaller, within the first. "Can they even afford to fly him to Hawaii?"

"Camp should pay. It's the least we can do. We'll pay for counseling, too, if Max goes."

"So you're telling the grandparents everything?"

"Fisher's decision. He's the pro."

Campers grouped around us, then dispersed, then grouped again, like thunderheads massing before a storm. "They're going down!" said Petey Wooster, all hothead cockiness. "Pretty soon we're gonna catch 'em all."

Caroline patted his butt. "Go for it." She toed a third circle in her sketch. "If all else fails, there's always you, right? Bring Max back to Cambridge as your pet?"

I gathered she was being ironic, and just in case I laughed a clunky laugh. But the idea took fierce hold of me.

Caroline ground her toe in what I saw now was a bull's-eye. "You're both just what the other one deserves."

Why shouldn't I be his guardian? I imagined myself packing Max's lunch before school . . . and the two of us, rollicking in Harvard Yard at Halloween, kicking up pumpkin-colored leaves.

A surge of sudden noise made us turn. A vigilante swarm of boys packed the English section. Past them, looking puny at the distant finish line, stood a final Amish pair: Max and Eli.

"You're goners," shouted Dylan, ringleader of his side, and indeed, the conclusion was foregone: a last boy would be caught, and his horse alone would win. But who would ride, and who would play the horse? The two holdouts crouched, negotiating. I guessed they might shoot: scissors, paper, rock. But Eli climbed, unfighting, onto Max.

In place of the previous mock-scriptural dogma, the banter devolved to vulgar hoots. The boys couldn't have cared less about Amish theology; who was avoiding whom, or why. But as I watched Max pacing, preparing for this last dash, I realized I'd gotten the game all wrong. When the Amish stay untainted, resisting their desires, they do so with redemption clear in sight: the fellowship of other yielded souls. (It's the selfish who are condemned to the loneliness of self, who end up discontented and denied.) But my silly summer-camp bastardization twisted the logic inside out. Max had avoided corruption all game long;

he had managed to stay unblemished. But now, consequently, he would be left alone. When he won, he would just as surely lose.

Eli sharply spurred his heels into Max's kidneys. "Move it," he said. "Pronto. Giddyap."

TWENTY-FIVE

—◄○►—

When Caroline took Max to Rutland to get his cast sawed off, I suffered a cramp of jealousy like the one (could it have been less than two months before?) when she'd driven him away to have it set. But this time the pang quickly passed. As the bone of his wrist had stubbornly mended, so had Max and I fused at our lines of fracture. He loved me. Nothing could shatter that.

My security was confirmed when he returned from the doctor's and bestowed on me half the cast. "Here," he said. "I want you to have it. It stinks, but they said that would fade."

It did smell: carnality and confinement. Flakes of skin caked the fiberglass.

"Only half?" I teased. "I'm not worth the whole thing?"

"I thought if I kept one half, and you kept the other, it would be like a promise to remember. You know, when we can't be together."

But maybe we wouldn't have to be apart. Caroline's jest had launched a rocket of possibility: my new life as Max's caretaker. I pictured his bed (we'd buy a new one) next to mine, his toothbrush in the jelly jar on my sink. The kinetics of imagination zoomed.

"It's a deal," I said, joining our halves at their seams. "Now let me see that arm."

The appendage was badly atrophied. Its skin, like yogurt left too long in the sun, was curdy and toxically gray.

"Flex," I said.

A ghost of muscle bulged.

—◄○►—

The official plan was for Max to take the bus to New York, where he'd get a quick visit with his mom. Then on to Honolulu to start the eighth grade. Ironwood would pay for both tickets.

With luck, though, all that could be averted. When I'd floated the guardianship notion to Don Fisher, he didn't laugh: initial victory. He said he would contact his counterparts in New York and investigate various arrangements. Meanwhile, the last week of camp rolled around—and I hadn't approached Max with the proposal.

The fourth-to-last night was Pie-palooza, an annual end-of-summer treat. Raspberries and blackberries were just coming ripe in the meadows along the camp road. We turned the boys loose in the late afternoon, and by dinnertime boasted bucket-fuls of fruit. After the meal, each cabin baked its own fresh dessert, and the Lodge filled with sweet, indulgent scents. What a mess! Flour clouded the air and landed on boys' scalps, aging them comically. Tabletops became abstract canvases. And on T-shirt after juice-dribbled T-shirt, stains multiplied in a joyful epidemic.

In the midst of it, I felt a tap on my shoulder. Max was poised, kung fu style, a pie in his hand. Before I could blink, he aimed at me. But with slapstick largesse he misfired his thrust and kept the pie miraculously balanced.

"Gotcha!" he said. "Want a taste?" He produced a spoon and gestured "dig in."

I was stoked from the jolt of the sneaky near-miss, and also from the knockout sight of him. His teeth were dyed vampirish, his chin obscene with juice. The gleam in his eyes was gluttonous.

I scored a spoonful. "Mmm. Tart but not too tart."

"Good. I made it just that way for you."

And I knew it was time for me to ask.

"I need you," was how my try emerged. I revised it fast. "I mean, to talk with you."

"Sure," said Max. "Shoot. I'm all ears." His grin revealed a seed stuck in his braces.

"Not here," I said. "Something more . . . private."

He seemed to remember his own code. "Roger. How about a walk?"

"Great. Let me just ask Caroline."

I had vowed to keep Caroline in the loop on everything; an assistant director deserves to know. She hadn't yet formally accepted my idea, but acted already as if she ran the place, strutting lieutenantly in her father's navy shirt.

When I asked if she would mind if Max and I ducked out, she said, "Bye-bye, Miss American Pie. See ya."

Max and I walked south on the camp road. Neither of us led; neither followed. There was a weightless momentum, a ski-lift sense of being carried to a common destination.

It had been another dazingly clear day, wild blue yonder as obvious as an advertisement. But without a single cloud to suspend the dying sun, a quick dusk had robbed the sky of color. In the canopy of shade maples, fearless squirrels flew, chittering in their squirrely projects. Farther on, a woodpecker knocked. The bruised smell of nightfall tickled in on gusts as fleeting as improper thoughts.

We talked about how unbeatable the Yankees were this season, how much hotter it must be in Manhattan. Max reenacted his Pie-palooza fake-out, and I complimented his acting. We crooned a verse of "Blueberry Hill."

We passed a knurly beech that had been struck by lightning when I was a camper, years ago. Half of the trunk had been singed and sheared off, but the rest remained standing, alive; new leaves grew vibrant and thick. I felt I should tell Max the tree's history, shape a story to illuminate something. But all I could manage was, "Lightning." The things I longed to say were like pieces of litter being blown across a parking lot.

And then we were at the apple orchard, its knoll a swath of black within the black. I wasn't sure I wanted to climb up. But Max said, "Let's go," and so we did.

We blazed a trail past where the fireworks had been launched (mortar holes still scarring the sod), then through spiny trees that huddled tight like gossips.

"Look," said Max. "There's actually apples."

There were, but they hardly qualified—stunted by neglect and too much rain.

"Can't eat them, though," I said. "They're still green."

"How can you tell in the dark?"

"We're only halfway through August, city boy. Apples don't ripen this soon."

But Max never could resist a dare. He picked one, palm-polished it, and chomped. "Yum," he said, followed by a moan so fervid that he almost tempted me to steal a bite—until he sprayed my face with apple mush. "Nasty! Like chewing soap," he said.

"You don't have to take it out on me!" I smeared the gob of pulp back on him.

"Eew," he squealed, and spat at me again.

In a flash, I tackled him to the ground. We wrestled in the tall grass, we pinned and dodged and rolled, one of us ascendant, then the other. I tasted soil, sweat, sour apple. Bloodrush drugged my brain to dizziness. Our manner of engagement was a cut-throat sibling love—each seeking to win, but not quite to defeat.

We ended side-by-side, hyperventilating, punchy, all grass stains and muddy-kneed forgiveness.

"You okay?" I asked.

Max panted a yes.

"Your arm?"

"No problem. Good as new."

There was a cut-open, appley smell about him. I suppressed a sudden urge to nip his neck.

I *could* suppress it, couldn't I? We could grapple and then lie like this, close but not too close—at least for now, till he grew old enough. In the telephoto, self-convincing way of fantasy, I detailed all the chaste fun we would have. I saw the Harvard sweatshirt I would buy him, extra large; the duplicate apartment keys we'd cut. On voice mail we'd record a goofy joint message. Was twenty bucks enough as an allowance?

Max sat upright. "Jesus! What the hell?"

"What?" I said. "What? I didn't see."

"Something flying. Like a bird, but kamikaze."

"Probably just a bat," I said.

"A bat? Blech. That creeps me out."

I shrugged. "Nighttime is when they feed."

"But what if they, like, want to feed on me?"

I laughed at his urbanite terror, and even more at his self-centeredness. "They don't want you. They eat bugs. Mosquitoes."

"No way. How do they find them? It's dark." Max still sounded dubious that one of God's creatures could pass up his own supple flesh.

"Echo location," I explained. "They send out a signal, and when it hits something it tells them where to dive. Watch."

I plucked a low-branch apple and arced it in the air. A bat's iconic form swooped into view.

"Zow," said Max. "He must have thought that was one huge mosquito. Let me try." He lobbed his own apple.

The bat appeared as an instant's interruption of calm sky. We heard the trenchant slicing of its wings.

"Apocryphal!" Max skied another apple. This time two bats met in a cruciform of hunger.

"All right," I told him. "That's enough." I had always admired bats' ingenious adaptation—how they could be, within their blindness, so acute. I didn't like to know how easily they could be fooled.

We lay back in the scraggle of grass. The night's fleecy hush filled my ears.

"It kicks butt," Max said, "all the different things you know. Apples, bats, the works."

"Thanks. It's just stuff I picked up. If you come here a few more summers, you will, too."

There was so much more, still, I could impart. A cooling

breeze coiled from the invisible lake, and I thought to explain temperature inversions. But it wasn't just scientific lore. I wanted to guide Max through the shoals of adolescence, to lead him to a free and open sea.

"You know," he said, "even with what happened? This has been the best summer of my life. And you're the best friend I ever had."

He was prone to teenage hyperbole. Everything, for him, was "to the Max." But just then I chose to believe him. In some ways, although it had also been the worst, this had been one of my best summers, too. Max himself had made it so.

"I wish it didn't have to end," he said.

I put my hand on his arm, emaciated but intact, the first part of him I'd ever held. There was sanctity in that touch—not for greeting or rebuke, not for anything more than touch itself. I was going to say, "It doesn't have to end." I would tell him about Cambridge, the new bed, the extra keys. I would say, "Everything of mine will be yours."

"Hey!" he cried. "Look. Exponential!"

"What? You see another bat?"

"No, a shooting star. Over there." He pointed to a bleak quadrant of sky.

I was still adjusting my focus to the infinite gloom when Max called out, "Zam! Another one." Seconds later, "Bombs away, they're everywhere."

"It's the Perseids," I mumbled.

"The whats?"

"The Perseid meteor shower. Comes every year, the second week of August." I couldn't bear to go on with the lesson. Any words I spoke would only be Ruff's words.

If it were daytime, I realized, I could see the Point from here—just over the hill, across the lake. I was twice as old, exactly, as I'd been that star-shot night. In all those years, had I only come this far?

"Dang," said Max, "they look like you could reach right up and grab 'em. Close enough to trick the bats, I swear."

I could just discern his face's complication: thin, elegant nose; gem-cut jaw. He sprawled so close that I could feel his heat. I loved Max; he'd told me he loved me. Why then was our closeness so perverse? How different was I now from Ruff? From Charlie?

The worst part was not that I thought I might do something, but knowing I could probably refrain. I would be at once the famished bat and the tosser of decoys, teasing myself cruelly to starvation. The Amish way—being shunned—would be more bearable; Beulah at least had no doubt where she stood. But my penance was being forced to make the choice myself. Only I held the power to condemn me.

"*Pshew*," said Max, narrating the shooting stars like gunfire. "*Pshew pshew.* They're coming in for the kill."

His arms were vee'd to the heavens as though awaiting deliverance. The meteors were flagrant, copious.

"Hey, Jeremy? Next year? I'll be, like, technically too old. But can I come back and visit anyway?"

"That's a pretty long trip from Hawaii."

"But if I can? We'll come right here? Just you and me?"

I felt the barren ache of appetite. My heart, painfully boxed. The thuggish dark.

"Max, what you said? About this having to end?"

He sighed mopishly. "Forget it. I'm being dumb."

"No," I said. "It doesn't have to end. I mean, this feeling— you can take it anywhere. So even if this isn't the right place for you . . ."

Max closed his delicate, sky-hugging arms and retracted them like a pair of wings. I heard him breathe once, twice, again.

"Why wouldn't this be the right place?"

I could have lied, could have protected him from yet one more burden. But we'd all been dissembling far too long.

"Max, Charlie did awful, awful things."

"I thought he was gone for good," Max said.

"He is. But it goes deeper than that." I blinked hard, blotting out the pell-mell storm of stars, then opened my eyes and looked at him. "Ruff," I said, half expecting the name to shake the ground, but like any human noise it disappeared. "The thing Charlie did to you, Ruff had done to him—something like it. A long time ago."

Max still looked fixedly upward. The edges of him blurred into the night. "Did Ruff do those things to *you*?" he asked.

"No. But I was there. I never told." A knifepoint of superstition grazed my neck. But I felt it, too, slicing the ties that bound me. "Ruff's a good guy," I said. "His whole life is kids. But that's what also makes him dangerous."

This was finally the story I could tell myself about Ruff. In fifteen years, what would Max say about me?

He readjusted himself on the ground. A chilling dew had soaked through my pants and to my skin; I imagined it had done the same to him.

"So screw this place," he said. "We don't need it. I'll just come up and visit you in Cambridge."

"I don't know," I said. "Max, I'm just not sure."

"What? We'd have a blast. Just us two."

A quickening, pastoral scent sifted from the trees, and I remembered my first taste of Vermont—half a lifetime ago, vital and revelatory. Like false promises, two meteors flared and died.

"This is hard for me to say," I told Max.

With a flimsy thread of breath, he shifted again: Was he moving nearer to me, or away?

"What Charlie did to you, I never would have done. Never. I never would have forced you." And I knew for sure, saying this, it was true. "But Max, if you'd agreed. If you'd asked."

Quiet. Our breath. The addled sky.

Did I expect him to cry, to scream, to spit at me? To jump to his feet and run away?

"Do you understand? I wanted to. I still do."

He turned to me. Starlight made a mess of his eyes. In a far-off voice he said, "I understand."

I was shaking, but beneath that was an unexpected calm, the way a spun top, within its wobble, stands still. I would always now have said what I'd just said.

"I want to," I whispered. "I do."

"Don't," he said. "Don't say anything."

And I didn't. I owed him at least that.

There came a tangle of silence that, like a strand of DNA, seemed to hold our full twist of destinies—our timeless, imperfect human code.

Max said, "I think I should go now."

"Yeah," I said. "You're right. You should go."

He stood and brushed hayseed from his pants. He appeared to wait for a head rush to pass. Then he faded off into the night.

When his image was invisible, I recalled the way he'd looked at the end of the recent all-camp game. Eli had been caught and joined the ninety-eight shunned; Max, the sole survivor, stood alone: tight-faced, arms lifted in the air. It could have been the gesture of hard-earned victory, or the pose of a thief conceding capture.

I realized Max didn't have a flashlight, and I thought to chase after him and help. But I'd forgotten my flashlight, too.

EPILOGUE

—◄○►—

How can I know the weather? My carrel is windowless, remote;
the air conditioner endlessly chugs. But Weather.com says certain thunderstorms, a bullying nor'easter's approach. Good news
for us city folk: the heat wave's coming end. But poor Caroline.
Poor kids. Poor camp! A deluge on the first night, strafe of lightning, thunder's snarl. Not exactly how you'd want things to
begin. At least by this hour all the parents are long gone, the
footlockers ferried down the hill. The boys are in their bunks,
scared but safe.

And in Hawaii? Typhoons, or volcanic eruptions, or a dol-
drum sky as empty as exile?

I take down my ragged half of Max's cast and sniff—nothing
but a glum, corpsey smell. "We'll share" reads the interrupted
hope of my handwriting before it runs off the fiberglass. At another spot, what said "Max" is now "ax."

I sip Thai iced tea—lukewarm, curdling. Time again to try
the dissertation. I nudge the mouse, and the screen wakes:
"Avoidance."

Beulah, I remind myself. Start with her, my first informant. I
key in the word "Introduction."

But it's been almost a year, and I've still not answered her.
Now at last, from this distance, am I ready? I replace "Introduction" with "Dear friend Beulah." Then I type. I type and
type and type.

I tell her about Ruff, Charlie, Max—everything—although it

will likely end our friendship. I need to divulge, to expose each twisted root, so she knows just how well I understand.

When at last I arrive at that dismal starry night when Max left me stranded in the dark, I want to end the recollection there. Nothing after that truly mattered. But there are questions Beulah might still have.

I never really talked with Max again. The ardent, knowing stares he used to train in my direction were replaced with darty, agitated looks. Like erstwhile sweethearts waiting for divorce papers to clear, we sidestepped in a lame-duck kind of love. Caroline didn't ask about his and my withdrawal. Perhaps she thought it our way of mitigating disappointment.

I saw him for the last time as he boarded the charter bus. He lifted his healed arm in an imprecise good-bye, then disappeared behind tinted windows. I could make out only waving hands and dim, crestfallen heads, the shadowy gestures of departure. The driver took his seat, Simon double-checked the count. The engine growled. We heard the air brake's cuss.

As the door was closing, one boy's contour moved—a specter behind the shaded glass. Max reemerged, a frantic worry in his look, as though he had misplaced something essential. He peered across the send-off crowd to me.

I wanted to do something—to raise my hand, to smile—but my body, ever wayward, failed to move. His eyes caught the strange crosswise colors of the morning: bittersweet blues, absolving greens. Bending down, he palmed a scoop of dirt from the camp road, then stood again and pocketed the grit. He pursed his pouty lips as if to spit, or blow a kiss, but did neither. He turned back to the bus.

I didn't resign till the beginning of spring, so Ruff's only choice was to promote Caroline—who else could he have found at such short notice? My excuse was the dissertation, mounting pressure from the deans, the threat of losing my fellowship.

At first, Ruff was paternalism run amok, said Caroline—now

infantilizing, now egregiously stern. He hawk-watched every tiny move she made. Finally she told him, "Listen, I've already got a father. You're my boss, not my dad. This is a job." Instead of rankling Ruff, her directness seemed to free him. His tyranny ebbed. They formed a team.

They asked if I'd visit once the summer was in swing—stay a week? Finally build that spruce shelter? But I haven't returned their calls or e-mails for a month. I've thrown out all Ironwood envelopes. I've done my best, like Charlie Moss, to vanish.

We never found out where he went. Maybe he's pumping gas on the graveyard shift in some godforsaken outpost. Would that please me? Do I want to see him suffer? Sometimes, yes. Justice should be served. Other times, I imagine that he's saving lives somewhere, driving an ambulance in Kosovo or Kenya. What a shame if all his caring went to waste.

The letter runs to twenty-four pages—too bad this isn't actually my thesis. Almost ten o'clock, says my computer. Closing time.

The lights flicker. Again. The nor'easter. Once more I think of camp, hammered by rain. A camper jolts awake, heart flustered by the storm, his very first night away from home. A counselor hears the noise, sits by the boy and hugs him. *Relax. It's okay. You're all right . . .*

The computer screen scrambles, then finds its form again, like water into which a stone's been tossed. Do I hear, outside, a muffled gripe of thunder?

The final things I need to say to Beulah are much harder. Without them, though, my story holds less sway. I confess, at long last, that I know her sister's family and lived with them even as they shunned her. That I understand their side, too. That I love them.

Beulah may conclude I'm a typical *Englischer:* relativist, exploitive, double-dealing. Knowing both sides, in the end, left me with neither.

◄○►

The day I mailed my resignation to Ruff, I jumped into the car and drove south. I longed for the patchwork precision of Peach Bottom. I wanted to go where I had family.

Crossing the Pennsylvania border, I imagined the joy of surprising the Yoders. Sadie would lay out "whoopee pies" and chow-chow for a party; the kids and I would romp and play Dutch Blitz. My only apprehension was Jakie: Was he living at home? Was he in jail?

The farm looked exactly as I remembered: sharp white house, fanatically clipped lawn. The fields were expectant, newly plowed. When I stepped from the car I was besieged by grabby hands, kids climbing the ladder of my legs. Pickle Joe, Dan, Lydia. Baby Sam, now old enough to walk.

"Kinn-ah, bleib weck!" came Abner's voice from the barn door. "Jeremy don't need your bothering."

"It's fine," I said. I scooped Pickle Joe into my arms. He smelled of soap and slightly turned milk. "I missed you guys. I missed you all so much!"

But Abner repeated himself—"Children, stay away"—and they dropped back and retreated to the barn. His broad-brimmed straw hat cast a shadow on his face. Almost all I could see of him was his beard.

"Sadie in the house?" I asked.

He nodded. "Go on in."

I found her in the living room, alone at the quilting frame. "Jeremy?" she said. "What are you doing here?"

"I had a hankering for some pie. This the place?"

She frowned. "Afraid I haven't any baked."

"That's all right," I said. "I was only joking."

She showed off the Botch Handle quilt she'd half-finished, introduced me to Malinda, the new baby. She fetched me a glass of lemonade. But in all of her actions she seemed nervous and scowly, a fire victim who can't stop smelling smoke.

"We had a rough patch," she said, as we sat at the kitchen table. "Jakie fell in with the wrong set." She fidgeted some crumbs on the oilcloth. "At least it wasn't like some of the young folks up-county. Did you hear about last summer? Cocaine!"

I told her that I'd read some articles.

"We're doing better now, thank goodness. Next month Jakie starts *die Gemee nooch geh*—the classes for baptism. Ain't so, Jakie?"

"Yes, Maem," a meek voice responded.

I turned and saw him standing at the door. Abner, wiping his boots, stepped in after him, followed by the rest of the Yoders.

"Jakie, did you see who's here?" said Sadie.

"Yes." With a scant lift of his chin, he greeted me.

He was a man now—at least well on his way. I could see where he'd shaved above his lip. His hair was cut Plain again, unparted, to his earlobes. His trousers were crusty with manure.

"So," I said. "You're getting ready to join the church?"

"Yes."

Was this the only word he knew?

He and Abner helped themselves to glasses of lemonade and slices of bread slabbed with smearcase. We talked about a neighbor's farm that had been turned into a golf course. We spoke of milk prices, the weather. Jakie ate with tentative, hamstrung movements, as though he feared reopening an old wound.

After ten minutes, Abner said, "We'd like to visit longer. But we've got some more choring yet to do."

"Tomorrow's *Ordnungsgemee*," Sadie explained.

I rolled up my sleeves. "What can I do?"

Abner's gaze dropped for an instant to my bad finger. "I believe we can manage on our own."

"I can watch the kids tomorrow," I said, "when you're away at church."

"Can he?" said Lydia.

"Please?" said Pickle Joe.

Abner pinched his lips into a frown. "I'm sure Jeremy's got plenty to do back where he comes from. Getting ready for that summer camp, ain't?"

I could have explained that I was never returning to Iron-wood, that I'd have all too much free time now. But I knew I was being asked to leave.

At the car, Sadie firmly shook my hand. "We have to look out for the children, is all," she said. "It's better if they stick with our own sort."

"Sure," I said. "I understand. Good-bye."

As I drove away tearfully I caught a glimpse of Jakie, hitching Brown and Betty to the harrow. He steered them in a straight line through the field. This fall he would kneel before his family and friends—all who'd known him since before he could remember. He would vow to renounce the world, even his flesh and blood, and pledge lifelong obedience to the church. Then he would rise and accept the Holy Kiss.

Will he be happy? I type. *Is happiness an option? For some people, maybe. Others not. A drowning man can open up his mouth and try to breathe, but he might just let more water in his lungs. Beulah, only you can make your choice.*

I wish you, my good friend, much patience and much grace. I wish patience and grace upon us all.

I'm debating how to close—does "Love" mean anything?—when the lights suddenly jitter and quit. Computer, too. Air conditioner. Everything.

In a second, it will probably all come humming back. I'll find the file, print it, sign my name. But now, in the dark, I'm not sure I saved it. I could be underground, so total is the absence.

ACKNOWLEDGMENTS

Thanks first and foremost to my agent, Mitchell Waters, my editor, Fiona McCrae, and all the other fantastic folks at Graywolf. I also appreciate the support of my family: Janet Wyzanski Lowenthal and Jim Pines, Abraham Lowenthal and Jane Jaquette, and Linda Lowenthal; and my friendly readers: Bernard Cooper, Tom House, Michael Kozuch, Vestal McIntyre, and most especially Rachel Kadish. The Massachusetts Cultural Council and the Bread Loaf Writers' Conference provided fellowships for which I am deeply grateful.

ABOUT THE AUTHOR

Michael Lowenthal attended Dartmouth College and graduated in 1990 as class valedictorian. Subsequently he worked as an editor at University Press of New England, where he founded the Hardscrabble Books imprint. He is the author of a previous novel, *The Same Embrace*, and the editor of many nonfiction collections. His short stories have appeared in the *Southern Review*, *Kenyon Review*, *Tin House*, and *Witness*, and have been widely anthologized in volumes including *Best American Gay Fiction* and *Men on Men 5*. Lowenthal's essays and reviews have been published in the *New York Times Magazine*, *Boston Globe*, *Washington Post*, and *Out*, among many other venues. A recipient of fellowships from the Bread Loaf Writers' Conference, the Massachusetts Cultural Council, and the New Hampshire State Council on the Arts, Lowenthal lives in Boston and teaches creative writing at Boston College.

The text of *Avoidance* has been set in Sabon, a font designed by Jan Tschichold. It is based broadly on the work of Claude Garamond and his pupil Jacques Sabon.

Book design by Wendy Holdman
Typesetting by Stanton Publication Services, Inc.
Book manufacturing by Maple Vail Book Manufacturing
on acid-free paper

Graywolf Press is a not-for-profit, independent press. The books we publish include poetry, literary fiction, essays, and cultural criticism. We are less interested in best-sellers than in talented writers who display a freshness of voice coupled with a distinct vision. We believe these are the very qualities essential to shape a vital and diverse culture.

Thankfully, many of our readers feel the same way. They have shown this through their desire to buy books by Graywolf writers; they have told us this themselves through their e-mail notes and at author events; and they have reinforced their commitment by contributing financial support, in small amounts and in large amounts, and joining the "Friends of Graywolf."

If you enjoyed this book and wish to learn more about Graywolf Press, we invite you to ask your bookseller or librarian about further Graywolf titles; or to contact us for a free catalog; or to visit our award-winning web site that features information about our forthcoming books.

We would also like to invite you to consider joining the hundreds of individuals who are already "Friends of Graywolf" by contributing to our membership program. Individual donations of any size are significant to us: they tell us that you believe that the kind of publishing we do *matters*. Our web site gives you many more details about the benefits you will enjoy as a "Friend of Graywolf"; but if you do not have online access, we urge you to contact us for a copy of our membership brochure.

www.graywolfpress.org

Graywolf Press
2402 University Avenue, Suite 203
Saint Paul, MN 55114
Phone: (651) 641-0077
Fax: (651) 641-0036
E-mail: wolves@graywolfpress.org